Toni was tir
with Nick.

"Why would you deliberately put yourself into the middle of a shooting match?" she asked him.

Nick caught her chin and tilted it up so he could stare down into her eyes. She hoped to God he couldn't see what caused the intense burning behind them. "Don't tell me you were worried about me."

She jerked her chin free, angry because she *had* been worried, no matter how much she wanted to deny it. "Dream on, Manelli."

"I will if you will, del Rio."

He was referring to her dream of last night, of course. She could have slapped him for that remark. She couldn't help it if her subconscious mind was unstable enough to conjure up images of him. Of them...

Dear Reader,

If you have children, it's back-to-school time for them—and that means more reading time for you. Luckily, we've got just the list of books to keep you enthralled, starting with *One Last Chance,* the fabulous American Hero title from Justine Davis.

And the rest of the month is pretty terrific, too, with titles from Suzanne Carey (a bit of ghostly fun to get you set for the Halloween season), Nikki Benjamin, Maura Seger, Clara Wimberly— an Intimate Moments newcomer whose Gothic novels may be familiar to some of you—and star-in-the-making Maggie Shayne. (Look for her next month, too—in Shadows.)

I'd also like to take a moment to thank those of you who've written to me with your thoughts and feelings about the line. All of us—editors and authors alike—are here to keep you reading and happy, so I hope you'll never stop sharing your comments and ideas with me.

So keep an eye out for all six of this month's books—and for all the other wonderful books we'll be bringing you in months to come.

Yours,

Leslie Wainger
Senior Editor and Editorial Coordinator

RECKLESS
ANGEL

Maggie
Shayne

Silhouette®
INTIMATE MOMENTS®
Published by Silhouette Books New York
America's Publisher of Contemporary Romance

SILHOUETTE BOOKS
300 East 42nd St., New York, N.Y. 10017

RECKLESS ANGEL

ISBN: 0-373-07522-7

First Silhouette Books printing September 1993

All the characters in this book have no existence outside the imagination of the author and have no relation whatsoever to anyone bearing the same name or names. They are not even distantly inspired by any individual known or unknown to the author, and all incidents are pure invention.

®: Trademark used under license and registered in the United States Patent and Trademark Office and in other countries.

Printed in the U.S.A.

MAGGIE SHAYNE

and her husband of sixteen years make their home in rural Otselio Valley, nestled in the rolling hills of Southern Central New York. Among her friends, Maggie is known for her quirky sense of humor, a tool she sees as essential in raising her five beautiful daughters.

Maggie has served for two years as secretary and conference coordinator for her chapter of Romance Writers of America. She has written articles for *Romance Writers Report,* and wrote features and humor for all but one issue of *Inside Romance.* In addition, she often writes for her chapter newsletter, *Prose and Cons.* More than anything else, she enjoys writing. She loves to create characters that come alive in her own mind and, she hopes, in the minds of her readers.

To Rick, whose belief in me never wavered,
even when my own did

Chapter 1

In the murky, rain-veiled light that spilled into the alley, Nick watched. The man who called himself "Viper" leaned over, his face alternately beige and bright orange in the flickering light of a broken neon sign. Viper grunted as he pulled the blade from the dead man's chest. Nick turned up his collar when the rain came down colder and harder than before. He was glad of the rain. There would be less blood.

Something moved and Nick gave a quick glance up and down the alley, simultaneously lifting the 9 mm automatic. The gun's muzzle moved in perfect unison with his eyes until he found the source of the sound in an overflowing trash bin. Red eyes glowed in a shiny black coat for an instant before the rat scurried away. Nick relaxed and turned back toward the little man with the pinched face and the intimidating nickname. In truth, he looked more like a weasel than a snake. "We can't have Vinnie

ID'ed right away," Nick reminded him. "You know the drill."

Viper shook his head, but his slicked-back hair didn't move. "I've done my part." He wiped the blade over the dead man's lapel and started to stand.

Nick worked the action of the Taurus he held, and Viper's head snapped toward him. "Lou sent me to witness the hit, not clean up after it. You don't want to do it, either—that's fine with me. Just let me come along when you tell Lou why Vinnie was ID'ed before he was stiff." Nick knew his voice was like cold steel. He wanted it that way. He pretended great interest in the blue-black barrel of his gun while Viper made up his mind.

After a long moment Viper knelt again to begin removing items from the dead man's pockets, taking the ring from his finger, ripping the tags from his clothes. He handed these to Nick and bent once more, this time intent on rubbing the limp fingertips back and forth over rough pavement until no trace of a print remained. Nick stuffed the victim's belongings into a plastic zipper bag and pushed it into the pocket of his raincoat. Viper pulled a small-caliber revolver from his own coat, held it two inches from the dead face and thumbed the hammer back.

A sound like a gag, or someone choking, made them both freeze and turn their heads slowly toward the entrance where a woman stood, frozen. For an instant Nick's gaze locked with hers. She stared right at him, and there was no doubt in his mind that she was memorizing his every feature, better to describe him to the local cops she intended to call. Viper leveled his gun at her as she tore her gaze away and whirled to run.

"No!" Nick swung one arm downward, knocking Viper's muzzle off target before the other man had a chance to pull the trigger. "Finish this job, dammit. I'll take care of her." He spun and ran for the opposite end of the alley. He knew she'd head that way—to the closest place with lights and people. He vaulted the mesh fence that blocked the alley at the nearest end and landed with a jarring thud on the pavement. He jogged over the sidewalk, keeping close to the buildings.

He stopped when he heard her heels smacking along the wet sidewalk and waited to step into her path when she came around the corner at breakneck speed.

She careened into his chest. He felt the heat emanating from her, heard her ragged breathing. "Thank God," she said on a noisy exhale. "Take me to a phone, fast, I—" She looked up into his eyes and she knew.

Before she could pull back, he clamped his hands on her shoulders. When her full lips parted, Nick said, "Scream and you die, lady." She didn't. She pressed her lips tight and swallowed hard. Nick saw her fear. He felt it. It surrounded her like a halo of light around a candle's flame. He watched her, ready to react to her slightest move.

She had a mane of wild black curls that hung nearly to her waist and glittered with the clinging raindrops reflecting the city lights. Her eyes—they looked black, too, but he couldn't be sure in the darkness—were wide with fear, but alert and intelligent. She was small, so she wouldn't be hard to handle. The top of her head didn't reach his chin.

He heard footsteps in the distance, half trot, half shuffle—Viper's unmistakable gait. If Nick didn't think of something fast, the little bastard would probably put them both on ice. He held the gun under her nose, so she could get a good look. She refused to glance down. She stared up at him instead, her eyes still afraid but defiant. He could see the wheels turning behind those eyes. It surprised him to realize that he knew what she was thinking.

She was weighing the odds, waiting for a chance. She'd bolt at the first opportunity and then she'd end up dead.

"Listen to me and listen good." Nick used his best street voice and most intimidating tone. "The guy you hear coming is a killer—a pro. When he gets here he's gonna make you his next job, then he's gonna do the same for me 'cause I didn't off you myself. Now, you have one chance to live beyond the next few minutes. You wanna see tomorrow, you do what I say, *to the letter.* You got it?"

She didn't acknowledge the question in the slightest, but just kept watching him with those unbelievably huge, liquid eyes. He blinked and made himself continue. "When I let you go, turn around and run. I'm gonna fire one shot, and you're gonna hit the pavement and play dead for all you're worth."

Viper's footsteps drew nearer. Her gaze flicked away from his to glance back over her shoulder. She looked up at him again, a little of the defiance gone. "What if I don't?" The words sounded as if they were forced through a space too small for them.

"If you don't, lady, then the second shot will be for real." He let the words fall heavily between them, saw her go a shade paler. She nodded once.

Nick drew a steadying breath, released her shoulders and stepped aside to let her go by him. "Go."

She ran from him. Nick waited to be sure Viper had a good view, then raised the gun, aiming well over her head. He closed his finger on the trigger. He never realized he'd been holding his breath until she went down and he released it all at once. She lay still, facedown on the sidewalk some forty feet away. Viper reached him a second later.

"You get her?"

Lights came on in apartment windows. Nick had no doubt that someone was dialing 911. "You got eyes. How could I miss?"

Viper looked toward the girl and started forward. "Damn, that broad looked familiar."

"Where's Vinnie?" Nick's barked question stopped the other man in his tracks.

"In my trunk."

"Get him the hell outta here. This place will be crawling with cops any minute." Viper looked toward her again, and Nick saw the doubt in his eyes. Viper needed more convincing. Nick dug into his pocket and emerged with his keys. He tossed them to the smaller man. "My car's around the corner. Get it over here."

"What do I look like, a damn parking attendant?"

A head poked from a window above, then ducked back inside. The window closed with a bang. Viper muttered a curse and dashed around the corner, moving unevenly but quickly. Within two minutes he brought Nick's car to a screeching halt at the curb. Nick was already bending over her. He rolled her onto her back, and she went like a wet rag. Perfectly limp. She was putting on one hell of a show. He grabbed her under the arms and pulled her up and over his shoulder. He wrapped one arm firmly around her thighs to hold her there and turned toward the car.

Her hands dangled loosely against his back. Her legs felt cold beneath his hand. Stupid woman, he thought, walking around in a skirt on a night like this. "Pop the trunk, Viper." His thumb inadvertently touched the garter that held up her stocking. Nick's mouth went dry.

He moved to the rear of the car as Viper hit the button inside and the trunk slowly lifted. He dumped her unceremoniously inside, hard enough so Viper could feel the car sink with her weight. He checked to be sure all of her was

in, then slammed the trunk hard. Viper got out of the car,
and Nick hurried to slide behind the wheel. "Where you
dumpin' Vinnie?"

"East River," Viper answered quickly. He was nervous now. A faint siren came wailing from somewhere,
and his eyes danced in their sockets.

"I'll take her somewhere else. We don't want any connections," Nick said. "Let's go."

Viper nodded and hurried into the darkness like a
cockroach when the lights come on.

Nick managed to avoid the police, taking side streets
until he was certain he hadn't been followed. He pulled to
the curb on an empty street, between a crumbling, condemned heap and a weedy vacant lot. Most of the street-
lights had been shot out or demolished with stones. He
thumbed the trunk latch button and ran to the rear of the
car as it lifted.

The rain fell harder. He tightened the belt of his raincoat and leaned inside. The only light was the tiny bulb
that came on whenever the trunk was opened. "Come on
out," he said softly, glancing around once more to be sure
he wasn't being watched. She didn't move. He leaned
lower, frowning. "Lady, you can cut the act now." He
pushed at her shoulder with one hand. She remained as
she was, a small, unmoving bundle. Nick's blood slowed
to a stop in his veins. Could he possibly have—

"Oh, hell . . ." He gripped her shoulders and shook her
gently. When she still didn't respond, he found himself
frantically pushing the damp, tangled masses of hair away
from her face in search of an exit wound or a trace of
blood. He bent so close to her, he could smell her per-
fume. It wrapped around his mind and tugged. He saw the
tiny beads of moisture clinging to her face.

When her feet suddenly slammed into his solar plexus it was like an explosion. He stumbled back, pain shooting outward in every direction from his middle. He doubled over, struggling to draw a breath, and so far failing. When he finally blinked enough moisture from his eyes to see straight and managed to unbend himself and actually inhale, he glimpsed her running like hell in the direction they'd come from. He swore violently and dove back into the car, pulling it around in a noisy doughnut and slamming the accelerator to the floor. The car overtook her in seconds, but she veered into the lot. Nick pulled over, got out and sprinted after her.

His legs were longer, more powerful, but God, she could run. Her feet flew and her hair billowed behind her. She'd kicked off her shoes somewhere along the way. The lot was thick with tall grasses and weeds, and Nick's legs were soon soaked to the skin. His shoes were so wet it was hard to keep from slipping. Still, he gained on her.

With one final burst he leapt on her, taking her to the ground in a tackle that was brutal. He came down on top of her and in two quick movements he rolled her over and clasped her wrists in one hand. He held them to the ground over her head. She struggled, and he dropped his body on top of hers, stilling her instantly. "You try that again and I'll tie you up so tight you'll be lucky if you can breathe. You reading me?"

Her eyes flashed anger at him, and her breath came in shuddering gasps. "I'm supposed to come along peacefully, is that it? You want me to load the gun for you, too, before you blow my head off?"

It was the most she'd spoken to him, and Nick was surprised that her voice was deep and sultry, not soft and high-pitched as he would have expected from someone her size. She had a voice like Hepburn or Bacall. A voice that—a voice that distracted him from the matter at hand, dammit. "If I'd wanted you dead, you'd be playing a harp by now," he ground out, irritated. His grip on her wrists tightened when she tried to pull them free. Her breath was warm on his face in contrast to the chill breeze.

She twisted beneath him, trying to wriggle out from under him—a futile attempt. He pressed himself harder against her, his chest jammed so firmly into hers that each shaky breath she drew lifted him. He knew he must be hurting her.

When she saw that her struggling was useless, she stopped. He eased the pressure of his body on hers. "What are you going to do with me?" she finally asked.

"Keep you quiet about what you saw in that alley tonight. That's all."

"That's all," she mocked. "You might as well shoot me and get it over with, then. You can't lie on top of me forever." The venom in her voice was real, and he was shocked she could do more than cower in fear and swear she'd never utter a word if he'd only let her go.

"You've got a smart mouth on you, lady. I don't need to keep you quiet forever. Just for a few days." His common sense whispered that it would likely be closer to a few weeks, but he ignored it. What she didn't know wouldn't hurt her—or him.

She seemed to absorb what he'd said and turn it over in her mind. A little more fear came into her eyes. "How do you plan to do that?"

It hit him then that, tough as she came off, she was probably more afraid of him than she'd ever been of anyone in her life. He eased his grip on her wrists and moved off her to let her sit up. He never let go of her hands, though, and he kept her feet in sight at all times. Her question was one he'd been trying to answer since he'd first seen her near the alley. No matter how he figured it, there was only one solution. He stood and pulled her to her feet. "Come on."

When he tugged on her, she resisted. Her bare feet braced in the wet grass, she refused to move a step. He turned to look at her. She squared her shoulders and met his gaze. "No."

His brows shot up as she surprised him yet again. "What do you mean, 'no'?"

"Do what you have to, mister, but don't ask me to make it any easier."

Nick shook his head, unable to understand her train of thought. He pulled the automatic from beneath his coat, intending to persuade her to be a little more cooperative. When he looked at her again he saw her swallow, stand straighter and close those huge dark eyes. Her lashes brushed her cheeks. She looked like a proud Gypsy princess about to be sacrificed for the good of her people or something. Her voice only shook a little. "Not in the face, okay?"

"What?"

"It will be easier on my mother . . . when she has to . . ." She broke off and opened her eyes again. They shimmered. "Just consider it a . . . last request." She blinked and met his gaze squarely. "Could we get this over with? I never thought I'd go out bawling, but if you drag it out much longer, I—"

"Hell!" He thrust the gun back into the shoulder holster and grabbed her again. "Will you get his through that thick skull of yours? I am not going to kill you. You have trouble with English or something?"

Eyes flashing wider, she exploded in a burst of Spanish, none of which he understood. He supposed he could probably guess at most of it, though. He hadn't meant his remark as a racial slur. He hadn't realized her Gypsy-like looks were due to a Hispanic bloodline until this moment. Did her exotic beauty come from her mother or her father? he wondered, then he wondered what difference it made.

Her stream of insults ended. She drew a breath and whispered, "I speak English better than you do, you overgrown thug. I was born ten miles from here. My mother teaches English lit—" She bit her lips as if to stop herself. That aroused his curiosity.

"Go on. Where does she teach?"

She averted her gaze. "What are you going to do with me?"

So she wasn't talking. All right. He could find out anything he wanted to know in less time than she would believe possible. "I'm taking you home with me." He said it slowly, watching her face.

She looked up fast, her shock in her eyes. "You're kidnapping me."

Toni shivered. She was soaked, she was barefoot and she was mad as hell. How dare the bastard make a remark like that when *he* was constantly sprinkling his speech with "gonna" and "wanna"? Her father may have been Puerto Rican, but he'd also been one of the finest surgeons at Saint Mary's. Her mother—as she'd very nearly blurted—taught English literature at NYU. Toni had grown up hearing both languages, and she spoke both fluently and flawlessly. Her English had no trace of an accent, nor did her Spanish. She was proud of her parents. The past had taught her that nothing was more dangerous than an ignorant bigot.

Unless it was being kidnapped in the middle of the night by a hit man. She shook her head slowly as she walked with him back toward the car. Months of lurking around courtrooms and reputed mob hangouts had given her a lot to work with. Nothing, though, had prepared her for this. When she'd followed Vincent Pascorelli from the jail, she'd expected to see him meet with one of Taranto's men, maybe even Fat Lou himself. She hadn't expected to get a front-row seat at a contract killing.

She glanced again at her captor. His London Fog trench coat hung open, and his tailored three-piece suit was soaked—ruined, she hoped. At least he still had his shoes on. If he hadn't been so damn big, she might have managed to get away from him. She supposed she'd have to make the best of it until she had another opportunity. She was beginning to believe he wasn't going to kill her. It made no sense, but he'd have done it by now if he were going to.

Her foot came down on something sharp, and she winced. The only things between her sensitive feet and the littered ground were the remnants of her stockings—not exactly prime footwear. She lifted her foot, jerked her hand from his and ran her fingers over the arch. No cut. She supposed she'd live. He watched her, his dark brows drawn together over his narrowed eyes, as she put her foot down again.

The next thing she knew, he scooped her up into his arms and carried her. When she tried to fight him, his powerful arms tightened and she gave it up. The guy was just too big. She sat still and grated her teeth. His jaw was set, she noticed. Did he find this as distasteful as she did, then? He carried her as if she weighed no more than that gun of his. She wished she was eighty pounds overweight. She wished carrying her would give him a hernia.

This close he wasn't as frightening. Big, yes, but that hardness to his face was only in the expression. He'd lose the hardened-criminal look the minute he smiled, she thought. She could see the shadow of a beard darkening his jaw. As they moved past the glow of the car's headlights, she saw his thick lips and the cleft in the center of the upper one, which gave it a sensual shape—when he wasn't snarling. He wasn't so mean, she told herself. He wasn't half as scary as he probably thought he was. He could've killed her. He hadn't. He could've roughed her up, slapped her around until she was ready to do whatever he said. He hadn't. Hell, he couldn't even make her walk barefoot over a lot of broken glass and litter.

When he dropped her onto the passenger seat, slammed her door and started around to his side of the car, she thought about yanking the door open and running again. He must've seen it in her face, because he tapped the window with the gun barrel and shook his head. In another second he was behind the wheel.

He drove fast, but not recklessly, away from the city. The headlights barely cut a path through the pouring rain. She watched him often. He didn't look her way at all.

He'd driven in silence for forty-five minutes before she drummed up the nerve to ask, "Where do you live? Tibet?"

His brows went up, and he glanced at her briefly before returning his attention to the highway. "It isn't much farther."

He took the next exit, and they spent ten minutes negotiating side roads before finally pulling up to a tall iron gate. He took a remote control from the dash and thumbed a button. The gate swung open and they drove through. It closed smoothly behind them. The house that loomed ahead was a fieldstone monstrosity. It towered, three stories of it, and all of them the color of mud.

He thumbed another button when they drew near, and an overhead door rose. The headlights pierced the black interior of the garage. He pulled the car in, shut it off and closed the door. They sat in total darkness. "Don't go nuts on me," he said, his voice very low, as if he thought someone might be listening. "This is for your own good."

She stiffened in anticipation, but he had her wrists quickly imprisoned in one huge hand. His other hand smoothed something sticky over her mouth. Tape! She heard his door open. He pulled her across the seat to get out the same side he had. He kept hold of her wrists and managed to stay far enough ahead of her to avoid her attempts at kicking him. A lot of good it would've done, she thought miserably. She was barefoot.

He hauled her forward, flung open a door and drew her through it. She was in a kitchen, dim but not dark. The impression she had was of shiny copper and chrome. He tugged her through another door and along a hallway. She glimpsed a huge formal dining room to the left, and what might be a library to the right. He moved too quickly, his long legs eating up the distance as she stumbled in his wake. Another doorway, and she would have gasped if she could, at the living room. A marble-topped bar with crystal glasses suspended upside-down from a rack above it. Brass-legged coffee tables and end tables with glass surfaces. White marble sculptures stood on every one of them: a rearing stallion, a Bengal tiger, Pan with his pipes. The ceilings were stucco, and there was a chandelier with crystal droplets turning slowly. *Money,* the place seemed to say. Not in a whisper, but loud and clear.

He pulled her at a frantic pace over the plush carpet that felt like heaven to her frozen, bruised feet. She saw a foyer beyond a mammoth archway and what she took to be the front entrance. She paused for a moment, frown-

ing, her body jerking forward again when he yanked her
hands. She'd caught an unnatural glimmer from the left
eye of the bear's head mounted on one wall. It caught her
attention immediately, and when she looked at it, she realized that the two eyes didn't quite match. Because one
of them concealed the lens of a video camera. She'd been
at this game too long not to spot surveillance devices as
obvious as that one. The question was, who did the big lug
want to watch? Or was someone watching him? Did he
even know the thing was there?

Her pondering was cut short when they came to a broad
staircase and he pulled her up it behind him. At the top
they veered down a hall and mounted still another staircase, this one steep and narrow. At the top of that, another hall, nearly pitch-dark, and through a doorway into
what might have been a study. There was a desk silhouetted in the darkness. Other shapes loomed, but she didn't
have time to identify them. He drew her right up to a
bookcase at the far end of the room and he did something to it. Suddenly it swung inward just like a door. She
felt her eyes widen in fear. Gangsters and hit men she
could deal with. Not secret passages in creepy old houses,
though. No way. She braced her feet and resisted, but he
pulled her hard and she stumbled through into total
blackness. The bookcase door closed.

What was this? Was she in some cobwebbed and rat-
infested partition between the walls? Was he going to en-
tomb her here and leave her to die where no one could
hear her screams? God, this was like something Poe might
have written. He dropped her hands and moved away
from her, and she shot forward, simultaneously ripping
the tape from her mouth, regardless of the sting. She
grabbed for his arm, and when she touched it with her

groping hand, she clung. "Don't leave me in here. You can't..."

She stopped when she heard the soft click and the room was flooded with light. She blinked and saw that she'd been acting like an idiot. She released his arm and looked around. This was a compact living room, with a small camelback sofa and a couple of chairs in a soft fawn brown, a carpet a shade lighter, a stereo system on a shelf near one wall and a good-sized television beside it. Off to her right was a tiny kitchenette. To her left was an open door, beyond which she saw a king-size bed.

She heard his deep sigh when he crossed to the sofa, no longer concerned about her getting away, it seemed. He sunk down as if exhausted and leaned his head back. His hair was no longer combed down gangster style. The rain, combined with wrestling her so many times in the past hour, had it curling over his forehead as crazily as her own. It was dark brown, like sable, and still damp.

She studied him, her fear nearly drowned out by her boundless curiosity. "What kind of a setup *is* this?"

"What's your name?" he asked as if he hadn't heard her question.

She hugged herself as a full-body shudder raced through her. She hesitated over that question. If he knew who she was, he'd change his mind about keeping her alive in a hurry. Still, it wouldn't hurt to tell him her true name.

"Antonia Veronica Rosa del Rio." She pronounced it with the smooth Spanish accent she used when she wanted to impress someone...or confuse someone. As far as recognition went, she knew there would be none. It was a far cry from her pseudonym, Toni Rio.

His stern expression changed. He seemed amused. The hard lines in his face eased, and his lips curved upward at

the corners. "I guess I don't need to ask if you're making
it up." He tipped his head back and regarded the ceiling.
"Antonia Veronica Rosa del Rio," he mused. "What do
your friends call you?"

"Irrelevant, since you're no friend of mine."

His head came down, and he fixed her to the spot with
deep brown eyes. In this light she could see the tiger stripes
surrounding his pupils. "Glad you realize it, Antonia."
He watched her for a minute longer. "You're shivering,"
he said at length. He nodded toward the bedroom door.
"Bathroom's through there. I'd suggest a hot bath and
some sleep. You can use one of my robes."

"¡Que cara!"

His brows went up. "Problem?"

"I'd sooner stay wet, than—than..." She was shaking
harder now, and it wasn't entirely from the cold. He was
big. Not big like some guys were big; this guy was big like
Schwarzenegger. When he started talking about baths and
sleeping and her wearing his robe... well, maybe she was
a little more afraid of him than she'd thought. After all,
they were alone here. They were isolated, cut off from the
world.

He stood slowly, and came closer until he was only
inches from her. He towered over her, making her feel as
small as a child. Her pride wouldn't let her back down.
Her gaze stayed on the tie he'd yanked loose. Her lungs
slowly filled with his scent and that of the rain on his
body.

"Look at me, Antonia." She did. She didn't like looking into those eyes from such a small distance, so she tried
focusing on the lips. The sensual curl of them made them
more disturbing. "If you don't get out of those wet
clothes," he told her, "you are likely to catch pneumonia. I'm not in any position to take you to a hospital, so I

can't allow that to happen. Now, are you going to take them off, or am I?''

She tried to swallow and couldn't. She wanted to move away from him, but her feet seemed to have grown to the floor. He took her inaction for defiance. She knew it when he shrugged as if it made no difference to him and reached up to release the top button of her blouse. She drew a calming breath and told herself to move. He released the second button. At the third, his fingertips brushed over the mound of her breasts, deliberately, she was certain. The way he slowed his movements, made them a caress, was a dead giveaway. The contact shocked her out of her momentary paralysis. She balled up one hand, drew back and let him have a left hook he wouldn't soon forget. When he rocked from the impact, she whirled and ran into the bedroom, slamming the door and leaning back against it. She was certain he'd come after her, and God only knew what he'd do.

Chapter 2

Nick stared at the door, rubbing his jaw. She'd surprised him more than she'd hurt him. A grudging smile tugged at the corners of his lips, and he shook his head slowly. Damned if he'd come across many men who'd slug a guy his size—let alone one who happened to be packing a 9 mm automatic. This mite of a woman didn't hesitate. She was gutsy; there was no denying it.

At least he'd managed to figure out what she reacted to. He'd been worried for a while. His gun hadn't seemed to intimidate her, or his size, or his best street-thug imitation. When he touched her, though, that was a whole other story. When he'd trailed the backs of his fingers over her breast, she'd gone three shades whiter. Her pupils had dilated until her irises vanished. Then she'd decked him. So he'd learned two valuable methods of dealing with his little Gypsy. He could intimidate her with sexual innuendo, and he'd better duck whenever he found it necessary to do so—because it scared her. He didn't imagine there were many things that did.

Nick tore his gaze from the door and glanced around the room. She'd be safe here, and no threat to his cover. He unplugged the phone, wound the cord around it and tucked it under the couch. He'd take it downstairs later, while she slept. He double-checked the door—the only way out of this hidden apartment. It could only be opened by pressing the right combination of numbered buttons on the panel beside it. A light would flash and an alarm would sound if anyone tampered with the lock, so there was no chance of her getting away.

He felt a momentary pang, but he forced it aside. It wasn't difficult. What he was doing was far too important to put it at risk just for one woman. So she'd be scared for a while. So her family would go nuts worrying about her. So what? Kids were dying every day, and Lou Taranto was as responsible for that as if he were choking the life out of them with his own fat hands. Nick's own brother... No. He wouldn't think about Danny—not now.

Too late, a voice whispered from within, and the memories crashed over his mind like a flash flood.

Nick squeezed the limp hand tighter, as though he could squeeze the life back into it. "Don't die on me, man. You're all I got, Danny, hold on. Hold on for your kid brother."

Blue eyes opened, but they were filmy—glazed. "S-sorry, Nicky... let you down... you kep' tellin' me... poison, man... poison."

Sirens screamed nearer, louder, until they tore Nick's brain apart with their noise. The wind blew like frozen death into the condemned, rat-infested heap the Cobras called their own. No one who stood there now wore the colors. Danny's "brothers" had run off, and left him

there to die alone. Nick didn't know what kind of gar-
bage Danny had OD'ed on, but he knew where it had
come from. He reached down to brush an auburn tangle
from Danny's forehead. Danny had all the Irish blood in
him, from their mother. Fiona had walked out two years
ago—just left. They didn't need her, though. They had
each other. Nick was the image of their father, but he
didn't want to be. A. J. Manelli was doing eight to fif-
teen in Attica. They didn't need him, either.

"Help's here, Danny. You hear me?" There were voices
and thundering feet now. Flashing lights bathed the still
face in color. Red and blue. The cops were here, too, then.
Nick felt the dampness on his cheeks and swiped it away.
"They're here, Dann-o. It's gonna be okay. You'll be
fine—home in time for your eighteenth. We'll party like
we planned. It's gonna be okay."

Only it wasn't.

Nick shook himself free of the rage he'd felt in the
months following Danny's death. He'd blamed the gang,
but he'd only been sixteen then. Street smart but naive.
Those kids, he learned later, had been just like Danny.
Young, cocky, following the pack. It was the filth responsible for bringing the drugs into the country—into the
streets—who ought to pay.

"And pay he will," Nick muttered. "If it causes an in-
convenience to one sloe-eyed spitfire, well that's just too
damn bad."

He realized that water was running into the tub. She was
going to take that hot bath he'd suggested. He frowned.
He hadn't expected her to comply quite so easily. Maybe
he'd scared her more than he thought. He told himself
that was a good thing. She'd be more cooperative, and a
hell of a lot less trouble, if she were afraid of him. God
help him if she ever got it in her head that he was all bark

and no bite. She was cocky enough as it was. She wouldn't be, though, if she had a clue about how much trouble she was in. Nobody—*nobody*—eyeballed Viper and lived to tell. That Lou Taranto had trusted Nick enough to send him along on one of Viper's hits was the best thing that had happened since Nick had come in. To think it had all nearly gone to hell because some dusky Latin beauty happened to be in the wrong place at the wrong time!

Nick's stomach growled, and he glanced at his watch. Midnight, and he hadn't had a bite since lunch. He wondered briefly whether she'd had dinner tonight. He shook his head and shrugged. It didn't matter to him if she was hungry or not.

The water gurgling and splashing into the bathtub covered any noise she might have made scrounging for items she could use to defend herself, if it came to that. She'd found nothing. Not a can of hair spray—he obviously wasn't the hair-spray type—or even a razor blade. The jerk used an electric one. It lay beside the basin, still dusted in tiny black hairs.

She stared at the shaver and frowned. Why in the world would he have shaved in here this morning? Third floor, hidden-away apartment tucked behind a wall in a mansion fit for a king. Why use this bathroom? She pondered if for a long moment, then had to hurry to shut off the water. The tub was nearly brimming.

Steam curled from the surface, and she had to admit it was tempting. There wasn't a muscle on her person that didn't ache from running, struggling with him or riding in his trunk. She was chilled to the bone, and her feet hurt. She regarded the bathroom door, its lock and its keyhole. She had no doubt he had a key. She'd been in here quite some time already, and he hadn't bothered her yet.

The robe that hung from the hook on the door was black velour. It probably came to his knees, but on her it would hover around her ankles. Still, it looked plush and inviting. Biting her lip, she turned the lock. She took a big towel from the pile in the closet and placed it within easy reach. At least she'd have something to cover up with if he decided to come barging in. She peeled off her wet blouse, shimmied out of her skirt and stockings. She exhaled as she sunk into the soothing heat.

The warmth seeped into her, easing her knotted muscles and chasing the chill away. She leaned her head back. She'd needed this, she realized as her eyes closed. Time to calm herself, assess her situation and begin to plan.

"I'm being held prisoner by a hit man," she mused very softly in case her overgrown ruffian was listening. "So obviously my first priority is staying alive. Ranks right up there with finding a way to escape."

She sunk until her head was submerged, soaking her hair. When she resurfaced she reached for the bottle of shampoo. It wasn't a new bottle, as you'd be likely to find in a seldom-used guest room. It was half-empty. She allowed that information to take up residence in her brain for possible future use.

"The question is, do I really want to escape? When am I going to get this close to the mob again? This is a research opportunity like nothing I've ever had."

Her last tell-all book, sold under the guise of fiction, had blown the whistle on several key members of a Colombian drug cartel. Government officials who, for one reason or another, had been dragging their feet on the investigation had been forced to act. Her sources for the book had all been genuine, her information checked to the last detail. She'd changed the names of the players but she'd made sure the people who mattered could guess the true identities. Of course, the story revolved around ex-KGB operative turned American agent, Katrina Chekov. All her books revolved around Katrina. The last two had hit bestseller lists nationwide.

"And this one will be the topper," she mused aloud. "Katrina infiltrates the Taranto crime family." She almost laughed. If Mr. Macho out there had any idea it was Toni Rio soaking in his tub, he'd probably have a stroke. Rumors about the subject matter of her next book were rampant, and the mob was getting nervous. Luckily Toni had always protected her identity. She accepted telephone interviews only, and everything else was handled through her agent. If her face became familiar, she'd never be able to move in the right circles and get the information she needed to make her books authentic. In a way, she *was* Katrina.

She shook her head. She'd like to be Katrina. Katrina had the courage to do things Toni could never do. While Toni snooped and eavesdropped behind the scenes, Katrina stormed the front gates and faced whatever was behind them. While Toni dreamed of finding the perfect man and having a home and a family, Katrina dressed in slinky gowns and seduced dangerous rogues. Katrina had all the courage Toni lacked. If Katrina had been Tito's daughter, she would never have watched in stunned silence as her father was slowly destroyed. She'd have done something about it.

Toni blinked her guilt away and rinsed the soap from her hair and face. It had trickled into her eyes and it burned. She ignored the impulse to rehash it all and relist all the things she should have done and failed to do. It was too late for that.

She needed to concentrate now on the matter at hand. Being who she was and what she was, she probably ought to stay and consider this a golden opportunity. She swallowed hard and thought again about the man in the next room. She was afraid. Hiding fear was something at which she'd become adept, but she felt it as much as anyone else. Maybe more so. She wished, not for the first time, that she had a fraction of Katrina's pluck.

She rinsed her hair again, just for good measure. It was so long and thick it required extra care. She leaned back against the cool porcelain to think. It didn't look as if she *could* get out of here at the moment. She would escape at the first opportunity, though. She couldn't write the book if she were dumped off a bridge somewhere. Even if the giant in the other room had decided to let her live, that could change in a heartbeat if he ever found out who she was. So, while there might be a good measure of cowardice in her decision, there was at least an equal measure of practicality.

In the meantime, she decided, there was no reason not to keep her eyes and ears alert. As long as she was stuck here, she might as well get something out of it. And she couldn't do that by cowering in a corner and shaking like a wet dog.

When the water began to cool, she stepped out, patted herself dry and pulled on the oversize robe. The sleeves were too long, and she had to keep pushing them up while she rinsed her underwear in the basin. The stockings were beyond help. She was arranging her panties on the towel rack to dry when he knocked on the door. She only glanced toward it and scowled, but he thumped again.

"Antonia? Did you drown yourself in there?"

She lip-synced his words back at him and hopped onto the counter to wait. It would be a good idea to know for certain if he had a key to this room. She heard him swear and move away after he pounded once more. Seconds later he returned and maneuvered a key into the lock. He flung the door open, saw her sitting there and frowned.

Toni tried not to show her disappointment. She tossed her wet hair over her shoulder, slid down to the floor and moved past him. He was behind her a second later. His hand touched her elbow, and she resisted the urge to pull it away. There was no sense in letting him see how intimidated she was by his touch—how it reminded her of his size and strength. He propelled her into the kitchenette, where a pedestal table held two plates of food. He waved to one of them, and warning prickles raced one another up her spine.

Steak oozed juices and columns of delicious steam. Plump baked potatoes rested beside the meat, and small dishes overflowing with leafy green salad completed his offering. He moved to the refrigerator and stood in front of it, holding the door open. "I have Italian, ranch or Catalina."

Right. And he expected her to buy into this?

"I'm not hungry."

He closed the fridge, a bottle in his hand, and turned to frown at her. "At least try the salad."

Toni's gaze slid from his tiger-striped one to the bowls on the table. "You must think I'm an idiot." She prayed her false bravado wouldn't fail her now. "Let me correct that notion for you. I won't be eating anything you push at me. You'll have to think of something more original." There was a numbing certainty in her mind that he'd put more than salad into the bowl reserved for her.

He stared for a moment before he understood. "You think I poisoned it, don't you?"

Her cold, level voice deserted her. She couldn't come up with a fitting rejoinder. A sickening mass writhed in the pit of her stomach when she thought of how easily she could have simply sat down and dug in. This was like walking blind through a pit of cobras. She'd have to watch her every step.

"I don't quite know how to get this through your head, Antonia, but I brought you here to keep you alive."

That really *was* too much. Her temper came into play, and her paralyzing fear was forgotten. "You brought me here to keep me quiet, so don't try putting any noble motivations on it now. I think we might as well dispense with this bull about a couple of days, too. We both know you have to silence me permanently. A few days won't make a bit of difference unless you've figured a way to resurrect Vincent Pascorelli from the dead!"

His eyes widened. He lunged forward, one long stride bringing him to her, and he gripped her upper arms hard. "How the hell did you know his name?" He asked the question softly, but his face looked dangerous.

Toni felt her heart flip over. She'd blown it with her damn temper again, and it wasn't the first time. Now what? "I must've heard you say it to the other guy while I was playing dead."

She watched him turn that one over, trying to remember if anyone had mentioned the victim's name. She waited. He must not have been sure, because he let the matter drop. He continued holding her arms, though. "I need to know if you have a family. Anyone who's going to miss you."

She thought of her mother, and her anger flared anew. "You think I'd tell you if I did? Would you have to silence them, too?"

He released a short breath and shook his head. "You mentioned your mother. How long before she realizes you're missing?"

She eyed him and she felt her defiance oozing from every pore in her. The day she'd breathe a word about her mother to this bastard would never come.

"I don't want to silence her, Antonia. I only need to—" He broke off there, released her arms and looked at the floor. "Hell, I don't suppose I'd tell, either, if I were you." He reached for one of the salad bowls and thrust it toward her. "I'm not going to poison you, Antonia. Eat your salad."

With an angry swipe of her hand, she knocked the bowl to the floor. Cherry tomatoes, lettuce, slivers of onion and cucumber chunks littered the place like confetti. His face turned murderous. He grabbed for her again, but she was faster. She ran into the bedroom and slammed the door as she had before. He came after her this time. He threw the door open so roughly that she was knocked away from it. He stalked toward her, rage marking his every movement. He grabbed her by one arm and jerked her toward him until her chest was pressed to his. He held that arm so tight his fingers burrowed into her flesh and she winced. His other hand went to the back of her head, and he twisted a handful of her hair around his fist. He yanked once, pulling her head back. She felt tears of pain and fear burning her eyes.

Then his mouth descended. He was brutal, making sure he hurt her, forcing his tongue into her mouth. She twisted away, but another tug at her hair forced her compliance. His tongue invaded her mouth, attacking, plundering. Her lips were ground between his teeth and her own.

When he finally lifted his head away, she knew there were tears pouring down her face. She tried to check them and found she couldn't.

"Have I made my point?" He let his hand fall from her hair but still held her upper arm, forcing her to face him.

She met his triumphant gaze with tear-blurred eyes. "Oh, yes. You made your point. You are bigger than I am, therefore, you are in charge. What you say is law and I am at your mercy. Is that the point you wanted to make?" She rushed on before he could say another word, angrier than she had ever been in her life—with one exception. "Now I'll make mine. If you close your eyes in my presence, I'll slit your throat. If you lose track of your gun, I'll use it to blow your head off. If you forget to lock the bathroom door while you're bathing, you might find a toaster landing in the water beside you—plugged in. And if there *is* any poison floating around this hole, you can bet you'll be the one who ends up ingesting it. Have *I* made *my* point?"

She doubted her words had much impact, since she blurted them as she cried uncontrollably. He released her arm, shook his head in exasperation and turned toward the door. "Get some sleep," he muttered. "I'll spend the night on the couch." He turned and left her standing there, feeling as if she really could carry out those ridiculous threats she'd hurled at him. She felt she could wring his neck with her bare hands, if she could get them around it.

Nick went to the table and attempted to eat, but the little witch had ruined his appetite. She was being about as uncooperative as was humanly possible and she was only hurting herself. His little show of aggression had scared her into submission—for a moment. His lips thinned and his stomach twisted when he recalled the sight of twin rivers of tears burning down her face. He'd scared her, all right. He'd terrified her, acted like a crazed maniac, made her fear and despise him. He had no doubt she'd meant what she'd said. She might very well try to slit his throat in his sleep, if he gave her the chance.

He sawed off a piece of steak and speared it with his fork. "Good, let her hate me. That's just the way I want it." He lifted the fork to his lips and paused. He threw it down in disgust. He rose and took two steps toward the bedroom door, then stopped himself. What am I going to do, go back in there and apologize? he asked himself. Tell her I'm not the bastard she thinks I am? "You have me all wrong, lady. I'm a *nice* slime bag." Right.

He *could* just tell her the truth.

Nick shook his head the minute that notion popped into it. No way. He was already beginning to wonder if her appearance earlier had been an accident. That alley wasn't in what he'd call a good neighborhood. So what was she doing there? How had she known Vinnie's name? She sure as hell hadn't heard it from him, and he knew she hadn't been close enough to see the man's face. He couldn't have mentioned the name. It was too well-known, had been plastered all over the papers since Vinnie had been busted on a trumped-up racketeering charge. The D.A. had put a scare into Vinnie, leaned on him until he'd agreed to testify against Lou Taranto. Then at the last minute, Vinnie the songbird had changed his tune. There wasn't a person in the city who couldn't guess why. Lou had got to Vinnie while he was inside. Lou scared Vinnie a little more than the D.A. did. Vinnie recanted. The D.A.'s bluff was called. He'd never had a stand-up case against Vinnie to begin with, so he'd turned him loose. Then Lou sent his top hitter to repay Vinnie for his loyalty. By the time Nick got to the alley to witness the hit, Vinnie was dead.

Nick remembered the fear in Antonia's face when she'd seen Viper level his gun at her. That had been Nick's first glimpse of her, standing in the rain, pale with fear and revulsion. No wonder she didn't want to eat. If he could guarantee the food was safe, she probably wouldn't be able to eat it.

Two hours later the light flashed near the door. Nick flicked on the big-screen monitor, reminding himself to hide the remote control when he was finished. The screen lit, giving him a view of the front gate and the pizza truck parked beyond it. Joey stood beside the truck, pressing the button there.

Antonia was asleep. Nick had peered in a few moments ago. He depressed the button on the speaker and spoke softly. "Yeah?"

"Pizza delivery, Mr. Manelli."

"Extra anchovies, kid?"

"Sausage and mushrooms, just like you ordered."

He'd given the right answer. Joey was alone. Nick used another button to open the gate and watched the monitor as the truck lumbered through and stopped near the front door. Nick used the remote to switch the view on the screen to that of the foyer as Joey came inside.

When Nick let him into the apartment a few moments later, Joey tossed the pizza box on a table and glared at him. "I knew you wanted him bad, Nick, but not this bad. How could you do it? She was just..." He swallowed hard and looked toward the ceiling. "She was such a little thing." He closed his eyes, cleared his throat. "The suits are gonna have a ball with this one, Nick."

"Then you were there," Nick asked.

"Vacant room over the bar. I saw the whole thing go down." His gaze was accusing. "I never thought you had it in you—"

Nick pressed a finger to his lips, and Joey instantly went silent. He glanced around as if he expected to see Fat Lou himself emerge from the shadows with an Uzi. Nick walked to the bedroom door, opened it slightly and looked through. Antonia lay on his bed with the covers pulled protectively up to her chin. Her hair spilled over his pillow, completely hiding it from view. Her thick black lashes touched her cheeks. He stood back and allowed Joey to peer through the crack in the door. Joey pulled back in shock, and Nick closed the door again, urging his friend away from it.

"What did you *do?*"

Nick sat on the couch, stretching his legs out fully and tipping his head back. "The only thing I could do. You didn't really think I'd shoot an innocent bystander, did you?"

"What was I supposed to think when I saw it with my own eyes?"

Nick shrugged. "She *was* convincing, wasn't she?"

"What, you just told her to fake it and she did?"

Nick didn't want to relive the tense moment. "I told her I'd kill her if she didn't."

"And she just came here with you? How much did you have to tell her?"

Nick's head came up. "I didn't tell her anything, Joey. She already knows too much. She saw Viper."

Joey paled visibly. "I was afraid of that. It's as good as her death warrant, you know that, Nick."

"Exactly. I brought her here because I had no choice. If I didn't have one, how the hell could I give her one?"

"You kidnapped her!"

Nick winced at the term. "I'm trying real hard to think of it as protective custody."

Joey shook his head, got up and went to the refrigerator. He took out two beers, tossed one to Nick and popped the top on his own. "Man, I'm relieved. I thought you finally went over the edge." Joey took a long drink from the can. "So do you think Lou trusts you, or was it a test?"

"No way to tell, although if anyone identifies Viper to the local cops in the near future, you can bet my body won't be found for months."

"You know how many people that bastard's killed, Nick?"

Nick nodded slowly. "I know. I want him put away as badly as you do. Now that I've been at the actual scene of a hit, I can give sworn testimony and take Viper out of commission. But we have to let him have his head a while longer if we want to take Taranto out, too." Nick sat a little straighter. "How's your part in the drama coming along?"

"I'm still just a flunky, running errands for the big boys. I did wrangle an invitation to a poker game tomorrow night at the Century. Word is there's something big coming up. I hope I can find out what."

Nick frowned at the news. The Century was Lou Taranto's nightclub—a place where most of the patrons were mob players and prostitutes. Private rooms were commonly set aside for invitation-only poker games. Every employee in the club was drop-dead loyal to the Taranto family. "I don't like it, Joey. You'd have no backup. What if something goes wrong?"

"What do you think I am, a rookie? I've been at this as long as you have. You know damn well the bureau's got guys watching Lou's place twenty-four hours a day, snapping cameras and taking down names. An extra plain-brown wrapper parked out front won't raise any eyebrows. Lou's so used to having them around he sends out sandwiches sometimes. They don't worry him any. I had Harry assign somebody. All they know is that if they see somebody stand in the window and light a cigarette, they raid the place. Bust everyone inside, me included, on a gambling charge."

"But the surveillance guys won't know there's a Fed inside," Nick said.

"They don't need to know, Nick. That's the drill."

Nick shook his head. "I still don't like it." He saw the determination in his friend's face and sighed. "At least you'll have a way out."

"Right. Now, what are we gonna do about the girl?"

It was just like Joey to change the subject rather than risk an argument. "I'm keeping her here," Nick told him.

"Not a smart move, my friend."

"Smarter than letting her go. The second she was spotted, Viper would kill her."

Joey sighed. "You're right on that count. If he knew she was alive, a whole army couldn't protect her from that bastard. But, God, Nick, how long can you keep her here?"

"As long as I have to." Nick frowned at a small noise from the bedroom. He met Joey's glance, his eyes conveying the message. Was she up and listening? They'd kept their voices low, and Nick wasn't concerned about his cover. Still, it wouldn't hurt to buy some insurance. His voice only slightly louder, he added, "I just hope she's not foolish enough to try and escape. She'd be digging her own grave."

Toni didn't close her eyes after that. She couldn't believe she'd managed to fall asleep in the first place, knowing he was just in the next room. All she had to do was think of him to feel his mouth possessing hers again— the way he'd thrust his tongue halfway down her throat. He'd enjoyed showing off his physical power over her. The truth was, she was glad he'd done it. There had been

odd moments when she'd actually found herself thinking
he was attractive, admiring his size and the hardness of his
body. Of course, she hadn't allowed such thoughts to linger. For all she knew, he was a killer. She knew she
wouldn't be bothered by the idea that the man was anything but repulsive from here on in. He couldn't have
done anything to turn her off more.

She pushed all of this analysis aside and tried to guess
who had been speaking to him just now. She'd been
roused from sleep by a man's deep laughter and she'd
quickly pressed her ear to the door. She'd heard Joey's
question, "What are we going to do about the girl?"

And the answer: "I'm keeping her here."

Nick. Joey had called her captor Nick. Then she heard
both men remark on her abbreviated life expectancy
should she be discovered by Viper. Was Nick telling the
truth, then, when he said he'd brought her here to keep
her alive? More likely to keep himself alive, she thought
glumly. He would be a marked man if Viper ever learned
of his little deception. Neither of them mentioned killing
her. She supposed she could take that as a good sign. And
the bit at the end about digging her own grave had obviously been tacked on for her benefit.

A few minutes later there had been absolute silence.
Either Nick had left her alone or he was asleep. She was
too afraid to open the door to find out which was the case,
so she went back to the bed, where she still lay, wide
awake, in the morning.

She knew she was a wreck when Nick flung the door
open. Her eyes were sore and felt puffy. Her head ached
from lack of sleep and nervous tension. All things con-
sidered, she'd had better mornings.

He stepped into the bedroom with a flash of straight
white teeth in that tanned face and a tray of food in his

hands. Toni sat up, clutched the robe tighter and watched him warily. His eyes scanned her face, and his smile vanished.

"You didn't sleep?"

"Did you really think I would?" She injected all the venom she could into the words.

Instead of getting angry, he only frowned harder and put the tray down on the bedside stand. When he sat on the edge of the bed, she intended to slide right out the other side, but he gripped her wrist, his hand capturing hers with the speed of a cobra striking. "You look awful."

"Sorry. Being kidnapped has that effect on me."

"More like no sleep and nothing to eat."

"Who's to blame for that?"

"Look, I'm trying to be friendly," he snapped. "Why don't you lighten up? I brought you breakfast in bed. How bad can I be?"

"I've already told you, I won't eat anything you bring me." She said it louder than she needed to, but the aromas coming from the tray were too cruel to bear.

"Use your head, Antonia. I could think of a hundred more practical methods of killing you than poison."

"That makes you an expert, doesn't it?" She averted her face to avoid the tempting scents. "Take it away."

"Maybe you think it's something other than poison. Is that it?" He caught her face in his hands and turned her until she faced him. "You think I dropped a tranquilizer in there? Think I want to knock you out and have my way with you?" She felt her cheeks blazing and tried to pull free of him, but he held her still and smiled.

"You are a bastard," she said slowly, enunciating each syllable.

"You may be right." He let go of her face. "But at least I've figured out a way you can eat." He pulled the tray of food nearer the edge of the stand. She couldn't resist looking. The brown sausage links and fluffy yellow eggs pummeled her senses. Her stomach rumbled and he laughed. "What would you say to a brief truce? Just long enough to eat breakfast?"

She glanced at him, her eyes narrow with distrust. He took a sausage and brought it to his lips, his eyes fastened to hers. He took a bite from the end. She couldn't look away as he chewed, swallowed, licked his lips. He held the same piece of sausage to her lips. "Eat, Antonia. You're hungry and you know it."

Ignoring her pride, she parted her lips and let him push the sausage between them. She took a bite. He smiled and she realized she was staring at him instead of the food. He was so different this morning, speaking softly and using good grammar rather than that horrible speech he'd used last night. His face was relaxed, not hard and scowling. His hair wasn't wet or slicked back as it had been, but dry and thick and wavy, with a shine to it that rivaled a mink. He wore a faded pair of jeans and an ordinary T-shirt—clothes that accentuated the well-developed muscles underneath.

He took another bite of the sausage and held the last tiny piece in his fingers. He pushed it into her mouth, and when she took it, her lips closed around his fingertips. A jolt shot through her at the sensuality of the contact, and she didn't miss the dark intensity in his eyes.

He looked away quickly, scooped eggs onto a slice of toast, folded it and took a bite. He handed it to her this time. He didn't try to feed her from his hands again.

Toni was famished, and more grateful to him than she cared to admit for thinking of a way to show her the food was safe. She shouldn't be. It was his fault she had to be suspicious of everything he said or did. She ate everything on the tray, always careful that he tasted first. She even made him sip her coffee after she'd spooned sugar into it. He grimaced but he sipped. He drank his own black and sugarless, she noted.

"This is much better," he said, relaxing now and sipping his coffee. "I think we got off on the wrong foot last night, Antonia. This will work out better if you think of yourself as my guest. I promise I won't keep you here a day longer than necessary."

She was shocked at his easy, almost friendly tone. "It isn't that simple. There's my mo—" She stopped herself.

"Your mother," he finished. He drew a breath and released it slowly. "I wish I could do something about it, but I can't."

"She'll be so worried." Antonia saw the compassion in his face and pressed him. "Couldn't I send her a note— tell her I've gone away—"

He shook his head. "She'll have you back alive. It's the best I can do. Sorry."

"Not the best you can do, only the best you will do, you lousy—"

"Nick," he told her. "It's Nick Manelli. Save yourself the effort of thinking up all those lovely nicknames, okay?"

He drained his cup, stood and left the room. When he returned he carried a large green plastic trash bag. "I brought you some things to make your stay a little more bearable." He dropped the bag in the center of the floor. "If I've forgotten anything, let me know and I'll do my best to get it for you." He stepped back into the living room and closed the door.

Curious, Toni got up and looked inside the bag. She drew back in shock. Her own clothes lay in neatly folded stacks. Her purse rested on top. Gaping and gulping air as her rage mounted, she flung open the door and charged him.

"You arrogant bastard! You broke into my apartment last night! You—"

He held up one hand, flat palmed. "Ah-ah-ah, I did not break in. I had a key. It was in your purse along with the address. If you recall, you dropped it last night when I, uh, shot you. The least I could do was get some of your things for you. It was no trouble. You don't need to thank me."

"Thank you! Thank you? I—"

"You're welcome, Antonia. I knew you'd appreciate it. Of course, I am beginning to think I shouldn't have bothered bringing a robe. You couldn't possibly look better in it than you do in mine." His gaze moved heatedly down her body.

In her fury, Toni hadn't tightened the cord. The robe hung loose to her waist, and the inner swell of her breasts had caught his gaze. She tugged the cord tight and moved toward him. "You are the lowest, most vile, son of a—" She'd lifted her hand in preparation as she spoke, but he grabbed it in midswing.

One ruthless tug, and she was flat against him. "Since I've already demonstrated what happens when you lose that hot little temper of yours, I can only conclude you want more of it."

Her eyes focused on his lips, and her anger began to turn to fear. "Thanks for reminding me what scum you are, Manelli. For a second there I thought you might have some crumb of decency."

"Never think that, Gypsy, because I don't. Push me too far, and you'll find that out." His eyes blazed down into hers, and Toni waited, trying not to let the moisture spring into her eyes.

Chapter 3

The tears were his undoing. She didn't let any spill over; she was too proud to do that a second time. He saw them all the same. They formed glistening pools that made her black eyes into rare and exotic gems. Something inside him came alive, and Nick dropped his arms and turned away, shoving one hand through his hair.

"I am doing my level best to make this easy on you, lady, but if you want it rough, make no mistake, I can make it rough." His voice was unnaturally gritty. He didn't care. He only knew he had to get away from her right now. He blocked her view of the panel with his body as he punched the numbers in. He went through the door without looking back once and he closed it hard behind him.

He just stood for a second on the other side. What the hell had just happened in there?

He went back over the confrontation in his mind, trying to pinpoint the moment when the tide had turned.

He'd been ready to kiss her cruelly, just to show her that she shouldn't be trying to slap a guy his size every time she got her dander up. He'd almost done it. But when he'd had her there, crushed against him, and he'd looked down to see her storm-tossed eyes, something had slammed into him. He'd felt her heart thudding inside her and had been suddenly, acutely aware of his own, pounding right back. He'd heard her short, choppy breaths, and his own caught in his throat. Her scent wafted up, enveloping him until he was aware of nothing else—only her. If he hadn't stepped away from her at the moment he had, he knew damn well what would have happened and he was not one bit happy about it. He would have kissed her—and not the way he'd kissed her last night.

In his soul, he knew he'd have slipped his arms around her until he could cradle her head in his hands. He could imagine the feel of all those silken, raven curls tangling around his fingers. He'd have tasted her lips first, drawing them between his own like he might a succulent cherry. He wouldn't have bruised them this time. He'd have worshipped them. He'd have—

Nick groaned and forced her golden skin and wild black mane from his mind. She must've lied about being Puerto Rican. She truly was a Gypsy. An elusive Gypsy enchantress capable of casting powerful spells over men. At least, over him. What was he supposed to do with her for the rest of the time he had to keep her here?

He shouldn't be having this problem. He'd worked in close proximity to some gorgeous women in the past. He'd *never* had a problem. He'd always been perfectly able to take them or leave them. Never had he felt so close to losing it—as though he'd been shoved off a cliff and was scrambling for a branch to keep from falling.

"Chemistry," he mumbled. "Major chemistry." He turned from the bookcase door and stalked down to the second floor and the master bedroom. Since she'd cycloned into his life, he'd had to use the bedroom often. Before, he'd only done so often enough to make it appear lived-in. He'd have to force himself to keep her out of his thoughts for the rest of the morning. Lou Taranto and Viper would be here to see him, and he'd damn well better be on his toes.

If sending him to witness the hit had been a test of Nick's loyalty, he'd soon find out whether he'd passed. If he'd been sent because Lou trusted him, he'd learn that, too. He grimaced as the third possibility entered his mind. If Viper or Lou had any idea that Antonia was still breathing, Nick would be a dead man in the next few minutes.

Joey knows she's in the apartment upstairs, he thought grimly. If anything happens, he'll come for her.

Still, his own particular preference was that nothing happen. He peeled his shirt over his head and tossed it carelessly as he moved into the adjoining bathroom for a shower. Despite his decision to keep her out of his thoughts, he recalled his late-night visit to her apartment as he stood beneath the pounding spray. He hadn't learned a lot. He'd had to get in and get out as quickly as possible and do it without being seen. His reasons for taking her things had been twofold. He wanted her to have everything she needed and he couldn't afford to be seen buying women's clothing and toiletries in a store. That was the first reason. The second was her mother. While it was necessary that the woman act worried about her daughter's disappearance, Nick had to give the poor woman something to cling to. With enough of Antonia's belongings missing, she could believe her daughter had simply gone away for a few days. The sickening worry could be put off for a little longer. It wasn't much, but it was the best he could do.

The apartment was nice, but not exactly spic and span. There had been a day-old newspaper spread on the counter that separated living room and kitchen. A stained coffee cup sat there, as well as a cereal bowl with the spoon still inside. A couple of blouses and a slip were slung over the back of the brocade sofa. Antonia wouldn't win any housekeeping awards, he thought.

Nick moved quickly to the bedroom to get the clothes she'd need. He found the bed made, but haphazardly. The comforter was neat, but the sheets underneath showed bumps and bulges. He took an empty suitcase from her closet but didn't bother packing it. It was faster to drop the clothes into the trash bag he'd brought along. Taking the suitcase was just to make her impromptu vacation a little more believable. He took the book she'd been reading, too.

He moved into the bathroom, where she'd left a damp towel slung crookedly on a rack and a pair of silk stockings hanging over the shower-curtain rod. He took her toothbrush and everything else she might conceivably need. As he left he noted a door he hadn't seen before, probably another bedroom. It wouldn't hurt to check, though. He tried the knob, but it didn't give. He frowned. Why keep a spare bedroom locked? He would have pursued the matter, but the sound of the telephone split the silence like an ax splitting a melon. It bleeped again, and Antonia's voice filled the apartment, so low and sexy it was as if she were in the room.

". . . can't come to the phone right now. Leave a message and I'll get back to you.''

Nick listened. Maybe he'd learn something about Antonia after all. A woman's voice came clearly.

"Antonia, my dear, sweet girl, if you do not call me the minute you get in I am coming over there. I loved reading about Katrina's latest. Can't wait to see what that vixen will be up to next." There was a long pause. "I love you, honey. I'm worried, it isn't like you to stay out so late." The woman sighed. "Call me." The line went silent, and Nick continued to stare at the machine.

I love you, honey.

Her mother. It had to have been her mother.

I love you.

Nick braced himself against the rush of scalding pain that threatened to crush his chest. It didn't matter. He was a grown man, not a little boy craving three meaningless words from an ice-hearted parent. It didn't matter.

He'd forgotten about the locked room and hurried to get out of the apartment. He refused to think of the message on the machine, except for the part about Katrina. Who was she?

But he couldn't spend any more time dwelling on this. He twisted the knobs, stopping the water flow, and stepped out. After toweling down, he dressed in one of the detestable three-piece suits and combed his hair back while it was still wet. Personally he thought it made him look as though he were stuck in a time warp, but he did it anyway. It was part of the image.

Toni paced the small living room and wondered if he was deliberately trying to confuse her. He'd been about to deliver another rapacious kiss, bruising her lips and devastating her mind. She'd seen it in his face—but then it had changed. He'd softened visibly. His painful hold on her had eased until it was an embrace. The anger in his eyes vanished, and the emotion that had taken its place, for the tiniest space in time, had looked like desire.

How would she have responded, she wondered, if his kiss had been tender, given in a passion based on desire rather than one based on anger?

Insane! Even the idea was insane. She wouldn't let herself think about it again. It was obvious that he was playing some kind of mind game with her—trying to convince her that, though he worked for the most powerful criminal in the state, maybe the country, he was really just a nice guy. Why else would he have taken the couch and let her have the bed, or hand-fed her just so she wouldn't go hungry? It was a ploy to confuse her—and it was working, she realized.

She forced the overdeveloped jerk out of her thoughts. Let him be as nice or as mean as he wanted. It wouldn't matter to her one way or the other. She occupied her mind fully with unpacking her clothes and finding places to stow them in the bedroom. She squashed his things to one side of the dresser drawers, trying but failing to picture him in the brilliant-colored tank tops she found there. She shoved his three-piece suits to the back corner of the closet and hung some of her blouses and sweaters in front of them. She glimpsed a pair of high-topped basketball shoes with neon laces in them and shook her head. They clashed with her image of him. She shouldn't be surprised, though. Anyone built the way he was obviously worked out to get that way. She hadn't thought about it before. There was a whole other side to Nick Manelli, associate to the mob. Toni's curiosity was thoroughly aroused. She chided herself for wasting time unpacking clothes when she should have been giving this place a complete checking out. Who knew what kinds of things the guy was hiding?

Dragging a chair nearer the closet, she stood on it to see what was on the top shelf. At first she noticed only a couple of spare blankets and a well-worn basketball. Then she poked around a bit, moving things, and her fingers met something hard. A photograph in a frame, she realized as she pulled it down.

She sat on the chair and studied the faded black-and-white snapshot. A man, a woman and two small boys smiled back at her. The woman seemed young and happy, and the boy on her lap resembled her more than a little. But it was the man who caught her attention. He was the image of her captor, in every way except one. He didn't have muscle bulging from every possible locale. She let her gaze move down to the little boy in the man's lap, and she knew she was looking at Nick. He couldn't have been more than six years old, with a wide grin and a tooth missing. His hair was a riot of dark curls beneath his father's hand.

She felt a lump form in her throat. How did an adorable child like that grow into a common criminal?

She was allowing herself to become distracted again. She stood and quickly replaced the photo, then completed her examination of the bedroom, noting little of interest except the twelve-inch portable TV. Why have two televisions in an apartment this small?

In the living room, the first thing she looked over carefully were the rows of books. It hadn't occurred to her to wonder if any of hers were among them, but it did now. Her heart was in her throat as she scanned the spines on the two shelves along the wall. Not that he could recognize her just because he'd read her book. It just made her uncomfortable to think he might have one here. As it turned out, he didn't. She sighed her relief and frowned. There was one small area where the books were not pushed back to the wall. A space had been left behind them. She had to stand on a chair once again, and in seconds she pulled a slender remote control from behind the books.

Why on earth would anyone hide their remote? She got down, pointed the thing at the television, noting for the first time the absence of any buttons or switches on the set itself. The image that lit the screen was even more confusing: a tall iron gate, standing motionless on a twisting drive. She stared, blinked slowly, and then the truth hit her. It was no TV; it was a closed-circuit monitor—probably hooked up to the camera she'd noticed in the bear's head, as well as several others. She tested her theory by hitting various buttons. Just as she'd suspected, each button gave her a view of another room within the mansion.

"He must have a camera hidden in every room," she whispered, still flicking one button after another. She stopped short when she saw the living room, with the black leather furniture and marble-topped bar. Nick stood at the bar, pouring whiskey into crystal glasses. He was, once again, the gangster she'd seen in the alley last night. He wore a dark suit, minus the jacket. His hair was tamed down. His stance, his very expression, were different than when he'd been here in the apartment.

Beyond him she saw Viper, his beady eyes darting constantly in his puckered little face. He stood near a fat man with white hair and flabby jowls. Toni knew him. She would have known him anywhere. Lou Taranto. She glanced at the remote in her hand, located the volume button and pressed it. She could listen to them, as well.

Nick forced a smile for his guests, but it felt stiff. All he seemed able to think about was that Antonia was upstairs at this very moment. Having Viper this close to her sent a chill through him, right to the marrow. He splashed Jack Daniel's into three glasses, despite the early hour, and handed them each one. Lou took his and held it up.

"To new associates."

Nick clinked his glass to Lou's. Viper didn't, he noted. Viper wasn't thrilled with new associates in the least. He was cautious. More so than Lou. Nick looked at him and felt the same bristle of aversion he'd felt from their first encounter. Trying to avoid becoming this man's enemy was essential if he were going to get the evidence he needed to put Lou away. It was also the toughest thing he'd ever done.

"You get Vinnie dumped okay?" Nick slipped back into his street-tough pattern of speech.

"No problem." Viper took a slug of the whiskey and smacked his lips.

Lou shifted from one foot to the other.

"Somethin' wrong, Lou?"

"The girl," Lou answered, his words clipped. "Where'd you dump her?"

"She's in the bay." Nick tried not to show his reaction to the question. Did they know something? "I weighted her. She won't turn up for months. Maybe never."

Lou nodded, looking fractionally easier. "Who was she?"

Nick shrugged as if it didn't matter.

"Dammit, Nicky, didn't she have any ID on her? Didn't you check?"

Nick took a long pull from his glass. The less Lou knew about Antonia, the better. "Didn't think it was important. She saw us, she had to go. There was no time to check her out before I hit her, and after it didn't seem to matter. Dead's dead, Lou."

Lou grunted and didn't say anything. Nick felt a cold finger of unease trace the curve of his spine. Finally Lou sipped his whiskey and sat down, his substantial weight noisily crushing the leather cushions. "Viper tells me Vinnie went down easy. You agree?"

"Viper didn't wait for me. It was a done deal by the time I got there."

"But you're sure it was Vinnie? You took a look at his face before it was . . . altered?"

"Sure did, Lou. No mistake. Vinnie the songbird in the flesh."

"He won't be singing anymore," Viper put in. He laughed aloud, and Lou did, as well. Nick forced himself to join in.

"What about the body?" Lou drained his glass, got up with an effort and refilled it without asking. He was speaking to Nick.

"Lou, I couldn't watch the dumping. I had to get the girl the hell outta there. Someone had already called the cops."

"You don't need to send witnesses on my jobs, Lou," Viper snapped. "You know I always come through. Vinnie's feedin' fish."

Lou nodded, still standing. "Let's hope he's a lesson to the next rat who thinks of squeaking to the D.A." Nick raised his glass and nodded heartily. He downed the rest of the whiskey in a slug that burned a path down the center of his chest.

Lou cleared his throat. "Things'll be hot in the city for a while—as soon as they miss Vinnie."

"It isn't like they didn't know what they were doing when they sprung him, Lou. Every official in office knew you'd order Vinnie snuffed. They didn't care. He wouldn't give the testimony he promised, so they just didn't care. And they call us the criminals." It was the longest speech Viper had ever made in Nick's presence. The worst part was, he was right.

"Sure, but no one's gonna admit that. It would be political suicide. Besides, it gives 'em a great excuse to hassle me. When did you know 'em to pass one up?" Lou shook his head, frowning. "At least it's what I expected. I don't like surprises. That's why I'm worried about that girl. She was a surprise."

"Too bad Nick was in such a hurry to off the bitch," Viper said slowly. "I could'a made her tell me her life story." He licked his lips. "She was a looker, Lou. We could'a kep' her awhile. Partied with 'er for days before we killed her off—the way we did with that uppity hooker that tried to put the squeeze on you. Remember her? But Nick, he has a hair trigger, this guy."

Nick's jaw clenched tight, and he felt a muscle work near the corner of his mouth. He turned slowly and glared at the slime standing across from him.

Viper met the scorching gaze with one of his own. Lou was quick to step between them. "I don't think Nicky likes you findin' fault with his work." His tone made the simple statement a reprimand. He glanced at Nick. "It's okay, Nicky. I think you done good. Hell, Viper said she was off and running when you popped her. If she'd have got away, all hell would'a broke loose."

"Funny, though," Viper said, slow and confident, his snake's eyes never leaving Nick's face. "I drove by there this morning and I didn't see no blood."

"You saying she didn't bleed, Viper? Or are you saying something else?" Nick took a step closer to the little weasel, his temper approaching the boiling point.

"I'm saying I'd feel better if I had a look at her before you took off with her. How do I know she's dead? She saw my face!'' Viper stepped closer, as well, and Lou's pudgy body was wedged between them.

"Maybe you'd like a trip to the bottom of the bay, pal. Maybe you'd feel better if you saw her up close and personal.'' Nick leaned over Lou, his voice level but tight with barely controlled rage.

"Enough, already.'' Lou's command cut the tension between them, and Nick backed off. "I have enough trouble without you two going at it like a couple of punk kids.'' He nailed Viper to the spot with his gaze. "Nicky says he killed her. That's good enough for me. I don't want to hear you talk him down again.''

"You're crazy, Lou. He's not even one of us—''

"But he will be.'' That statement earned stares of disbelief from Viper and Nick. Lou turned and encircled Nick's shoulders with one beefy arm. "Next commission meeting is this weekend, Nicky. When it's over, you'll be a made man—officially.''

Viper rolled his eyes toward the ceiling and swore. He downed his whiskey and slammed his glass on the bar. "You really think the others will go for this, Lou? No way. Nick isn't proven.''

"He took the broad out.'' Lou slapped Nick's shoulder repeatedly. "For me, he did this. He acted from loyalty, and loyalty to Lou Taranto doesn't go unrewarded. You should know that.'' His arm tightened, and he grinned until his fat face puckered. "What do you say, Nicky?''

"I'm honored, Lou. I—I wasn't expecting this.''

Lou reached into a pocket and extracted an envelope that appeared stuffed to the bursting point. He pressed it into Nick's hand. "For the girl, Nicky. You done good.''

Nick accepted the money, thanked Lou, but his thanks were waved away. "I need a favor,'' Lou told him. "As I already said, things'll be hot in the city. The Century won't be practical, and we need this meeting. This place—" he waved an expressive arm to indicate the entire room "—this place would be perfect."

Nick swallowed and tried to appear bowled over with joy that the leaders of several organized crime families would be meeting here. The idea shook him. These guys were sharp. But he had no choice. You didn't thumb your nose at an offer like this. It was an honor. To refuse would be taken as a personal insult, and Viper was already suspicious of him.

"My place is yours, Lou."

"Good, then. Saturday night. And don't worry about the vote. I'll speak to the others." He gave Nick one last slap on the back, put his glass down on the bar and turned for the door without another word.

Viper glared at Nick. "Don't get too cocky, Manelli. The vote isn't over yet, and if I have anything to say about it, you'll come out on the short end."

"Lucky for me you don't have anything to say about it, then, isn't it, Viper?"

Toni fought a surge of nausea when she heard Viper talking about how he could've "made her talk." Thank God Nick had been there. She brought that thought to a grinding halt. Nick was no hero. He was only the lesser of two evils. He'd taken part in a murder. No, she corrected herself. He'd arrived in the alley after the fact, if she could believe what she'd just heard. Still, he was about to be inducted into the mob.

She watched him after the others had gone. He spun around, pushing one hand through his hair and rumpling its slick perfection. He looked stunned and more than a little bit worried. He ought to be, she thought. If those two found out what he'd done—that he'd lied to them and hadn't killed her at all—he'd be a dead man. He really *had* taken a risk in not letting Viper shoot her that night—or letting him take her alive and do far worse. There was no way she could deny it. Nick had saved her life. According to the slimy Viper, he'd saved her from more than just death—a lot more.

But why?

He moved as if deep in thought, picking up glasses, replacing the whiskey bottle, wiping the bar with a soft cloth. Toni was certain of only one thing. She wouldn't leave here now—not even if he left the doors wide open and offered her a ride to the bus station. The bosses of at least three major crime families would be meeting under this very roof. She had this wonderful setup to watch them and listen in. To turn her back on a research opportunity like this would be nothing short of pure cowardice. She turned in a slow circle. She couldn't let her lack of backbone scare her away from this. She'd leave here somehow, but after that meeting. She ought to be able to survive four more days here. Nick obviously wasn't planning to kill her. He wouldn't have risked his life to keep her alive, only to kill her later. She'd be fine as long as he never guessed who she really was.

She glanced at the screen, stiffening when she saw only an empty room. She hurriedly shut the monitor off, leapt onto the chair and replaced the remote in its unoriginal hiding place. She placed the chair exactly as it had been before and rushed into the bedroom to finish unpacking so she'd appear busy when he returned.

She pulled the last armful of things from the bag and stuffed them into an already crowded drawer. That done, she bent to pick up the bag, surprised to find there was still weight in the bottom. She bent and pulled out the last items in the bag: two brand-new spiral notebooks and her own copy of *On Being a Writer*. She'd left the book on her nightstand beside her bed.

Did he know? My God, had he been inside her office? The door was locked, but there were copies of every book she'd ever written in there—and in the safe behind the framed painting of her first cover, there was enough evidence to put Lou Taranto behind bars for the rest of his life. If he'd found it, he would kill her. There was no chance he'd do otherwise. She should have turned it over to federal authorities, she moaned inwardly. She'd known that was the thing to do, and she'd come perilously close to handing it to one man who she later learned was on Taranto's payroll. She'd been terrified to make the same mistake again.

Did Nick know now that she was Toni Rio? He must. Bringing the book and the notebooks were his way of telling her the game was over. She held the books in hands clenched tight and white knuckled.

"I found it in your bedroom." She jumped as if jolted and spun to face him.

Chapter 4

Toni stood motionless, unable to utter a word, waiting.

"Look, the truth is, you might be here for more than a few days," he went on. "I figured if you could get something out of this forced vacation—spend some time writing, if that's what you want to do—it might be easier."

She opened her mouth and closed it again, still unsure.

He shrugged. "You've got to start sometime, Antonia, or you'll never know whether you're any good."

She thought he must have felt the air currents stirring when she sighed in relief. He'd bought the notebooks so she could try her hand at writing.

Pretty nice thing for a morally bankrupt criminal to do.

He's probably still trying to confuse me, she reminded herself.

"I could've sworn you just smiled," he said slowly. "Did I finally do something right?" As he spoke, he turned toward the dresser, snagged the tie loose and tossed it down. He looked tired—drained. His gaze met hers in the mirror, and his lips curved slightly in response to her alleged smile. She caught just a trace of the whiskey's aroma clinging to him.

"I suppose, if I had to be abducted and held against my will by a two-bit hood, I could've done worse than you."

"Don't heap such extravagant compliments on me, lady. You'll swell my head."

She smirked at him, her relief that he hadn't discovered her secret making her feel easy for once in his presence.

"Before I forget again," he continued, facing her. "Who is Katrina?"

She felt the blood drain from her face. "K-Katrina... who?"

"Damned if I know. You had a message on your machine last night—a woman. She said something about wanting to know what Katrina was up to."

There were only two possibilities that crept into her mind. Her agent or her mother. She swallowed hard, wishing she could hear the rest of the message. "Katrina is, um, an old friend. I've known her since I was a little girl." That much was true. Before Katrina had developed into an ex-KGB supersleuth, she'd been the imaginary friend of a four-year-old. Later she'd been a fictional big sister Toni used to threaten bullies. She'd even had occasion to blame Katrina for her own offenses, when she'd had guts enough to commit any. "She's a rather adventuresome lady." She glanced up to see if he believed her. He seemed to be accepting what she said. "Did the caller say who—"

"I think it might have been your mother."

The air all left her lungs. Toni sunk slowly to the edge of the bed, her eyes on the floor. She'd hoped her mother wouldn't miss her right away. "Did she...did she sound worried?"

His gaze slid away from hers. "A little. For what it's worth, I took enough of your stuff to make it look like you'd gone away for a few days. If she checks, she'll think—"

"Mom knows I'd tell her if I were going away." Toni closed her eyes slowly and tried to remind herself that Kate del Rio was not exactly a fragile, elderly parent who needed protecting. In fact, if she knew where her daughter was right now, she'd probably kick the door in, grab Nick Manelli by the scruff of his neck and give him a swift kick.

"You're *that* close?" Nick's voice made it sound as if she'd just claimed the impossible.

Toni opened her eyes slowly. "She's my *mother.*" He scowled and shook his head. She had the distinct impression that he did not believe her. She could have kicked herself for the overwhelming urge to convince him, and still she found herself doing just that. "Maybe we're closer than most, but that's because we need each other. For a long time, we haven't had anyone else. But it's more than that, because we *enjoy* being together." She paused and drew a shaky breath. "She's my best friend." She sought Nick's face and found it with an expression of bewilderment, his gaze still focused on her. He was listening— *raptly.*

He pulled his gaze away and tried to sound casual. "What kinds of things do you do together?"

His voice had come out minutely tighter than before, and Toni wondered why. "Everything. We do a lot of shopping. Mom has a wonderful sense of style. We both love the theater—we saw *Phantom* three times." Toni laughed softly. "Mom loved that musical. If we get really bored, we sometimes go to a nightclub."

"With your *mother*?"

Toni realized how ridiculous that might sound to him. "You've never seen my mother. When we're together, people usually think we're sisters." She saw the skepticism clearly on his face. "You don't believe me?" She glanced around the room, spying her purse on the stand where she'd left it. She reached for it and tugged out her wallet, flipping it open and slowly turning photographs in their holders until she came to the one she wanted. Her mother smiled back at her from a smooth, unlined face with skin as tight and clear as it had been when Toni was a little girl. High cheekbones always dusted with a hint of blusher, and clear, sparkling blue eyes beneath perfectly arched brows gave her a regal appearance—but her long blond hair, curlier than Toni's was, right to the ends, softened that look with a touch of wildness.

Toni handed the wallet to Nick and had the pleasure of seeing his eyes widen. "*That's* your mother?"

"Umm-hmm."

He shook his head. "She looks great."

"She *is* great. She's been great to me, and I don't want to cause her all this worry. She's had enough grief in her life. She's going to worry herself sick about me if she doesn't hear something...." She broke off as he handed her the wallet, and looked skeptical again. "For God's sake, wouldn't *your* mother worry if you dropped off the face of the earth without a word?"

"Not only would she not worry, she wouldn't know. If she did, she wouldn't care." His voice held more bitterness than Toni could believe. He went on, his voice devoid of any emotion, his expression shuttered. "She walked out when I was thirteen, and I haven't seen her since," he said.

Toni swallowed hard, thinking of the pretty young woman in the photograph. How could she have walked out on her own son—two sons? "I didn't know. I'm sorry." She closed her wallet and dropped it back inside the purse.

"I'm not." He released the top buttons of his shirt and stalked into the living room. Toni followed.

"Then your father raised you alone?" She shouldn't be so curious about his background. She certainly didn't care. But he'd lost his mother—she'd lost her father. The only difference was, he pretended not to care.

He walked to the stereo system, chose a CD without hesitation and dropped it in. In a moment Ray Charles's voice moaned "Georgia on My Mind," and Nick sunk into a chair. He leaned back, hands behind his head, legs stretched in front of him. "Last I knew, my old man was doing eight to fifteen in Attica. He went up in sixty-nine."

"Then he should have been out almost ten years ago, shouldn't he?" Toni felt her stomach turn over. Had his father gone to prison before his mother had abandoned him or just after? She couldn't help seeing the sweet, dark-haired little boy in the photo, with his front tooth missing, and feeling the incredible hurt he must've felt then.

Nick shrugged. "I never bothered to find out."

"What was he—"

Nick's head came up. "That's enough, Antonia. I'm not up to telling you my life story, and I can't imagine why you'd want to hear it." Again he tipped his head back and folded his arms behind it.

Toni took a seat on the sofa and studied him. The tension in his body seemed to be ebbing. He'd been wound up and nervous from his encounter with Taranto when he'd first come in. Now the mellow piano and the sooth-ing voice coming from the speakers seemed to be calming him.

"You like the blues," she said, unconsciously keeping her voice low in respect for the music. "I never would have guessed."

"Relaxes me."

She shifted, feeling anything but relaxed. "Was it whoever was here before that got you all tensed up, or talking about your parents?"

He didn't move. "You don't know when to quit, do you? Okay, I'll bite. How'd you know someone was here?"

"It was a guess. I saw the red light come on, by the panel."

His head moved enough to nod. "Sharp lady."

"Are you going to tell me who it was?"

"What do you think?"

Antonia sighed and got to her feet. He'd given away all he was going to. Her stomach protested softly, and she realized it must be nearly noon. "Am I allowed to help myself to some lunch?"

He nodded. "Can you cook?"

"It is not one of my more highly developed skills. I was thinking along the lines of a sandwich or some cottage cheese." She walked to the refrigerator and scanned its contents. "Or some yogurt," she said, spying the row of containers.

"Help yourself."

Toni hesitated, then shrugged. "You want one?"

His eyes opened and focused on her. "Why not?"

She picked peaches and cream for her, strawberry ba-nana for him, located two spoons and carried them to the living room. She held the plastic cup out to him, and he took it. Their fingers touched and for a moment that seemed eternal, Toni didn't take her hand away. When she did, she felt flustered and not sure what to say.

Something had passed between them. Some unspoken agreement or understanding. He wouldn't hurt her. She'd be safe as long as she was with him. He'd been saying so all along, but she was suddenly sure of it. She didn't quite hate him anymore. She was beginning to see that there were reasons he'd become what he had—strong emotions that had shaped him into the man he was. If he was bitter, it was no wonder.

He seemed content to relax there with the music filling the room. Toni was eager to write down some of the interesting discoveries she'd made here and begin to fit them into her plot and Katrina Chekov's world. She hesitated, though. The fact remained that she was Toni Rio and her book would ruin Lou Taranto. If Nick found out, all bets were off.

She finished her yogurt. "You speak any Spanish, Nick?"

"Not a word," he said, taking his last bite. She couldn't seem to take her eyes from him as he licked the pink cream from his lips. "Although I can tell when you're swearing at me." He got up at long last, carried the cup to the kitchen sink and rinsed it. "I have to go out again. I might be a while."

Toni sighed loudly.

"Don't tell me you'll miss me." He was mocking, but not cruelly.

"In your dreams, I might." She took her cup to the sink as he had, rinsed it, then turned, leaning her back on the drain board. "I don't like being locked up here alone. There's not a window in the place, not a soul to talk to—"

"There's the stereo," he said, pointing. "There are all those books." He pointed once more. "Besides, you can use the time to do some writing. If you get sick of that, there's a TV in the bedroom—"

"What's wrong with this one?" Toni couldn't resist asking.

"Not working right now," he replied without missing a beat.

Toni chewed the inside of her lip. "If I spend every day sitting in this apartment, I'll gain twenty pounds inside a week. I run every day, for God's sake. I can't vegetate for God knows how long just because it's convenient for you."

He crossed his arms over his chest and leaned against the fridge. "Piling it on a bit, aren't you? It's only been one day."

She smirked at him. "I thought you'd understand. *You* obviously work out—"

His brows shot up. "Not much slips by you, does it?" His amusement stirred her anger, but not for long. "How about a deal?"

Her curiosity rose on its hind legs. "What kind of deal?"

"I have a gym downstairs, in the basement. You behave yourself while I'm gone, and I'll take you down there."

"When?" She sounded too eager, but she couldn't take it back now. She truly was beginning to feel like a caged animal.

"As soon as I can. But right now I have to go." Toni sighed in resignation, while his tiger-striped eyes perused her face.

He stepped closer, looked down at her, smiling slightly. "I wouldn't be averse to a kiss goodbye if you're interested."

"Since when do you ask permission?" She tried to make her answer sting, but her eyes went to his full lips the minute he asked the question.

He shrugged. "Is that a yes?"

"Only if you'd like to kiss my knuckles, Manelli."

He nodded, his face splitting in a broad grin. "Atta girl. For a minute there I was afraid you might be losing your spunk." He tousled her hair playfully as he spoke, then his hand stilled, buried in her hair. He took it away slowly so the long tendrils slipped between his fingers. Toni pushed off from the sink, ducked under his arm and moved quickly to the bedroom, where she'd left the notebooks.

She picked them up. "I'll take your advice and do some writing, then. See you later." She closed the bedroom door.

A moment later she heard him leave and she relaxed again. She'd have to be careful or she'd wind up liking the man. She'd have to keep reminding herself that no matter what kind of horrible childhood he'd had, it was no excuse for what he did now. Lots of people had lousy family lives and still managed to grow up and become productive citizens.

She was surprised that she was able to put him from her mind and concentrate on writing. The words flowed from her at a remarkable rate. Time slipped by without her being aware of it. Pages filled, one after another. She wrote in Spanish so he wouldn't be able to read it and guess what she was doing.

Nick couldn't explain why he'd told her the things he had. He talked to no one about his family. He didn't even allow himself to *think* about them. None of it mattered; it was in the past and that's where it should remain. It had no bearing on his life today. With one exception. Danny's death was at the core of his need to end Lou Taranto's reign as king of the underworld. The man had been getting rich on other people's sufferings for too long. It would end. Nick would be the one to end it.

He ran the errands necessary that afternoon, taking the money Taranto had given him to three different banks to exchange it for clean bills. It wouldn't be surprising if Lou had somehow marked the bills and was keeping track of them. He then went to a small gym and left the money in an envelope in one of the lockers.

He told himself he shouldn't be thinking about the little Gypsy alone and restless in his apartment. He shouldn't allow Antonia to haunt his thoughts the way she was. He shouldn't keep catching phantom traces of her scent on every wayward breeze. He shouldn't unconsciously rub his fingertips together, remembering the feel of her silken hair. He certainly shouldn't keep imagining how it would feel to hold her—to wrap his arms so completely around her tiny body that she'd be enveloped in him.

Nick blinked fast, shocked at the path of his thoughts. They'd come to a tentative truce, if he'd read her right this morning. He couldn't revert to total animosity between them by coming on like a cave man again. He'd get a lot more cooperation from her if he could keep things friendly between them, but not too friendly.

By the time he returned to the hulking mansion, it was dusk. The sky beyond the house was only a shade lighter than the house itself. The place looked haunted. Big and dark and ugly. It wasn't a home—not anybody's home, but least of all his. It was just a cover. Something the government set him up with to help convince Taranto he was a productive criminal. The truth was, Nick didn't have a home. A small apartment in Brooklyn served as a base when he wasn't undercover. He wasn't sure he wanted a home. It would be too damn empty.

He picked up the white paper bag with the cartons of Chinese food inside and hurried up the two flights to the apartment. When he went in, Antonia was on the couch with her legs curled beneath her. She bent over a notebook, and her pencil was flying over the lines. She was so engrossed, she didn't even hear him. He quietly set the food down and went back through the door to pick up the telephone he'd left in the study. He carried it inside and closed the door, and still she didn't look up.

His curiosity got the best of him, and he walked up behind her and glanced over her shoulder, frowning when he saw line upon line of Spanish words. So she didn't want him reading what she wrote? Interesting.

"Productive afternoon?"

She looked up fast and slammed the notebook closed. Her eyes had a spark in them that he hadn't seen before. It was like the effect of certain amphetamines. He had the feeling as she looked at him that she wasn't really seeing him, but was instead still at least partially immersed in whatever she'd been writing. "I didn't mean to interrupt. You look...driven."

"It's going pretty well," she told him. Her gaze fell to the telephone tucked under his arm, and the zealous gleam left her eyes entirely. "I've heard of portable phones, but isn't that a bit much?" Her attempt at humor was lame, at best. It didn't fool him for a second. He set the phone down, cursing himself for bringing it in now when he should have waited until she was distracted in another room. It was cruel to let her see it when he couldn't let her use it.

He grabbed up the bag and took it to the kitchen. "I brought food. You like Chinese?"

"It's fine." Her voice sounded dead.

Nick sighed hard. He walked to the couch and sat close beside her. "What is it?"

"Nothing." She looked everywhere but at him.

He cupped her chin and pulled her head around so he could see her eyes. His thumb traced her jawline of its own will. "You might as well say it, Antonia. Your face is too expressive."

She pulled her face from his grasp. "You have the telephone," she said slowly. "It would be so easy to let me call her." She got to her feet, restless.

Her mother again. He'd actually thought he'd won that argument. "I would if I could. I'm not doing this just to be cruel, you know." He stood, as well.

"You could let me call if you wanted to. Just plug the damn thing in—stand beside me with your gun to my head. Blow my brains out if I say one wrong word. I just want to let her know I'm okay—"

He gripped her shoulders, silencing her tirade. "Use your head, will you? If your mother doesn't act worried, it will be obvious to Taranto that you're still alive."

"Taranto doesn't know my name," she whispered. "How can he watch her if he doesn't know who I am? Unless...you're going to tell him."

He released her and threw his hands in the air. "Of course I'm not—dammit, I thought we were past this stage. I'm not going to tell him anything about you, but that won't stop him from finding out. And when he does, you can bet he'll watch your mother. If she acts suspicious, he'll do more than just watch her. It would be just like Lou to assume she knew where you were and try to make her tell him, and if that happens—"

He stopped when he saw the change in her. Her eyes narrowed. Her jaw twitched and she stepped closer to him. Her voice shook with pent-up anger. Her breathing was faster and shallow. "If anything happens to her, Nick Manelli, I swear you will pay. If I have to wring your neck with my bare hands, you'll pay, and that goes for your precious Lou Taranto and that snake, Viper, as well!"

He felt the return of that grudging respect for her just before he felt the shock. "How do you know Viper?" She said nothing, and Nick saw her courage waver. He saw the fear behind it. He stared at her, shaking his head and wondering how he'd been so stupid. "It was no accident that you were in that alley that night. What were you doing there, Antonia?"

She met his gaze. She stood inches from him and tipped her head back to pummel him with her tear-glazed eyes. "I can't let anything happen to her," she said. Her voice was hoarse. "It would be my fault. God, I never stopped to think I would be putting her at risk. I can't let anything happen. Not this time. I can't stand by and do nothing, like before. I won't. I'll do anything—"

She was approaching panic; he could see it swirling in her ebony eyes. He gripped her shoulders again. "Antonia, I didn't say—"

The tears spilled over and he choked. Antonia's small fists came up to grip his lapels. "Don't let them hurt her. For God's sake, Nick don't let that happen."

He didn't intend to slide his arms around her or to hold her tight against him. It wasn't something he thought about doing. It was something he couldn't help doing. He cradled her head against his chest and he rocked her slowly. Her shoulders quaked. She was stiff in his arms but she didn't pull away. "I didn't mean it to sound like a threat. I just wanted you to understand why I couldn't let you call her. No one's going to hurt your mother, Antonia." He held her harder, his arms tightening almost against his will. A lump came into his throat, and he closed his eyes. "I swear to God, I won't let anyone hurt her."

She shook her head as much as his grip on her would allow. Her voice was muffled by the fabric of his shirt, and her breath warmed his skin right through it. "You have no control over what Taranto might do. No one does."

She sounded so hopeless. It tore at his emotions—emotions he hadn't known he could still feel. "Don't be too sure about that."

She sniffed, pulled herself away from his chest but not out of his arms. She blinked her eyes drier and frowned up at him. "What do you mean?"

"I mean I may not control Lou, but he can't control me, either." He saw her brows lift, the need in her eyes. *Make me believe,* she seemed to be begging him. *Take this awful fear away.* "There are things I can do," he said softly. "Things Lou never has to know about. You can trust me on this, Antonia. No one will touch her."

She stared up at him, her huge black eyes like bottomless pools. But a moment later they clouded, as if she'd only just remembered who was speaking to her. "Trust you?" She whispered. She looked at the floor and shook her head slowly. *"Buena suerte."*

Reassurances leapt into his throat, but Nick swallowed them forcibly. To convince her she could trust him would be to destroy his cover. He didn't answer, and when she gazed up again he couldn't face her imploring eyes. He let his arms fall away from her and shrugged. "Fine, don't trust me. You'd sleep better if you did, but that's your problem. In the meantime, why don't you tell me what you were doing in that alley, in the middle of the night, in the pouring rain?"

"I was watching a contract killing," she said softly. "Why didn't you let your pal Viper shoot me? It would've solved all your problems. I saw him lift the gun. He never misses, or so I've heard. What was going through your head when you knocked the muzzle down? Any other thug would've just..." Her head came up slowly, her wide eyes narrowed, and her brows pushed at one another. "Why did you stop him from killing me?"

Nick didn't like the look in her eyes. He wasn't sure what was on her mind, but it had him squirming like a worm on a hook. He tried to keep the offensive. "How do you know Viper? No one knows his face."

She acted as if she hadn't heard him. She turned slowly, looking at the apartment as if she were seeing for the first time. "Why do you stay here, in this hidden apartment? Are you hiding from someone?"

Nick's temper began to simmer. He didn't like the way she was trying to take charge of the conversation. His jaw tight, he demanded, "When did you hear the dead man's name?"

She shook her head slowly as her gaze fell on the phone. "Why do you bring the phone in here every time you want to use it?"

He turned and paced away from her, more uncomfortable than he could remember ever having been. He could barely believe it when she followed, her hand on his shoulder trying to turn him to face her.

"When do you drink the beer I saw in the fridge instead of that expensive whiskey downstairs? And when on earth do you pull on your high-tops and shoot a few

hoops? In between dumping bodies and snuffing witnesses for Lou Taranto? Why do you talk like a thug and
dress like a gangster when you're with him and speak
perfect English when you're with me?''

Nick was stunned by her barrage of questions and the
direction they were taking. He tried to force a scowl instead of showing the shock he felt. ''You seem to have
forgotten your position in the scheme of things, Antonia. I'm in charge. Your life is in the palm of my hand.
You'd be on a slab in a morgue by now if I hadn't dragged
your cute little butt out of the trouble you stepped into. *I*
ask the questions. *You* answer them. Is that clear?''

She stared up at him a moment longer. She raked her
fingers through her hair and shook her head. ''No. I'm
crazy to think... Look, I've had all I can handle, okay?
I'm going to bed.''

She turned and walked away. As soon as the door
closed, Nick slammed his fist on the table hard enough to
send the cup that sat there two inches from the surface.
She was one giant pain in the backside, and if she was
thinking along the lines he thought she was, she was going to be trouble. He no longer doubted that her presence
in the alley had been no accident. That theory was out the
window. She knew way too much.

''Yeah, way too much,'' he muttered. She knew just
how to look at him to make him forget about protecting
his cover—to make his stomach tie itself into a knot while
he broke his back to try to tell her what she wanted to
hear. Her tears worked better on him than automatic
weapons would. He paced the room and wondered if he
should give in to the urge to kick the damn door in and
make her tell him the truth.

He had to remind himself that her reasons for being in
the alley were probably the least of his problems. She was

beginning to see holes in his story. Holes no one else had seen. She looked at him just now as if she could see right inside his brain and read his mind. It was damn nerve-racking. It reminded him of—

He wasn't prepared for the reality that hit him. It reminded him of the way Danny used to look at him whenever he tried dishing up a line of bull. Nick sucked air through his teeth at the sudden pain, like a yard-long saber, running him through. He saw his brother's knowing expression. Danny always knew when Nick was lying, used to say he could see it in his eyes shining like a beacon. It drove Nick crazy. He'd been the best liar he knew. He'd had to be, or he'd have wound up in foster care somewhere with Danny somewhere else. He'd made up some of the biggest piles of crap ever, and people bought it; the wild excuses he invented for school officials whenever they wanted to see one of his parents, the line he'd fed the manager at the High Spot when he scammed his way into his first job.

He'd always been big, so it was easy to convince them he was older than he was. But the club owner wanted an experienced bouncer, not a rookie. By the time he was hired, Nick had convinced his new employers that he was the greatest bouncer in the city. Nick had gone home and tried to tell Danny his new job was at a convenience store, and Danny had seen right through it. Nick had been afraid his brother would try to make him quit, and he loved the job. Tossing guys twice his age out on their butts when they got out of hand was the most fun he'd ever had. He used to fantasize that his father would come in some night. He planned to put the bastard through the door without bothering to open it first.

He'd kept working in that dive for two years after he'd lost Danny, and the entire time he'd been in constant training. He told himself it was because he had to be tough to keep the job. Deep down, though, he knew he was bulking up so he'd be ready to take on the Cobras. At that time he'd still blamed the gang for Danny's overdose.

Nick forced the mismatched memories from his mind. Why had he thought about his past so much lately—about Danny? Was it just having *her* here that brought the memories on? Was it because he felt, even from his first glimpse of her standing terrified at the edge of that alley, an irrational urge to protect her? Just the way he'd wanted to protect Danny.

He'd known his brother was in trouble, and he'd tried every way he knew to talk him back from the edge. Danny ignored Nick's warnings and walked face first into the fire. He'd left Nick alone, just as their worthless father and mother had. Just as little Antonia would do if he gave her half a chance, he thought, even if it was likely to get her killed.

He wouldn't let her do that.

He shook himself and plugged the telephone in to dial Joey. He was already late.

"Yeah, Joe's Pizza, whaddya want?"

"Sausage and mushrooms to go," Nick replied, to let Joey know that he, too, was alone and free to talk.

"Where've you been, Nick? On vacation?"

"Couldn't be helped. You forget I have myself a new roommate?" Nick glanced up at the door and wondered if the little snoop was listening. "You have enough money for that game tonight?"

"Not unless I win the first few hands."

"That's what I figured," Nick said. "Go down to the gym. I left a package in your locker."

"Greenback? Thanks, Nick."

"Thank Taranto. It's what he gave me for handling that little problem the other night."

Joey hesitated. "You—uh—think he might've marked the bills, Nick? If he connects us—"

"I did some banking today. The money's clean."

"Perfect. How's your guest, by the way?"

"Just beautiful. What do you say I send her to your place for a while?"

Joey laughed. "Uh-uh, pal. You caught her, you keep her."

"I was afraid you'd say that. Listen, I need you to call Harry for me. I never know when she has her ear pressed to the door."

"Curious, huh?"

"A little too curious. She knows stuff she shouldn't. She's got a mother, and I'm uncomfortable with the lady's security. I want you to have Harry assign a man to her, twenty-four hours. I want to be informed if one of Taranto's guys gets within ten blocks of her."

"Got it. Anything else?"

"Yeah. A background check on the lady herself. She's holding back."

"I'll call Harry right now. Then I have to head over to the Century. I'll see you after the game if there's anything worth telling you."

Nick hung up, unplugged the telephone and took it with him when he left. The tension coiled tight inside him hadn't eased any, and he needed to work it off. If he didn't, he thought he was likely to wring Antonia's pretty neck for keeping so much from him. Even then a little voice whispered that wringing her neck wasn't at all what he'd like to do to her.

He felt a pang of guilt on the way down. He had promised her a crack at the basement gym...and he would give her one. To have her with him now would defeat the purpose. She was the source of the tension he needed to get rid of.

Toni hadn't heard his telephone conversation because she'd locked herself in the bathroom to pace and try to work through her sudden suspicion. It had seemed so obvious all at once. Nick didn't just switch personalities arbitrarily. It had to be deliberate. He was like two men in one body, entirely different with Viper and Taranto than he was with her. She'd been confused by him before. How could he point a gun at her head one minute and buy her notebooks the next? She wasn't confused anymore. She thought she knew the answer.

He wasn't working for Lou Taranto at all. He was undercover, just as she was. He was probably some kind of cop.

Joy at her newfound theory bubbled in her chest, and she caught herself grinning. Wait a minute, she thought, pulling a mental emergency brake. Just why does this idea make me so damn happy?

Why shouldn't it? It certainly would improve my odds of surviving this mess.

It would also ease the guilt she'd been feeling for allowing herself to be physically attracted to a man whose moral values were roughly equivalent to those of pond slime.

Am I saying that it is now perfectly all right to feel slightly attracted to him?

No way, she realized. She could easily be adding two and two and coming up with eighty-nine. She might only be seeing what she wanted to see and not what was truly there. Still, she couldn't help but feel a hint of relief that he'd made that promise about protecting her mother. If he was a cop, the offer made perfect sense.

And what if he's just a great liar?

She had no idea how much time had passed, but she finally realized she was too wound up to sleep and that her stomach was too empty to relax anyway. When she emerged from the bathroom, Nick was nowhere in sight. She located the two cartons of Chinese food in the fridge and helped herself to a little bit of it. She no longer feared he'd try to poison her. Besides, he'd eaten from both cartons. She took her plate to the coffee table and wondered if he'd left the house or just the apartment. If she were going to find out who Nick Manelli really was, she would have to keep a close eye on him.

She retrieved the remote control and flicked the monitor on, getting comfortable on the sofa. She used the buttons to move from room to room, but didn't see him in any of them. Then the gym filled the screen. A small choking sound came from her throat, and she dropped the remote when her fingers went limp.

She'd found him. He lay on a bench, knees bent, feet flat to the floor on either side. He wore only a pair of baggy yellow shorts with an elastic waist. His chest was bare except for the mat of kinky black hair and the beads of moisture clinging. He pressed a bar with several disks at each end. His face contorted as he pressed. Sweat made a sheen over his nose and forehead. He clenched his teeth, his lips pulling away from them each time he pushed the bar up, away from his body.

Toni stood slowly, her gaze magnetized by the image on the screen. His arms bulged with each repetition. His chest muscles expanded, his pectorals rippling with the effort. She dropped to her knees and felt around for the remote, found it and thumbed the volume control without looking. She heard him grunt now, with every repetition. He didn't count, only emitted a guttural "ummf." The sound seemed forced from him.

She'd known he was big. She'd felt the hardness of his body whenever she'd had physical contact with him. She'd felt the bulge of those muscles beneath his clothes when he'd held her close to him—but, dear God in heaven, she hadn't imagined he looked like *that*. She could only imagine how he'd feel. . . .

Her eyes rounded and Toni flicked the power button off and sat there, blinking at the now-dark screen. Her stomach had a tiny lead ball resting right in its center. God, her throat was dry. She couldn't swallow.

She went to the kitchenette and opened a cupboard for a glass. She needed to drink something. When she glanced up, the rounded, amber-colored glass caught her gaze. It lay on its side, bottom facing out, on the top shelf—an extra bottle of that Jack Daniel's Nick was always feeding to Lou Taranto. Toni pulled a kitchen chair closer and told herself it was only to help her sleep.

Chapter 5

Nick stretched his hour-long workout into two and then some. He hadn't realized just how much he needed it until he got started. By the time he began to feel a little of the tension slip away, he'd pretty much exhausted himself. He spent another hour in the pool trying to cool down and relax.

When he finally showered and went back upstairs, the apartment was silent. He opened the bedroom door and peeked in. Antonia was curled on his bed, breathing deeply. There was a glass with a bit of amber liquid in the bottom on the stand beside the bed. Frowning, Nick moved quietly across the room, picked the glass up and sniffed. Whiskey. The little Gypsy had been snooping again.

He looked down at her and wondered why she felt in need of a shot. Was she that wrought up over her mother? She stirred and sighed. The light from the living room spilled through the slightly opened door and shone on her hair, so it gleamed like a raven's wing. For one wild instant, he had the insane urge to bend over her and kiss her lips—to taste the flavor of the whiskey on them and the flavor of her behind them. He shook himself and turned to leave the room. God knew what she'd think if she woke and found him standing over her.

It was tough to leave, though. He wasn't sure why it gave him such a rush to look at her as she slept. It couldn't have been that glorious hair all over the place, or that she hugged his pillow to her like a lover. It couldn't be because, in this light, her skin was the color of cinnamon or that he could see the dampness and smell the soap from her recent shower.

He made himself take a step toward the door. She moaned softly in her sleep, and he stopped.

"Mmm," she mumbled again. And then, in a whisper, "Nick."

She could have hit him with a hammer and done less damage. She'd whispered his name in her sleep—and she'd said it as if . . .

He stepped closer and sat down gently on the edge of the bed. He smoothed the hair away from her face and looked at her. Her eyes opened slowly, and for an elastic moment she gazed up at him, a lazy smile curving her lips. Her hands came up to cover his, where it rested on her cheek. She blinked.

Her eyes flew wide. She yanked the covers to her chin and moved as far from him as possible. "What do you want?"

Nick shrugged innocently. "You called me, Antonia. I thought something was wrong." He watched her face, making no move to get off the bed. "Was it a dream?"

Her eyes were huge and darker than midnight as she searched her memory. Deep color flooded her face.

"No!" She shook her head fast, so her hair flew. "I mean, not a dream. A—a nightmare."

He frowned. "That's funny. You were smiling when I came in. Looked as if you were about to start purring." He tried to sound genuinely concerned. "What was this... *nightmare* about?"

She shook her head once more. "I don't know. I really don't remember." She said it quickly, not even bothering to try.

"That's the thing about dreams. They're so vivid and then they're gone." He touched her chin with the tip of his forefinger. "The real thing, Antonia, you'd never forget."

He got up, chuckling, and strolled out of the room. He could feel the daggers she was shooting at his back before he closed the door. As soon as he finished grinning, he asked himself why it gave him such an absurdly huge sense of satisfaction to know that he wasn't the only one having impure thoughts. It certainly wouldn't make things any easier. He couldn't just hop into bed with her and go on about his business.

Why the hell not?

The question stopped him cold. Why not? He'd done it before. What was so different about her?

Dumb question. Everything about Antonia was different. So damn small, she seemed fragile as crystal, and so damn intrepid she was always on the brink of disaster. She was a giant in a tiny body. She was a Gypsy sorceress, dancing through his mind but always just out of reach. Her eyes were black quicksand. A man could disappear in those eyes and never find his way out.

He paced for a while, then reclined on the couch knowing full well he'd never close his eyes. How could he, when he knew she was just in the next room, as wide-awake and restless as he was? He shook his head, trying not to think about a sure cure for both of them.

It was a relief when Joey showed up later. Nick reached for the remote, checked to be sure Joey was alone and let him in. The smaller man was flushed right down to the bald spot in the middle of his head. Nick had to keep reminding him to keep his voice down.

"Okay, Nick, okay. But this is hot. It's going down tomorrow night and I'm in. I can't let it go. Not this time."

Nick took his friend's arm and urged him into the kitchen, as far from the bedroom as possible. "Now slow down. *What* is happening tomorrow night?"

"Cocaine. A big shipment of it, coming into Taranto's warehouse sometime after 9:00 p.m. Four guys have to be there to unload and I'm one of 'em."

Nick schooled his face into an emotionless mask. It had been cocaine that had killed Danny, cocaine imported by Lou Taranto. "So?"

"Come on, Nick, you know what I'm saying. That stuff will hit the streets in a matter of days, if not hours. Lou has a crew waiting to cut it up, and we both know they'll be selling it by the gram in no time. I can't let that go." He shook his head and ran one hand over it, front to back. "We have to look the other way all the time when we're under. I can't do it this time."

"It's your tip, Joey. Call it. We'll play it your way."

Joey looked at Nick for a long moment, his blue eyes thoughtful. "If we let the stuff get inside the warehouse, we might as well forget it. The place is like Fort Knox. A lot of cops would go down in a raid."

Nick nodded. "True enough. So what do you want to do?" Nick thought he already knew the answer, and he knew he wasn't going to like it. Allowing Fat Lou's poison to hit the streets was unacceptable . . . but so was losing his best friend. His only friend.

"I'm dropping an anonymous tip to the local cops. Letting them know when the truck is due in and what it's hauling. They'll probably be there waiting."

Nick expelled his breath in a rush. "They'll be there, all right, they'll be loaded for bear. There's no way you can tip them that there's a Fed with the suspects. You'll probably end up getting your head blown off."

"Forewarned and all that crap, pal. I knew the risks when I signed on. Besides, better I buy it than some kid who ought to know better than to try that garbage but doesn't. Some kid like Danny." He paused to let that sink in. "I figure this way I give the cops a pretty fair chance, with only four guys and the driver shooting back at them."

"Five guys and the driver," Nick said softly.

Toni leaned closer to the door. She had to strain to make out what they were saying because they spoke so softly. They must be in the kitchen. She recognized Joey's voice, but so far, hadn't understood half of what they'd said. She opened the door a crack.

"Oh, that's brilliant, Nick. You come along, that way we can both get shot full of holes."

Nick's eyes looked like Toni had never seen them. Possessed or something. "How long's it been, Joseph? Hmm?" He was almost whispering. "What, twenty years now? You remember when you lost Gina and crawled into a bottle headfirst? It took some doing, but I snapped you out of it."

Joey sniffed. "Smashed every damn bottle I had and wouldn't let me out of your sight for a week."

"Even further back than that," Nick went on, and his voice was gritty. "The night Danny OD'ed. I lost it. I wanted blood and I was ready to get it with my bare hands. If you'd let me go that night, I'd never have come back alive. You remember? You had to sit on me to keep me from going after the Cobras alone. You ended up with a black eye by morning—"

"Hold on, Nick. The way I remember it, you weren't too pretty the next day, either."

"Hell, I had twenty pounds on you even then, Salducci."

"Yeah, but I had ten years on you, you muscle-bound punk."

Toni edged nearer and peered through the door. Nick moved and put one hand on Joey's arm. "You stuck by me, Joey. You're the only one who did. It's gonna hit the fan tomorrow night, and I'm damn well gonna be there to tell you when to duck."

"More like *I'm* gonna be there to carry *your* oversize butt home when it's over." Joey stepped more clearly into Toni's range of vision. He was at least four inches shorter than Nick and sported some excess flesh that wouldn't dare attach itself to Nick's body. His face was shadowed with beard, and his black hair grew in a horseshoe pattern around a bald center. When he looked at Nick again, she saw the resignation in his face.

"You think you can manage it? I mean, you can't just show up—"

Nick held up a hand. "If I work this right, it'll be Lou's idea to send me along." He slapped Joey's back. "Get yourself a vest, GI Joe."

"I'll just borrow one from you. That way I'll be covered clear to my knees."

Toni closed the door soundlessly when they returned to the living room. She crept back to bed in case Nick should check. She'd heard only a minute's worth of their conversation, but it was enough. More than enough. Nick had lost a brother to drugs. He couldn't possibly be working for the biggest importer of narcotics in the state. It just wasn't possible. He had to be one of the good guys.

She'd heard enough to know that there was a tight bond between the two men, and more than she wanted to know about what was going on tomorrow night. They were going to walk into a situation that could get them both killed.

She spent the remainder of the night awake, turning their words over and over in her mind.

In the morning, when she rose and showered and dressed, it wouldn't leave her alone. The image of bullets flying toward Nick—toward both of them—haunted her constantly.

He wasn't there when she walked into the living room. Did the man ever sleep? She dragged herself into the kitchen for some coffee, following the rich aroma that had reached her the second she'd opened the bedroom door. It smelled great, but the way her stomach was churning, she wondered if she could even handle a single cup. She filled a heavy stoneware mug despite her doubts and held it with both hands as she paced the room.

She shouldn't be wondering where Nick had gone this morning. She shouldn't worry that he was already embroiled in a late-late-show-style gunfight. She swallowed. She shouldn't be worried but she was. She took the remote and checked the mansion, but she'd already known she wouldn't find him. She felt the sense of emptiness that pervaded the place with his absence.

God, what if he'd already gone on this suicide mission of his?

No. She'd heard them say that whatever was happening would happen tonight.

But would he return before all of that? Was he somewhere right now, preparing for it? Would he go directly to that hell of crisscrossing bullets?

She stood still, closed her eyes and took a bracing gulp of hot coffee, then grimaced. She hadn't put sugar in it.

"Enough, already." She moved purposefully to the counter and spooned sugar into her mug, then stirred. She vowed to keep from imagining all sorts of melodramatic nonsense and decided to distract herself by writing.

An hour later the coffee was stone-cold and her mind was nowhere near Katrina Chekov's world. Her efforts ended when she tore a sheet from the notebook, crumpled it into a tight ball and threw it across the room. The pencil followed, as soon as she'd snapped it in half. The entire notebook sailed through the air a moment later to join its companions in a corner. Toni got to her feet and paced the room. The confinement made her claustrophobic. The knowledge that the door was sealed and that the only person who knew how to open it might get himself killed before he came back here to let her out had her chewing her nails. Sitting here doing nothing, while he might be out there getting shot at, had her crazy.

She stopped pacing when her agitated gait took her right up to the door. Her gaze fixed on the numbered panel beside it, and a new thought made itself heard above all the others.

The panel had ten numbered squares. She was fairly certain it took three to open the door. But which three? Did it matter? She'd have to hit on it eventually.

She began with 1-1-1.

* * *

Nick had phoned Lou at the crack of dawn and arranged to meet with him at a truck stop off I-95. Always on time, Lou was waiting in a booth near the back of the place when Nick arrived.

He stood, clapped a hand to Nick's shoulder and waved him to the padded bench seat. Lou let his gaze sweep the place when they were both sitting, and Nick followed suit. There was a long counter facing the doors, and a line of stools with deep red upholstered seats. An old-fashioned cash register sat on one end of the counter, and a man who looked as if he ought to be in a boxing ring moved back and forth behind it. Booths like the one they were in lined the other three walls. The open floor was a maze of stackable shelving, all of it cluttered with snack foods, magazines and toiletries. The air was thick with the smell of hot grease.

"Nice place you picked, Nicky." Lou couldn't keep the worry from his voice. "What's wrong? Why'd you call so early?"

Nick sighed and tried to look tormented. He glanced at the waitress, whose parents had done a disservice by not getting her braces when she was young. She hurried toward them, pulling a pad from her apron pocket and a pen from her nest of limp brown hair. "Coffee," Nick told her. "You want some breakfast, Lou? It's on me."

Lou shook his head once. "I'm on a tight schedule."

"Just coffee, then," Nick told the girl. "Bring the pot."

She nodded, replaced the pad and was back in less than a minute with a bubble-shaped carafe. She turned over both their cups, filled them and disappeared again, seeming to sense that the two men did not want to be bothered.

Lou sipped and waited. Nick cleared his throat. "I've been thinking about what Vi—" He broke off, glancing around the place with feigned nervousness. "What our friend had to say the other day."

"He said a lot of things. He talks too much, that one."

"About the vote," Nick clarified. "I'm afraid he might've been right. I'm not proven."

"You took the broad out, Nicky. That's proof enough for me."

"You only have one vote."

Nick watched Lou's expression gradually go grim. Finally the fat man nodded, causing his flabby jowls to sway slightly. "Truth is, Nicky, they aren't sure about you yet. It might not go the way I wanted it to. But I'll keep backing you. Sooner or later—"

"I don't want it sooner or later, I want it now!" Nick made a show of forcing his temper back down. "Look, can't you set me up with something, give me some kind of assignment that would show my loyalty?"

Lou frowned and squeezed his chin in one hand. "There's nothing big enough going on—"

"Then it's hopeless." Nick leaned back hard and stared into his coffee cup.

Lou released his chin and drummed his fingers on the table. "There *is* a shipment coming in tonight. It isn't a big enough deal to earn you much clout—then again, it can't hurt."

Nick brought his head up fast. "I'll take anything you can give me, Lou. I want this so bad I can taste it."

He tried not to grin as Lou began to tell him about the cocaine that would arrive by truck at his warehouse that night.

He whistled as he drove back to the mansion good old Uncle Sam had provided for him. This thing was going smoother than he'd hoped.

Toni was all the way up to the possible combinations beginning with 3 before she realized she'd made a big mistake. 3-1-1 had no effect on the security system. When she tried 3-1-2, a bell started ringing—a high-pitched jangling that refused to stop stabbed at her ears and pierced her brain. The red lights beside the numbered panel flashed at her like scolding eyes.

She jumped back, barely suppressing a yelp when the door flew open and Nick's broad frame filled her vision. His face taut with anger, he stepped inside, slammed the door and rapidly punched a series of numbers on the panel. The alarm died at once, leaving a leaden silence in its place.

"What kind of asinine stunt was that?" He didn't raise his voice, but each clipped word made his displeasure perfectly clear.

She was so relieved to see him back in one piece that his ill humor didn't faze her. She turned her back to him so he wouldn't see it in her face. She still attempted to convince herself that her gnawing worry had been for her own sake, not his. If something happened to Nick, she'd be imprisoned here indefinitely. She hadn't truly cared that he might get shot—or killed. She wouldn't allow herself to care. She was not yet sure who the true Nick Manelli was.

"Well?"

She pressed her fingertips to her temples and closed her eyes. "I . . . had to try."

"Why, for God's sake? Antonia, you are safe here. You wouldn't be out there. I thought you understood that."

She turned to face him, feeling a bristle of anger that chased away her limp relief. "You can't expect me to sit here, docile as a lamb, while life-and-death decisions are being made for me by a man I'm not even sure I can trust!"

His brows came together. "*Not sure* you can trust me? Isn't that a major change in attitude? I thought you had me pegged as the next Hitler."

She averted her gaze and shrugged.

"As for sitting here, docile as a lamb, that's the last thing I expect from you, lady. 'Docile' is not an adjective I'd use to describe you. But you are here and you are going to stay so you might as well resign yourself to the fact. This place is buttoned up tighter than a spinster's corset. You're here until I say otherwise."

To Toni's ears it was a challenge. "Is that so? Well, I guess that's right. I'm here and I've got nothing but time on my hands. If I can't find a way out of this hole, then my name isn't Toni—" She stopped herself just before she blurted "Rio."

Nick's eyes narrowed and he studied her face. His gaze swept the room, falling on the crumpled paper and abused notebook in the corner. She shook her head and spun away to pace to the kitchen. He drew a long breath and let it out slowly. "Confinement is making you a little crazy, hmm?"

She turned, then dropped her gaze before his because he seemed to see so much. It was making her a lot more crazy since she'd overheard that conversation last night.

"Sit down . . . Toni."

She didn't argue. She was too tired. She went to the sofa and curled on one end with her legs tucked beneath her. Imagining him caught in the cross fire, cops firing at him from one side, criminals from the other, had taken a lot of energy. The relief left her weak. Nick sat down close to her. She felt his lingering gaze but didn't return it. She braced her elbow on the cushioned arm and rested her forehead in her upturned palm.

"I need you to promise not to mess with the security system again, Toni. I can't have the alarm going off every time I leave the house."

"I don't believe this," she murmured. "My life's turned inside out, my mother is being made to think I'm dead, and you're worried about your precious security system." She glanced sideways at him.

He pursed his lips, dropped his gaze and seemed to consider his next words carefully before speaking. Finally he looked at her again. "For all I know, the house could be wired. Do you know what that means?"

Toni's curiosity rose to the surface like a shark at the scent of blood. It swallowed her frustration in one bite, her anger in the next. "Wired by whom? The police?"

He looked away. "Maybe."

"No," she said softly. She turned to face him fully. "It's Taranto, isn't it? You think Taranto might be listening in." She knew she was right because the slight flicker in his eyes gave him away.

"The point is, those alarms would seem curious to *anyone* who might be eavesdropping. What if it was Taranto? If he finds out you're here..."

He didn't finish. He didn't have to. Toni was well aware what her fate would be if Taranto discovered her. That Nick thought Taranto would trust him so little—that was interesting to her.

"Why don't you just sweep the house?" She asked the question only to prolong the conversation. She'd hoped he'd say something that would confirm her suspicion that he was not what he pretended.

He watched her as he spoke. "The house is too big to sweep daily. I'd miss some nook or cranny."

Unconsciously chewing her thumbnail, Toni looked up suddenly. "That's why you stay in this apartment. It's small, easy to sweep, and no one knows it's here so it's unlikely they'd bug it anyway." She paused, looking around the room with new understanding. "The phone must be secure, too. Probably has a bug signal, doesn't it? What if someone tries to trace a call? Does it give them some sham number in Brooklyn?"

He stared at her for a long moment, and finally shook his head. "You seem to know a lot about this stuff, Toni. You want to tell me why that is?"

She'd allowed herself to get caught up in her own excitement and run off at the mouth, she realized grimly. She tried to look nonchalant and shrugged. If he was a cop, she must be making him hellishly uncomfortable. If not, she might very well have put herself at risk. "I read a lot of spy novels."

His jaw was tight, and his brown eyes probed hers like surgical instruments. "Then you ought to be able to see why it would be a big mistake to mess with the panel again. That alarm going off when I'm not even in the house is as good as a flare going up on a dark night. The wrong people notice it, it will be as bad for you as it will be for me." His tone was calmly dictatorial—as if he expected no disagreement on her part. As if he would not tolerate any disagreement.

He had a way of putting things so they made perfect sense, even in this crazy situation. She found herself feeling guilty for setting off the alarm. "I'll promise not to try it again if you'll stop disappearing without a word. I was wor—I was scared when I got up this morning and you were gone. What was I supposed to do? I wasn't even sure you'd be back. I couldn't just sit in front of the television and wait for a news report to tell me your body had washed up on a beach somewhere—"

"What the hell are you talking about?" He shook his head, puzzled. Then understanding crept over his face. "You were listening last night?"

"Not long enough," she shot back. She was tired of playing games with him. "I didn't hear a word to explain why two seemingly sane men would deliberately put themselves into the middle of a shooting match."

He caught her chin and tilted it up so he could stare down into her eyes. She hoped to God he couldn't see what caused the intense burning behind them. "Don't tell me you were worried about me."

She jerked her chin free, angry because she had been, no matter how much she wanted to deny it. "Dream on, Manelli."

"I will if you will, del Rio."

He referred to her dream last night, of course. She could have slapped him for that remark. She couldn't help it if her subconscious mind was unstable enough to conjure images of him, of them . . .

She shook her head and pretended she didn't know what he was talking about. "I just don't care to be left in the cell when the jailer checks out." She glanced at him again, sensing a chance to get a clue to the truth from him. "Why would you risk your life for Lou Taranto? Don't you realize he is personally responsible for seventy percent of the cocaine in this city?" She shook her head. "I would think that when you lost your own brother to that garbage you'd—"

"You *are* a good listener, aren't you?" He kept a tight hold on his anger, but she could see it there. It flashed in those deep brown eyes. "My brother is none of your business." His gaze wavered. He looked at his hands. "He's dead and buried. He has nothing to do with me or what I choose to do with my life."

The raw agony in his voice was like a whip lashing her heart. It also gave the lie away. His brother had everything to do with his life. She couldn't stop her hand from going to his arm. "That was hitting below the belt. I'm sorry." He didn't look at her. "Nick?"

"Go change," he told her. "I'll take you down to the gym for an hour."

All day Nick tried to shake the feeling of impending doom. The damn woman was hiding something from him; he was sure of it. She knew about bugs and sweeping for them. She knew about phone taps and bug signals. Worse than that, he was sure she suspected his "good-fellow" routine was the sham it was. She wouldn't let it drop. She was like a dog with a three-day-old bone. She had to keep gnawing at it.

And the ways she had of getting at him! When she looked at him with those giant, black-jewel eyes, he wanted to tell her everything. When she'd mentioned his brother, he nearly had. To let her think he could work for Danny's killer was too much—but he had to do it.

He'd left her alone in the gym for over an hour. When he'd finally interrupted, she was doing transverse sit-ups on an incline bench. For a moment he just watched her. Her face was red. Her hair was damp and sticking to her face. The T-shirt she wore had wet spots beneath her breasts and between them.

He felt bad for having kept her cooped up the way he had and he tried to make up for it. He took her swimming, then served her lunch in the formal dining room, warning her first they'd have to remain quiet. He took her on a tour of the entire mansion and found himself enjoying it, although neither of them could speak above a whisper.

The day passed quickly. She was soaking in a hot bath now to ease her muscles after the workout she'd inflicted on herself. While she was occupied, Nick plugged in the phone and dialed Harry's number. He needed to know what the background check on Toni had turned up. He was told that Harry was "unavailable." He could be reached later tonight, but then Nick would be unavailable. He'd have to wait until tomorrow.

She emerged from her bath with all that wild black hair, still damp, pulled back in a ponytail. She wore a pair of baggy gray sweats and a matching pullover with Yosemite Sam on the front. How was it possible, he heard himself wonder, for a woman to look so alluring with Yosemite Sam spread across her chest?

"What's the matter? Do I have something caught between my teeth?"

Nick shook himself. "What?"

"You were staring," she told him. She moved through the living room, into the kitchen, and yanked open the refrigerator. She took out a can of cola, popped the top and took a long drink. Nick watched her throat move as she swallowed. He had to force his gaze away from her.

When he glanced up again, she was the one staring. Her eyes were focused on a point just beyond him, and her face was slightly pale. He turned to see what had caught her attention. The bulletproof vest he'd dug out was slung over the back of the couch. She looked at it as if she thought it might come to life and bite her.

"You're really going to do this, aren't you?"

"I don't have a choice, Toni, and if it's all the same to you, I'd just as soon not spend the next hour and a half talking about it."

She blinked fast and averted her face. "But you could be killed—"

"Only if you pray real hard."

Her head snapped around, her eyes hard as coal chips. "I wouldn't pray for that! How could you think—"

"I was kidding. Lighten up, will you?" He stepped closer to her. "Look, I'd rather think about something else until it's time to go."

He saw her eyes narrow as she regarded him.

He pointed to the box on the coffee table. "I was referring to that. Of course, if you'd rather—"

"A jigsaw puzzle?" Toni frowned and went to the table, picking up the colorful box and shaking it so the pieces rattled. "You're ready to walk into a shooting gallery disguised as a duck, and you want to put a jigsaw puzzle together?"

"It's a ritual." Nick shrugged. He took the box from her and dumped the pieces in a chaotic mound on the carpet. "Helps me to stay focused."

He didn't mention that it would also—he hoped—help him keep his mind away from the thought that had been recurring all day: that if he were to die tonight, and if he'd been given a last request, it would have been to spend several hours in bed with his little Gypsy. Visions of her small, firm body, unclothed and crushed against his, crept into his mind unbidden. Whenever he touched her or caught the barest hint of her teasingly erotic scent, he had to restrain himself from taking her into his arms and kissing her breath away. When had this obsession with having her taken over? He was about to go into battle, for

God's sake—yet all he could think about was how it would feel to love every inch of the ebony-eyed minx.

He sat cross-legged on the floor and began sorting the outside pieces, forcing himself to concentrate on the task at hand.

Toni stopped arguing the sanity of doing a puzzle at a time like this as soon as she thought about how nervous he must be. She tried to imagine how she would feel if she knew that in a short time people would be shooting at her. She'd go along with the puzzle thing, she decided, if it would help Nick not to think about what was ahead of him tonight.

She watched the intense concentration make a furrow between his brows and ignored the urge to put her finger there and smooth it away.

"I probably had a hundred jigsaws when I was a kid," he said softly.

"I had a couple," she responded. "But my favorite pastime was paint-by-numbers. You remember those black velvet ones? Took forever to dry, but they were so pretty they were worth the wait."

He glanced up at her, and his relaxed smile took her breath away. "I'll bet it killed you—the waiting."

"Drove me crazy! I could only do one color, then wait and wait for it to dry before I could do another. I used to prop the picture on a chair and point an electric fan at it."

"Wouldn't a hair dryer have been faster?"

"Who has patience enough to stand around holding a hair dryer for hours on end?"

"Not you, that's for sure." He held her gaze with his, then looked down again and fit a corner piece to another. "When did you start writing?"

"I don't know exactly. It's just something I've always done. First it was journals and silly poetry and fairy tales. It wasn't until high school that I got into the serious stuff."

He looked up again, his gaze intense. "Such as?"

She frowned for a moment before deciding it wouldn't hurt to be honest with him. "Social injustice, corruption, that kind of thing." She wondered if he would get bored with the subject. He leaned forward, the puzzle momentarily forgotten.

"Okay, so what was the first so-called serious thing you wrote about?"

"Prejudice."

She didn't elaborate. Nick studied her. "Tell me about it."

Toni looked at him. She hadn't talked about it in a very long time. It was a painful subject. In her entire life, the only person who'd been allowed to glimpse just how painful had been her mother. And even she didn't know the extent of Toni's guilt. She was struck all at once with the urge to share it with someone—with Nick.

She cleared her throat. "It was during my senior year— a nurse was raped and murdered, her body found in the hospital parking lot. There were no witnesses, no fingerprints. The blood type was so common it was practically useless. And this was long before the advent of DNA fingerprinting."

She couldn't go on with his eyes focused unblinkingly on hers. She got up and walked a few steps away. "The only clue was a tie clip found at the scene. It was one of three that had been awarded to three of the hospital's outstanding surgeons something like twelve years earlier."

"That must have narrowed it down," Nick said. He sounded puzzled, and in a moment she heard him get to his feet, as well. "Did you know the woman?"

She shook her head. "No."

"One of the suspects, then?"

She nodded. "My father."

She heard Nick suck in his breath. She hurried to continue before he could say something that would make her change her mind. "None of the surgeons were able to produce their tie clips. It had been twelve years, after all. They all had alibis for the time of the murder, but people lie, so none were rock solid. My father was home that night. I know because I was home that night, too."

She glanced at Nick and found him frowning. "What happened?"

"The other two were Caucasian," she said softly. "My father was one hundred percent Puerto Rican. What do you think happened?"

Nick shook his head. "The blood type—"

"Could have been any one of them."

"But they didn't convict him—not with evidence that flimsy."

"No," she told him. "It never went to trial." She shook her head. "I saw what was happening. Dad was ostracized. The hospital suspended him. He was shunned by the community. We started getting hate mail and crank calls." She shook her head. "He was dying inside. I could see it happening right in front of me and I wouldn't admit it. I just kept thinking everything would be all right. Then the day came. He kissed me goodbye..." She looked down and shook her head again.

Nick stood in front of her, his hands on her shoulders. He searched her face when she looked up, not understanding. "Where did he go?"

She squared her shoulders. "They found his car at the bottom of a ravine. It was ruled an accident. But it wasn't. I knew. I knew before he left, but I wouldn't believe it." In her life she'd never uttered the confession to anyone else. It had been eating at her soul for thirteen years. "I could have stopped him, Nick. But I didn't have the courage to do it."

"My God." He pulled her into his arms and held her to him. "It's okay, cry." She did, letting the hot tears soak into his shirt and absorbing the utter strength of him.

"This is stupid. I'm not a little girl anymore." She sniffed and tried to straighten.

He looked at her, shook his head. "You've been living with a heap of guilt, Toni. It had to come out sometime. It wasn't your fault. You might have seen the signs afterward, but hindsight is always clearer."

"I should have stopped him," she repeated. "God only knows why I'm telling you all this."

"Maybe for the same reason I told you about my parents," he said slowly.

"Maybe," she whispered. She thought it might be the most honest moment to have passed between them since their first encounter. She blinked her eyes dry and cleared her throat, allowing the pain to slip away. "I guess that's why my mother and I are so close. We leaned on each other after that. Anyway, when my grief subsided enough to vent some of the anger, I wrote a lot. Scathing editorials about prejudiced bigots who see everything according to its color. The focus broadened gradually, until I was writing about anything I saw as unjust and exposing those responsible."

Nick nodded and then his eyes narrowed. "Is that what you were doing in the alley?"

She was surprised by his insight. She hadn't intended to give herself away by revealing some of her past. Her face must have confirmed his suspicion because he let the arms that had been giving soothing comfort fall to his sides. "Tell me the truth, Toni," he said slowly. "For God's sake, don't keep secrets that could get us both killed."

She looked at him for a long time and then at the floor. "You want the truth? Truth is, I'm some kind of fool, Manelli. Truth is, I'm getting used to having you around and I'd really hate to see you riddled with bullet holes. So much so that I'm willing to tell you all of it...if you'll call this off." She made herself face him. "I don't want you to go."

He swallowed hard. She saw his Adam's apple move. His hands flattened themselves to her cheeks, and he tipped her face up, searching it with his eyes. She felt his warm breath on her lips. When his lips parted, she thought he would kiss her. Instead, he whispered, "Then there is something you're not telling me."

Disappointment rinsed through her. His look had been so intense—but she banished that thought. "No more than what you aren't telling me." She would have pulled her face from his hands, but the look on his face paralyzed her. For an instant she glimpsed pain and raw longing. Then his lips came down to hers. He kissed her softly, parting his lips to capture hers between them and sipping at them like a fine wine.

Toni's knees trembled. Her heart fluttered in her chest, and before she'd made a conscious decision to do so, her hands had slipped across his broad chest, then slid around to press against his back. Her body seemed to have melded to his. Her lips relaxed open at the first gentle nudging of his tongue, and when its warm, velvet length plunged into her mouth, she welcomed it. She moaned around it.

Nick's hands left her face to cradle her head. His fingers tangled in her hair. His stroking tongue set her on fire, and the subtle movements of his hips told her that he was just as aroused. When he lifted his mouth away, she stood on tiptoe and caught his lips to her again. With a low groan, he complied with her unspoken request and kissed her once more. He kissed her until her breathing was broken and ragged, until her head was spinning and her entire body throbbed with wanting him.

Finally he straightened and held her to him. Her head rested against his chest. His heart hammered like a drum. He was breathing as erratically as she was. His voice was barely more than a whisper when he spoke. "You're seeing things that aren't there."

She frowned and would have looked up, but he held her where she was.

"You'd rather believe a fairy tale than to admit the truth, Toni," he went on. "I'm not hiding a damn thing. I'm exactly what I seem. Your problem is you can't stand to admit that you're hot for Lou Taranto's right-hand man."

Toni stiffened, and this time he let her step away from him. He turned his back on her, picked up the vest and put it on. His words were like knives in her heart—mostly, she realized, because they were true.

"You want to pick up where we left off when I get back, I'll be happy to cooperate," he said. "I just like my women to know who's taking them." He slammed a clip into his gun with the heel of his hand and worked the action. He never even looked at her. "Right now I have to go. Lou's counting on me."

Chapter 6

Toni's face burned with humiliation as she stared at the door he'd just slammed. She'd made an utter fool of herself. She'd let herself believe in something that was pure fantasy. Like a little girl dreaming of a knight in shining armor, she'd let her imagination twist the truth. She'd seen everything exactly the way she'd wanted to see it. Nick had nailed the reason, in his crude way. She couldn't allow herself to feel what she was feeling for a criminal, so she'd built him into a hero.

"How could I have been such an idiot?" She turned from the door, and her gaze darted around the empty room, not really seeing anything. "My God, I almost told him..." She bit her lip, unwilling to complete the thought aloud. Hadn't he just warned her about listening devices that might be in the house? Who was to say he hadn't planted a few of his own right here? She'd come perilously close to admitting her alter ego tonight. She'd almost told him she was Toni Rio. If he truly worked for Taranto, that would be suicide.

She grimaced, when she realized she'd mentally injected an *if* into the thought. Was she still determined to think he was some kind of a saint? Her eyes burned, and a stabbing sense of betrayal twisted inside, even deeper than the humiliation. It made no sense, that feeling. He'd never claimed to be anything but what he was. Yet she'd told him her most painful secrets. She'd bared her heart's deepest wounds to him.

He'd seemed to care, she thought miserably. The way he held her and spoke softly...

So what? Even a morally bankrupt bastard was entitled to noble impulses now and then.

What about all the other things that don't seem to fit? What about all the surveillance equipment, and his fear of being monitored by Taranto? Why the hidden apartment—the traveling telephone—the late-night meetings with Joey?

More than that, her mind whispered. There was his brother, who'd died of a drug overdose. Just the mention of his brother brought Nick extreme pain. How could he be working for Taranto?

She sighed hard and shook her head. She was at it again, trying to make a case for what was probably no more than wishful thinking. She couldn't tell if her theory might still be valid. She was too close to it. It was like a work in progress at the moment. She wouldn't be able to look at it objectively until she was able to distance herself.

The fact was, she'd allowed herself to begin to care about the big lug. The lines between realistic theory and whimsical fantasy had faded until she could no longer see them. She had to get the hell out of here. Tonight. Before she let herself forget his cruel words and started seeing him as a character from one of her books.

She paused as she realized that was exactly what she'd been doing. Nick was exactly the type Katrina would go for. Built like Atlas, arrogant and dangerous—that air of mystery about him.

But she was not Katrina Chekov, she reminded herself. The things she'd seen in him had been different. His inability to hurt her or even let her go hungry. That well-hidden gentleness, which wasn't nearly as well hidden as he thought. And while she'd exposed her secret pain to him, she remembered that she'd seen his, as well. The pain of being abandoned by his parents and of losing his brother, the pain he pretended didn't hurt at all.

Toni shook her head slowly. No, she couldn't stay here another night. She had to leave before she did something she might regret for the rest of her life.

He'd only glimpsed the hurt in her eyes briefly before he'd looked away. If he faced her, he was sure she'd see right through his act. He wanted to tell her the truth so badly it was eating him up from the inside out. But he couldn't. Taranto was an expert at getting the truth out of people. He was damn good, too, at sensing when a person had something to tell or when they were ignorant. If he ever got his filthy hands on Toni, it would be far better for her if she knew nothing.

Damn, the effect that woman had on him was like a wildfire on a tinder-dry forest. He could still taste her on his lips, feel her small body straining against him. Every move she made, every breath that mingled with his had been a plea. *Tell me... trust me...*

Trust her. He couldn't do that, dammit. Trusting other people had never brought him anything but disappointment. He'd be stupid to trust her when he knew she was hiding something. She had her own agenda. Who was to say she wouldn't get whatever information she could from him and then just walk away? And why the hell shouldn't she? Everyone he'd ever cared for had. He'd learned to depend on no one but himself. Leaning on others brought nothing but pain. It made you weak, vulnerable.

Since Danny's death, the finale in a series of desertions, Nick had existed in a virtual vacuum. No one got close to him. When he needed sexual release, he found it with strangers. He rarely even asked their names. His encounters with women were always cold, preplanned exchanges. He was consistently sober, consistently protected and never really satisfied.

The only one to breach his self-imposed seclusion was Joey. But Joey had been close to him before his mother had walked out, before his father had been caught running from that liquor store with a six-pack, a wad of money and a loaded gun, and before Danny had died. In all that time, Joey had never broken faith. He'd always been there. But even with that, Nick lived with the constant certainty that Joey would disappear one day. He tried not to need his best friend. People never abandoned you when you were aloof. As long as you could take them or leave them, they tended to hang around. The minute you needed them, they vanished like a magician's trick. Poof! *Voilà!* You're on your own again, pal.

"Here it is." Joey's voice shook him out of his brooding thoughts. Nick watched the red taillights come closer as the semitrailer backed up to the loading dock. The only other light was a single bulb overhead, just enough so they could see what they were doing. Besides Nick and Joey, three others waited to help unload the shipment.

Rosco, an old faithful employee of Lou's who'd never had the ambition to move up through the ranks, stood a few feet away, an automatic rifle gripped in a two-handed, ready-to-fire, hold. He was the lookout. The other two were younger, barely out of their teens, but already loyal lackeys to Lou's machine. One called himself Sly, the other, Jake. Nick figured their names were something like Howard and Irving.

When the truck came to a halt, Nick went to it and lifted the lever to release the rear doors. He swung them open and glanced inside. The crates looked for all the world like an innocent cargo of coffee. The cocaine was buried in the fragrant beans. The aroma would help to throw trained dogs off the scent.

The two kids rushed past him and grabbed a crate each to bring out and stack on a waiting pallet. Joey pulled up on a forklift. When the pallet was filled, he'd pick it up on the tines and take it inside the warehouse. Nick glanced out into the darkness. Somewhere out there police officers must be waiting. Any second the night could explode with muzzle flashes and lethal bullets. Still his mind kept wandering into the zone he'd deemed forbidden. He was thinking of Toni, wondering if his cruel words had caused her any tears. She'd had enough pain in her life. Damn little Gypsy was systematically chipping away at the walls he'd so painstakingly erected . . . and that scared him.

When the spotlight blinded him, Nick jerked in surprise, though he'd known it would come sooner or later. The bullhorn-enhanced voice drilled through the white glare. "This is the police. Step away from the truck, keeping your hands—"

And then Taranto's men started shooting. The kids dove for the weapons nearby, dropping crates and spilling coffee beans all over the place. Rosco squeezed off the first rapid burst of fire. The police shot back without missing a beat, and Nick knew that the men on the dock, himself included, were sitting ducks.

He bent low and charged across the dock, slamming into the two kids and knocking them to the ground five feet below. He almost went over the edge of the platform himself. When he whirled, he saw Rosco lying on the wood, unmoving, limp. He must've been hit in the first volley. Nick lunged toward him and grabbed up the Uzi he'd dropped when he fell. He pointed it, squeezed the trigger and held it, straining to keep the barrel from lifting skyward with the incredible force of the recoil. He put the spotlight out.

Joey had hustled his butt off the forklift and taken cover behind it. He didn't need to be told that the light above them made them perfect targets. He pulled his handgun and shot the bulb. Nick made his way toward him, bullets flying around him like a rainstorm. At least they had the benefit of darkness now. He and Joey crouched low, raced to the edge and over it, joining the two youths on the gravel-covered ground.

A searing in his left thigh drew Nick's hand to it. It came away warm and moist. With the adrenaline pumping, he hadn't even felt the bullet rip into him, but he sure as hell felt it now. The two kids were still firing back at the cops, but Nick knew they couldn't see enough to hit any of them. He tapped Joey on the shoulder. ''We better try for the car. They won't wait long to move in.'' The unspoken conclusion to the sentence was in both pairs of eyes. *And then one of these crazy punks might kill some of them.*

Joey nudged the other two, and the four of them ran for the nearest vehicle. Nick had left his car close for this very reason. They had a precarious three-second start before the police realized what had happened. Nick slid into the passenger seat, and Joey took the wheel without asking why. He slammed the pedal to the floor, sending a shower of loose stones behind them. Seconds later screaming sirens came to life.

Nick glanced over his shoulder at the two in the back seat. "You two all right?"

"Yeah," Sly replied. "Damn, I thought we were all goners! I could feel the freakin' bullets whizzin' past me. I could *feel* 'em. Damn!"

Jake said nothing. He sat still, his eyes dilated and his skin pale in the dim interior of the car. Nick had a feeling he'd think twice before he decided to devote his remaining years to working for Lou Taranto.

Joey's stream of fluent cursing brought Nick's head around. "You're bleeding, Nick. You're hit."

"Just drive," Nick told him. "It's nothing." He looked down now and saw that his pant leg was soaked in blood. The warm trickle along his outer thigh told him it was still flowing. He slipped the belt from his waist, wrapped it around the wounded thigh, just above the injury, and pulled it tight.

Joey rounded a corner, tires squealing, and came to a rubber-burning stop. "Out, you two," he ordered the boys in the back. "Stay out of sight for an hour, then get your butts home." The two clambered out the same door and vanished into a vacant building just as Joey pulled away from the curb.

"I'm taking you to a hospital Nick. You're bleeding like—"

"Forget it!" Nick yanked the belt tighter and held it mercilessly. "It's stopping. You let Jersey's finest catch up with us, and we'll be tied up for God knows how long. I can't leave that little Gypsy to her own devices for more than a couple of hours. You don't know what kind of hell she'd raise."

"Little Gyps—You mean Antonia? What damage can she do? She's under lock and key."

"You don't know her."

Her plan was simple. He'd open the door, she'd give him a healthy dose of hair spray in the face and then she'd run like hell. She'd wrapped a change of clothes and her notebook in one of his spare blankets, since there was no telling how long it would take her to find help. The bundle rested close enough so she could grab it as she fled. She watched for his car on the monitor, sighing her relief when it finally pulled up at the gate. She'd begun to think something might really have happened to him. She flicked the set off and tossed the remote over the row of books on the shelf. In case her attempt failed, it wouldn't do to have him aware that she knew about the monitor. She positioned herself near the door, lifted the hair-spray can and waited.

It seemed to take an unreasonably long time for him to come upstairs. She grew restless. Her feet itched and she shifted her weight back and forth from one to the other.

Finally the door moved and Toni braced herself. It opened. Her finger touched the knob on the top of the can. Joey came through with Nick's arm anchored over his shoulders. Nick's head was bowed. Toni's eyes widened as her gaze moved downward and she saw the scarlet blood dripping from his pant leg. His head came up. He met her horrified stare, and she could see the strain on his face. The can fell to the floor, forgotten in her rush to his side. She pulled his free arm around her and tried to take some of his weight. "To the bedroom," she instructed, and she and Joey half carried Nick there and clumsily eased his huge body onto the edge of the bed. Toni released him long enough to tear the covers back, then gripped him again and pressed him down into the bed.

"What happened?" Toni tried not to look at Nick's face. Instead, she grabbed up her purse and rummaged for the tiny pair of foldable scissors. She couldn't stand to see the pallor of his skin, the lines etched at the corners of his mouth. She found the scissors, dropped the purse to the floor and bent to begin snipping the material below the belt he'd twisted around his leg.

"It's just a flesh wound," Nick ground out. He wasn't lying flat, but holding his head and shoulders off the bed. She could hear the effort he made to keep his voice normal. She could hear the way he struggled to breathe deeply and regularly. The man couldn't admit to weakness at all, even with a quart of blood soaking his clothes. He was infuriating.

"He was shot," Joey finally answered. She realized it had been a stupid question. Of course he'd been shot, what else? She peeled the material away from his skin. A mottled chasm in his flesh still pulsed blood, but at a slower rate. She couldn't see the wound well until she cleaned some of the blood away.

Her gaze pinned Joey. "Find something to prop his feet on—they ought to be elevated. Get the wounded leg higher so it'll slow the blood flow." She got off the bed. "You can take his shoes off, too."

Joey's quick nod assured her he'd do what she asked. She hurried into the bathroom, dug into the medicine cabinet and gathered everything she thought might be of use: gauze pads and a roll of gauze, a tube of antiseptic ointment, some aspirin tablets, adhesive tape. She carried all of it into the bedroom, dumped it on the nightstand, then rushed back for a basin of warm water, a washcloth and a bar of soap.

She was faster than Joey—then again, the poor man was shaking so hard it was amazing he could move. She hurried into the kitchen for the bottle of whiskey she'd found there before and a small glass. As she headed back, she glanced out the wide-open bookcase door. A little shudder passed through her. Could the one who'd done this to Nick have followed them? She closed the door and breathed a sigh of relief, then went back to the bedside.

She had to swallow hard before she could speak. All of this was nearly too much. Seeing that much blood, knowing it was his . . . She twisted the cap from the bottle and poured with an amazingly steady hand. Leaning over him, she supported Nick's head with one hand and held the glass to his lips with the other.

"Hell, I'm not dying." He took the glass from her and swallowed the contents. Toni poured another shot as soon as he'd emptied the glass. "Will you quit with this, Toni? I'm all right."

"Shut up and drink," she snapped, her fear for him making her voice sharp. "And then you can quit this macho bull and lie back. It's a strain to sit up and you know it."

Again Nick downed the whiskey. But he didn't lie down. Toni sat on the bed and began gently cleansing the wounded thigh. The blood flow had slowed to a trickle.

"Joey, go close the door," Nick said, watching her. "Before my bird decides to fly the coop."

She didn't pause in her removal of the blood with the wet, soapy cloth. "I already closed the door. I was afraid you might have been followed. Didn't want whoever did this to walk right in and finish the job." She dipped the cloth and squeezed it several times. God, there was a lot of blood.

"Your mistake," Nick said slowly. "I was shot by a cop. If he had followed me, he'd have been your ticket out."

"I'd pretty much figured that out," she replied. "And if I'd wanted out, Manelli, I wouldn't be here. Don't kid yourself about that." She'd removed most of the blood by now. The bullet's path had dug a furrow along his outer thigh. He was lucky it hadn't been fractionally more to the right. It could've cost him his leg. She took the whiskey bottle and removed the cap again. "Another shot?" He shook his head. She took a folded towel and slipped it beneath his leg, then she tipped the bottle up and rinsed the wound in alcohol. She felt his body stiffen, heard the air he sucked through his teeth. Joey turned away, clapping a hand to his mouth.

Toni used a gauze pad to absorb the blood-colored whiskey that ran from the gash, down the sides of his leg, and prepared to pour a bit more over the wound. She glanced at Joey. In another minute he'd be green. "You two left some obvious footprints to this apartment. Maybe you ought to clean them up."

"Yeah, right. I hadn't thought of..." He stopped and glanced at Nick. "If you guys don't need me."

"It's not as bad as it looks," Toni told him. "He'll be fine, and I can handle this alone."

Joey's sigh filled the room. He sought Nick's nod before he turned and left them alone.

Toni rinsed the wound again, then began pulling the edges together and taping them to hold them tight. "I know it hurts," she told him. "Hold on and I'll get it over with as fast as I can. If you want another shot, for God's sake say so." He said nothing. She finished closing the wound, coated it in ointment and then several layers of gauze. She wound the roll of thin material around his entire thigh several times and taped it there tightly. Then she met his gaze.

He was still sitting up, and his expression was peculiar: puzzled, as if he couldn't quite fathom what she was doing. She hoped he hadn't lost a lot more blood than she realized. She gently released the belt and watched the white gauze, waiting for—half expecting—a red stain to appear. It didn't. She sighed hard and let her chin fall to her chest.

"It will be okay. We'll have Joey get some more bandages and some antibiotics if he can manage it. I don't want to risk infect—"

She stopped short when his hand shot out to encircle her wrist. He was staring intently, frowning, not angrily, when she looked up.

"The door was wide open, Toni. Why didn't you leave?"

She shook her head. "That has to be the stupidest question I've heard in a year."

"Not from where I stand," he went on. "I saw the hair spray, the little pack you had ready. You were planning to leave."

"That was before I knew you were hurt."

"What difference does it make?"

She looked at him and frowned. "I couldn't leave you like that. You needed me, for God's sake. You think I could just turn my back and walk out and leave you bleeding all over the floor?"

"Plenty of people have." He let his head fall back to the pillows.

Toni heard the double meaning behind the remark, and again she saw behind the facade of toughness to the real hurt inside him. "Not me, Nick," she told him softly. "I don't walk out on people—even when they deserve it." She got up and carried the basin of rose-colored water into the bathroom to pour it down the sink and rinse it clean. She refilled it, grabbed a clean cloth and returned to the bed.

"You mean what happened before I left?"

She nodded, trying not to feel again the hurt his words had inflicted.

Joey's voice from the doorway reminded Toni of his presence. "Bloodstains are all taken care of." His anxious eyes never left Nick's face. "You gonna be okay, pal? I still think you should've gone to a hospital."

"I told you it was nothing."

"Yeah, well, I'm spending the night just to be sure."

"You can't do that, Joey. We're acquaintances, don't forget. We start acting like bosom buddies and—"

"But I thought you two had known each other for years?" Toni's question brought a sudden wariness to both men's eyes. Nick's gaze held hers, tired but unwavering. Joey looked at her, then away, then back again.

"Maybe—uh—Nick and I ought to discuss this in private, if you don't mind, Miss—"

"It's Toni. I suppose you want me to believe you're another one of Taranto's hired killers? Shouldn't you just grab me by the hair, shove me through the door, call me a few choice names and threaten to kill me if you catch me listening? You probably don't realize it, but I've seen the way Taranto's men conduct their business. I don't believe the words 'If you don't mind, Miss' exist in their limited vocabulary."

"Don't ask her to leave, Joey. She'd just press her ear to the door." She glanced at Nick again. He sounded drained.

"I'm sorry," she said quickly. "I'm a little stressed out. Look, if you want to talk, fine. But he really ought to rest. He's lost a lot of blood—"

"Go home, Joey. I'll be fine."

"If it starts bleeding again, what're you gonna do? The door's locked, you can't leave the phone in here. How could she even get help for you?"

Toni felt a shiver go through her. "He's right, Nick," she whispered.

"He can't stay." Nick's eyes looked puffy and leaden. He was obviously wrung out. It would do him no good to waste energy arguing. Still, Toni knew it would be stupid for her to stay alone with him, with no way to summon help in an emergency. Nick sighed loudly. "Joey, punch the combination into the door before you pull it closed. That way the lock won't engage. If something happens, Toni can go downstairs and call an ambulance. Okay?"

"And if Lou's got the phone tapped?"

"I'll tell him it was just a hooker. He'll buy it. I know him."

Joey glanced uneasily at Toni. "And if she decides to take a walk?"

"I won't." She saw the doubt in Joey's eyes. "For God's sake, you guys are the ones claiming to be cold-blooded killers, not me. I said I'd stay and I will."

Joey glanced at Nick. Nick shrugged. "You heard the lady."

He sighed hard. "I'll go. But I damn well don't like it."

"Duly noted, Salducci. Now get the hell outta here."

She didn't miss the affection in Nick's eyes, and once again her certainty that he was no criminal outweighed the doubt. In fact, she didn't believe either one of them was working for Taranto. She'd never come across a gentler man than Joey.

He left, albeit reluctantly. Toni scrutinized Nick's face from her perch on the edge of the bed. "He cares a lot for just an acquaintance."

"Don't miss a trick, do you?"

She sighed at the tautness in his voice. "It's odd, but I'm not entirely comfortable with the door unlocked. I can't tell the good guys from the bad guys."

"You don't want to tell," he replied.

"You're wrong about that."

He dropped his gaze. "If you hear anyone coming, pull the door open and close it again. The lock will take automatically." He closed his eyes, then forced them open. "If you leave tonight, Toni, take my gun with you. Get on the first flight out of the country and—"

"I am not going anywhere! What is it with you? Don't you trust *anyone?*" His lips tightened into a thin line. "You don't, do you?"

"No. I don't."

She looked at the floor, then at his face again. "Is that why you won't tell me the truth?"

"Are you still fantasizing, Toni? Look, I need to get some sleep. I can barely keep my eyes open."

It was frustrating the way he kept her guessing. Still, he had admitted to a weakness rather than discuss whether he was or was not being honest with her. Maybe that should tell her something. "Okay, so sleep."

She leaned closer to him and unbuckled the strap that held the shoulder holster around his body. He stiffened, and his eyes flew open again. "Easy, big guy. I'm only trying to make you comfortable. You can't go to sleep as you are."

He relaxed and let her take the holster from him, gun and all. She put it aside, then began unbuttoning his shirt.

"Just how 'comfortable' are you planning on making me?"

"Still have a sense of humor, I see." She helped him sit up a little and tried to ignore the feel of his firm biceps as she pushed the material down them and eased his arms from the sleeves. She refused to look at the crisp black hair that swirled over his chest. She wasn't lying to herself anymore. There was a strong physical attraction here. But just because she admitted it to herself didn't mean she had to give in to it.

She eased him back to the pillows, located her discarded scissors and attacked the outside seams of his trousers. They were ruined anyway. He watched her without comment. "Brace with your good leg," she told him. "Lift your hips just a little." When he complied, she slid the pants from beneath him. He wore white boxers underneath. She kept her eyes averted and grabbed up the clean cloth from the basin of soapy water. Deftly she washed the blood from the length of his leg and patted it dry with a towel. She took the whiskey-dampened towel from beneath his leg and swiped the wet cloth over the back of his thigh. "Almost done," she told him, taking the basin to dump it again. "Then I'll let you sleep."

When she returned, it was with another clean cloth. This time she wiped a streak of blood from his face. She put the cloth in his hand. "Here. You can do your own hands." He did. Toni gave one last, worried glance at the patch of white on his thigh and pulled the covers over him.

"You going to read me a bedtime story, too?" His voice was heavy with sarcasm but heavier with exhaustion.

"I'm not going to fight with you tonight, so you can quit trying to bait me." She tucked the blankets firmly around him. "Now, is there anything else you need before you go to sleep? Another shot of whiskey? Some aspirin?''

"No. I'm fine."

"Okay, then." She gathered up the bandages, the discarded wrappers, the soiled clothes and towels. She dropped his ruined clothing into a plastic bag. She looked down at her sweats and saw they were smeared with his blood. Her hands were, as well. A shower was definitely in order. "I just need to clean up, but I'll turn the light off so you can rest." She snatched an oversize shirt from the back of a chair. "I don't want you to move, Nick." She chewed her lip, hating to leave him alone in case the bleeding should start up again. "I'll leave the door open. Yell if—"

"It's my thigh, not a damn kidney or a lung. I've hurt myself worse than this playing basketball."

She ignored him and rushed into the bathroom for a record-fast shower. She put the baggy shirt on after drying off and tiptoed back into the bedroom. She hoped he was asleep. She pulled a chair nearer the bed as quietly as she could and sat down in it.

"What are you doing?"

She saw his head turn in her direction as he spoke. "I'm sitting. What does it look like I'm doing?"

"You don't have to sit there all night. I'm okay. Go sack out on the couch."

"No thanks. I wouldn't sleep a wink out there, anyway."

"Why, for crying out loud?"

She shook her head. "Because you might need me. Whether you'll admit it or not, Nick, that is more than a scratch. You lost a lot of blood and you are not out of the woods yet. If you need me, I want to be close by."

He blew a short sigh. "I won't. I don't need anyone. I never freaking have."

"Well, I'll be here, just the same, in case you ever freaking do!"

Chapter 7

Nick lay awake for a long time, despite his feeling of having been wrung like a wet rag. He watched her, certain she'd get up and walk out before long. The door was wide open now. If he'd thought she could've made it off the grounds without his knowledge, he wouldn't have had Joey leave the door unlocked. If she got away, she'd end up dead. He wasn't sure why he'd blurted the warning he had, about taking his gun and leaving the country. He supposed it was because he'd lost so much blood and wasn't thinking too clearly. Or maybe because he had to admit there was a slim chance she could escape. She was resourceful. And gutsy.

He never for a minute thought he'd take a turn for the worse and need help. Leaving the door unlocked was completely unnecessary the way he saw it. He'd done it only to see her leave. He wasn't even sure why, but he needed to see her do it. He needed to be reminded, in no uncertain terms, that people couldn't be trusted. They left you the minute your defenses were down.

She didn't leave, though. He watched her tiny form silhouetted in the half light for as long as he could stay awake, and she never left. After a while her head fell to one side. Her breathing grew deeper and took on the rhythm of sleep. He couldn't believe it, wouldn't have if the proof hadn't been right there in front of him. When he fell asleep, it was in a state of confusion. She hadn't left. But she still might. Maybe she hadn't got from him all that she wanted just yet. Maybe she'd wait until morning.

For a time his mind relaxed in blissful darkness, but then something changed. The lights came up slowly, and the stage was set. Danny lay on the rotted wood floor, pale and blue lipped. Nick shook him, but he barely had strength enough to do so. He felt incredibly weak and clumsy and colder than he could remember being in his life. Still, he recited the lines he knew by heart. "Don't die on me. Hold on, Danny, hold on. Don't die…don't leave me, damn you!"

The young Nick in the dream thought he must have caught his leg on a nail on the way into this dump. His thigh was screaming. It felt hot and it throbbed like a toothache. He didn't care—he didn't care if the damn thing fell off, not when Danny's life hung in the balance. "You're all I got, man. Don't do this—Danny? Danny!"

The scene faded, but he knew it was there, just out of sight. Something cold and wet lay across his forehead. Another cold thing pressed to that spot on his thigh. God, it felt good. His head was pulled upward, small things between his lips…pills, then the lip of a glass and icy cold water.

"Drink, Nick. Swallow the aspirin, you have a fever."

He followed the instructions of that musical voice. The glass moved away, and he muttered something. He wasn't sure what. But it came back. He drank and drank. He couldn't remember being this thirsty. When the water was gone, his body moved until his head was cradled in a pillow of warm flesh, familiar scent. He knew that scent. "Toni," he muttered.

"I'm right here." Cool hands stroked his cheeks and his hair in soothing, slow movements. The cloth left his forehead, and he heard water trickling. It came back colder.

"You . . . didn't leave?"

"I told you I wouldn't."

He hovered between the reality of the woman who held him and the memory of the dream. "Danny—"

"I know." The hands stilled on his face. "It was a long time ago, Nick. Danny is gone. I'm here with you now, though, and I won't leave."

"You will." Nick let his mind drift back into the comforting blackness. The pain from his thigh had lessened. It no longer burned. "They all do."

Nick woke with his head in Toni's lap. Her palm rested motionless on his cheek, and he realized with a start that she'd been in that same position for several hours, stroking his head and his face as he drifted in and out of sleep. A glance at the clock's luminous dial told him there was still over an hour before dawn.

She sat with her back against the headboard, her legs curled beneath her. Nick's head lay on her uppermost thigh. Her chin touched her chest, and a frown had etched itself between her brows, even in sleep. Without moving, Nick shifted his gaze. On the nightstand a basin of water sat beside an opened aspirin bottle, an empty glass and two soaking-wet cloths. He tried to remember what had happened during the night to get Toni from her chair beside the bed to where she now slept. Only fragments came to him. He remembered pain and pills being pushed between his lips and the welcome coldness of the water. He remembered her voice—her touch . . .

My God, she's still here.

He studied her face as she slept and realized fully what she'd done. She'd held him all night and she'd done her damnedest to keep the pain at bay. She'd spoken softly to him, words of comfort. His own mother had never treated him with the tenderness she had. And she'd promised not to leave.

He was still regarding her face when the heavy lashes lifted, revealing to him yet again the glistening, fathomless jet eyes. He saw them narrow at once, felt the hand on his face tense and move to his forehead as it had done many times during the night. Finding no more than a normal amount of heat emanating from his skin, she smiled.

"How do you feel now?"

He shrugged. "All right, I guess." The silken warmth of her bare thigh under his cheek was distracting. He lifted his head so she could slip out from under him. She moved slightly to the side, stretched her legs out fully beside him. She hooked one hand at the back of her neck and rubbed. "What happened last night?" he asked.

"Your temperature spiked. I'm afraid that leg has a nasty infection trying to set in." She met his gaze. "You don't remember?"

"Bits and pieces."

She nodded thoughtfully. "I'm not surprised. You were quite . . . disoriented." She swung her feet to the floor. "I ought to change that bandage, see how bad it is."

"Not yet." Nick sat up, and she turned to face him. "What do you mean by 'disoriented'?" He hadn't liked the emphasis she put on the word.

She tilted her head to one side. "You did a lot of talking. Do you want some of that whiskey before I unwrap—"

"What did I say?"

She looked away from his eyes. "You told me everything. I know you're a cop. Don't worry, your secret is safe. I just don't know why you didn't tell me in the first place. This whole ordeal would've been so much easier if you'd just..."

Nick felt the blood drain from his face as she rambled on. He couldn't believe he'd been that feverish...that he'd blurt something like that and not even remember. He caught himself then and watched her as she spoke. She was talking too fast and she never met his gaze.

"What kind of cop?" She broke off at his interruption.

She looked at him slowly, her face blank. "Well—I—um—I guess you didn't say."

He smiled and shook his head in silent admiration of her brass. "Nice try, Toni. I didn't say anything like that. I know because it's bull. A figment of your creative imagination."

To his surprise she smiled, too, like the cat leaving the pet store with feathers in its whiskers. "I don't think so. You believed me for just a second. You wouldn't have if there wasn't some slight chance you might've said what I just told you you did." The smile died slowly. She held his gaze, her own eyes going softer. "It was a mean trick to play on a guy as sick as you were last night. I'm sorry. It was either that or go on questioning my sanity—not a healthy alternative."

"Your sanity isn't an issue here. It left the day you started with this imaginary secret identity of mine."

She shrugged, stood up and carefully peeled away the tape that held the bandages. "You are one stubborn SOB, Nick Manelli."

He didn't answer her. He couldn't just then. The concern that clouded her face as she unwound the bandage and gently peeled away the gauze pads was too convincing. Maybe even real. She cleaned the wound once more, applied an abundance of smelly ointment and rewrapped it, taking great care not to hurt him. "Tell you what," she said as she worked. "Since you are in a weakened state, I will drop this subject—for now—if you'll do something for me."

"To drop this, lady, you could damn near name your price."

Her dark brows shot up. "Well, now, that will require some thought. Normally, when I'm told I can have anything I want, I demand chocolate, but—"

"Chocolate? Chocolate what?"

"Oh, anything. I'm a confirmed chocoholic." She taped the gauze down and looked at him seriously. "But in this case I'd prefer conversation." Nick's wariness returned in force, but she hurried on. "Not about what you're not telling me or what I'm not telling you. I want you to tell me about *you.* The way I told you about me last night. About my dad, and—"

"What do you want to know?" He still wasn't sure this was anything but another attempt to get the truth from him.

She turned from his thigh, pulling herself fully onto the bed and facing him. "You did talk last night, when the fever shot up. You talked about Danny." Nick felt the old pain twist within him but concealed it. "Your brother, right?"

Nick nodded. "My brother's death is not my favorite topic of conversation."

"Of course it isn't. I heard enough about that last night." Compassion made her voice thick. "It must have been awful for you." He said nothing. "But what was it like before all that?" He frowned at her. "I never had an older brother, but I always wanted one."

What was she doing? Why did she want to stir up his most painful memory? Didn't she realize that he couldn't think of Danny without thinking of that horrible night in the condemned building? He hadn't—not from that day to this. His only memory of his brother was of those last few minutes in the filthy building with the sirens and flashing lights outside. Of his pasty skin and lifeless eyes. It wasn't possible to remember anything else. Was it?

"Or a sister," Toni was saying. "I had an imaginary sister when I was very small, you know. She walked me to school that first day. When I was afraid of the dark, she was always in my bedroom with me. Sometimes we'd talk all night long—or it seemed that way."

Nick frowned. "He was the one who brought home all the jigsaw puzzles." He hadn't intended to say the words. They'd slipped out, from some unseen crack into his subconscious. "There was never a lot of money—puzzles were cheap. Some nights we'd sit up until two in the morning trying to finish a new one." He felt something tugging the corners of his lips upward, suddenly recalling the two of them sitting on the bedroom floor trying to do a puzzle by flashlight and fighting off attacks of laughter that were sure to wake their mother.

"He was a year older," he went on. "He had the greenest eyes, and Fiona's red hair. If you'd seen the two of us together, you wouldn't believe we were related."

He shook his head slowly, in awe. But Toni didn't give him time to think about what had just happened to him. "I got one of those circular jigsaws for my birthday one year," she said. "Remember those? They were tough."

Nick's mind returned him to that bedroom floor, with a circular jigsaw in front of him depicting Superman in flight, an adoring Lois Lane in his arms. And Danny, wondering aloud why one of Superman's hands wasn't visible in the picture and whether or not it was inside Lois's skirt. They'd laughed so loudly over that one, they were sure they'd be caught. And every time one boy managed to stop laughing, the other one would start again and in seconds they'd both be rolling on the floor, red faced and breathless.

He didn't even realize he was telling her about it as he remembered, and a minute later Toni was laughing. *Nick was laughing.* He was laughing. And when he stopped, he looked at her and shook his head. "How did you do that?"

She smiled at him and parted her lips to speak, then stopped. The smile died and her gaze focused beyond him, through the doorway into the living room. "Nick, the light—the little red light on the panel—"

He looked over his shoulder. "Someone's at the front gate." He glanced again at the clock and could think of only one person who'd show up at this hour. "You'd better grab me some clothes."

She nodded and hurried to the closet, taking down a starched white shirt and a pair of the pleated trousers. Nick swung his legs over the side of the bed and felt the instant return of the pain in his thigh. Toni knelt and slipped the pants over his feet and up his legs. She made him lean on her when he stood to pull them up. She held the shirt for him to slip his arms into its sleeves.

He thought of the monitor as he buttoned the shirt, but before he'd decided whether it would be safe to share that secret with her, the little Gypsy was in the living room, tugging an armchair toward the bookshelf. She clambered up and grabbed the remote, pointed it at the big screen and turned it on. Nick limped into the room to glance at the screen and then, incredulously, at Toni. "When did you—"

"Within the first twenty-four hours. It's Taranto, isn't it?"

Nick looked at the gray Mercedes at the gate, its wipers beating uselessly against the slashing rain, its headlights pale in the storm's darkness. He nodded. He wanted nothing more right now than to sit Toni down and make her tell him how she knew about high-tech surveillance devices, but he had to deal with Lou first. "I'll have to go down and talk to him." He took the remote from her.

He started for the door, but her hand gripped his shoulder with surprising force. "You can't go down all those stairs on that leg."

"It's either that or invite him up here." He saw the worry in her dark eyes and knew it was genuine and for him. He reached down and touched her face, trailing the backs of his fingers from her delicate, high cheekbone to her impertinent chin. She'd given him a precious thing in the hours before this dawn: the knowledge that he could remember Danny as he'd been before—when they'd been brothers in every sense of the word. When they'd been happy. How could he tell her what that meant?

His fingertips in the hollow under her chin, he tilted her head up and lowered his own. His lips brushed over hers.

She didn't pull away. He kissed her again, pressing his lips fully to hers, parting them with the tip of his tongue. He still held only his fingertips to her chin. He wanted to sweep her into his arms—to pick up where they'd left off last night before he'd said the things he had.

She stepped away, avoiding his eyes. "Taranto," she reminded him.

He nodded and went to the door. She didn't even try to see the numbers he punched, but when he pulled the door open, she was at his side again, her hand on the knob. "Be careful on the stairs," she warned. "Don't put too much weight on the leg."

He closed the door with her still muttering that he at least ought to have a cane of some sort. And she was right. The stairs were torture, but he made his way down both flights and let Lou Taranto in the front door a few seconds later.

Lou burst in, hugged Nick like a long-lost son and urged him down onto the leather sofa. He moved behind the bar as if he owned it, poured two shots and waved a fleshy hand toward the mousy man who'd scurried in his wake. "My personal physician, Nicky. Also my nephew. I put him through med school. He returns the favor when I need him." He slammed a shot glass into Nick's hand. "The kid, Sly, filled me in. Down it, Nicky. Then drop the pants. David! Get over here and take a look."

Nick glanced at the guy who jumped when Lou bellowed his name. He was pale, thin, and the round wire rims perched on his nose made him look ten years older than he probably was. He had a facial tick that tugged one side of his mouth sporadically. His hair was rumpled, as if he'd been yanked out of bed for the occasion. He stepped up to Nick, black bag in hand. Nick swallowed the whiskey, stood up and lowered his trousers. You didn't argue when Lou Taranto offered to do you a favor. He sat down again, ignoring the small man who began to unwrap the wound.

"The boys say you got them outta there against the odds last night."

Nick affected a derisive snort. "A lot of good it did. We lost the shipment. And Rosco."

Lou swallowed half his whiskey and shrugged. "Too bad about Rosco. But I prefer dead to jailed. He went out with honor—not like Vinnie, eh?" He laughed, a low rumble that seemed to gain momentum as it moved through him. "As for the shipment, what the hell? Easy come, easy go, right, Nicky?"

Nick frowned, an uneasy suspicion settling in the pit of his stomach. "You don't care about the shipment?"

"It's gone. Whining about it won't bring it back. I can afford the loss."

Nick studied Lou's face and realized he couldn't care less about the cocaine that had been confiscated. "How much blow did we lose?"

Lou pursed his lips. "What difference does it make?"

He was wondering about all Nick's questions. Nick shrugged quickly. "Not a damn bit to me. How many cops did we take out, anyway?"

Lou drained his glass and slammed it on the polished surface. "Not a damn one."

"Good."

Lou's head snapped around. Even David stopped what he was doing and looked up quickly. "What the hell do you mean, 'good'?"

"Think about it, Lou. This way the cops think they've won one. They grabbed a major haul—didn't they?" Lou frowned and didn't answer, so Nick rushed on. "They took out one of Lou Taranto's men to boot. They'll be so busy patting themselves on the back, making speeches and taking interviews, they won't have time to bother us for a while. On the other hand, if we'd shot a cop or two—"

"They'd be out for blood," Lou finished. "You're a sharp one, Nicky. I'm glad you're not working for the enemy."

For once Nick's smile wasn't forced. David was already rewrapping the leg and not doing half the job Toni had, Nick thought. He was glad when the man finished and rose.

"I don't know who tended this for you," he commented, "but they did a nice job. Slight infection trying to take hold. I'll leave something for it." He rummaged in his bag as Nick stood and righted his trousers.

"Who fixed you up last night, Nicky? You holdin' out on me? Got a woman stashed around here?"

The question startled him. He hadn't anticipated it and he should have. Any hesitation would arouse Lou's suspicion, and his answer might well be checked out. "Joey—the new guy you sent along last night."

"Joey?" Lou's brows lifted, two silvery arches above a bulbous, slightly red nose.

"Hell of a man," Nick told him. "Drove like a pro, dropped the kids where it was safe, lost the cops. Then he stuck around long enough to patch me up. I would've bled to death if he hadn't."

"Salducci, right?"

"That's right."

Lou puckered in thought. "I'll see he gets a bonus, then." He looked down at David, who was bent nearly double, squinting at the label of a small brown bottle. "You about done?"

David jumped as if someone had pinched him. "Uh, yes. Here." He set the bottle on the coffee table. It tipped over. "Antibiotics. Directions are on the label." He pulled a tube of ointment from his bag, set it beside the toppled plastic bottle, snapped the bag shut and hurried to the door. He couldn't seem to get out of there fast enough.

Nick glanced at Lou. "You scared him."

Lou shook his head. "So does his shadow. I wanted to talk to you alone."

"About?"

"The girl. I know who she was."

"The girl?" Nick feigned ignorance.

"The one that you popped. She's trouble."

"She's dead, Lou. How's she trouble?"

"You're sure?"

Nick released a deliberate bark of laughter. "Damn, don't you think I can tell a dead woman from a live one?"

Lou smiled at that. "Sure I do, Nicky. I just wish you'd have asked her name first."

"Like I told you before, she saw the hit, she had to go. Who she was was irrelevant."

"Yeah, well, maybe not so irrelevant as we thought. Viper thought he'd seen her somewhere before. When they flashed her picture on the local news, he realized where. She'd been hanging around the club the past few weeks." Lou blew air through puckered lips and shook his head. "Big headline, you know. Missing, Antonia del Rio. Only they aren't saying who she really is. Not yet anyway. I wondered—checked with my informant inside NYPD."

Nick shook his head, not following at all. What would Toni have been doing at the Century?

Lou reached inside his voluminous coat and pulled out a hardcover book. On the front of the glossy black jacket was a lamppost with a shadowy figure leaning against it, feminine calves outlined beneath a trench coat, ending in stiletto heels. Huge red letters marched across the top:

Poison Profits. Across the bottom was written in equally large letters, Toni Rio.

The truth slammed into Nick like a freight train. He came to his feet so fast it jarred his thigh. "You've got to be kidding me."

Lou tossed the book down as if it were dirty. "No joke. The bitch wrote this last year. Raised so much hell with the drug trade I had to drop my Colombian supplier. Took me six months to set up a new partnership. She knew stuff about the business I didn't even know. She was good."

Nick didn't need Lou to tell him about the elusive Toni Rio. The bureau had a file on the woman that read like *War and Peace*. Her works were fiction, but the stuff she used to sweeten those plots was real and the whole world knew it. The lady sleuth she'd created—Katrina Chekov—waltzed from one taboo subject to another, shattering myths along the way and always putting the bad guys on ice.

That was no more than every Fed knew. If he'd actually read that file of hers, he might have known before now that her full name was Antonia Veronica Rosa del Rio—and that she looked like a tiny Gypsy princess. Rumor had it she was working on a new fictionalized exposé, one that would blow the lid off the Taranto crime family. Lou had to know that.

Nick cleared his throat. "Dead is dead, Lou. Even if she was some kind of celeb—"

"Don't you follow, Nicky? She was writing a book about me! She wasn't in that alley by accident. And if she knew enough to be there, she knew way too much. Who the hell knows what she has down on paper, just waiting for some nosy damn Fed to find—"

"It's fiction, for God's sake!"

"The book, maybe. But what about the notes—the research, or whatever the hell she'd call it? Man, to know about the hit, she had to be into us deep." Lou shook his head. "I'm sending some toughs to her place tonight—tellin' 'em to tear it apart. And if they don't find everything she had on us there, I'll have 'em lean on her family. She must'a had a family, right?"

"Wait just a damn minute," Nick barked. There was no more time to feel his way. He had to take the offensive here and now or lose the chance. "This was my mess. I should've wrung the truth out of her before I took her out. For once in his worthless life, Viper was right. *I* loused this up. *I* oughtta fix it."

"Like how?" Lou was listening. Nick knew he'd better make it good, or the game was over.

"I can get in and out of her place without anyone knowing I was there. If there's anything to find, I'll find it. Hell, I'll bring it to you. I'll personally light the match for you, and we'll watch it burn over drinks at the commission meeting. Be the highlight of the night."

Lou nodded once, then pinned Nick to the spot with an intense glint in his eyes. "And if you don't find anything? You got the stomach to rough up the family?"

Nick smiled slowly. "I got ways of getting information that Viper doesn't even have nightmares about. Let me handle it, Lou. I'll let you watch when things get nasty."

Lou's grin split his face. Nick knew the man's perverse appetite for watching people suffer. He was a sadist once removed—too soft to inflict the pain himself.

"All right, Nicky. All right. But I gotta have results by the meeting. I can't let it go beyond that. The others are nervous as hell. If you can't get what I need, I'll send in someone who can."

Nick nodded. "I'll get it, Lou. It'll be the finishing touch for my initiation, don't you think?"

When Nick had left the room, taking the remote with him, Toni had followed, shouting motherly warnings as a distraction and holding the doorknob in her hand as he pulled it shut. She hadn't let the handle turn, so the lock did not engage. As soon as Nick's footsteps had faded, she opened the door and silently followed. She would not sit still while he went down there, wounded and alone, to face Lou Taranto and whoever was with him. She didn't like the odds. Besides, she had to hear this conversation. She'd convinced herself again that Nick couldn't possibly be in Taranto's employ. The man he was when he was alone with her was not that kind. Granted, he was entirely different when he was with Taranto. She had to know, once and for all, which Nick was the real one.

She sat just out of sight and well within earshot at the top of the curving stairway. All the air left her lungs in a rush when she heard Nick make the offer he just had. Her throat tightened until she couldn't swallow, and her eyes were scalding. He'd sounded ruthless, vicious.

Not the Nick I know, she told herself as she struggled to contain the panic she felt spreading like ice water through her veins. *He wouldn't hurt her—he promised. This is just an act.*

Maybe, she thought. And maybe not. She wanted to trust Nick. More than anything, she wanted to believe her instinct that he wasn't capable of such cruelty, that he truly was the gentle, caring man she'd come to know. She felt it so strongly she would have trusted him with her life.

But can I trust him with my mother's? And if there's even a one-in-a-million chance I'm wrong . . .

She shook herself. She couldn't think objectively about Nick. Her attraction to him always got in the way. And her mother was obviously in jeopardy now, if not from Nick then from Taranto himself. She had to get out of there, get to her, warn her.

Nearly frantic as she fought with images of what the filthy Viper might do to her mother, Toni jumped when Nick stood to walk Lou to the front door. Then she saw her opportunity. She slipped down the stairs as soon as they were out of sight and ducked into a small room off the opposite end of the living room. She had only one thought in mind now. She had to protect her mother. She'd failed one parent; she wouldn't repeat the mistake.

She held her breath and waited, giving Taranto ample time to drive away and Nick time to remount the stairs and, she hoped, reach the third floor. It would take him longer than usual, due to the bullet wound. She tried to be patient. She knew he'd try to stop her leaving, no matter which side he was truly on. She couldn't let that happen.

When she thought enough time had passed, she moved to the nearest window. It faced the rear of the house, and beyond it she could see only darkness and slashing rain. It was locked, naturally. She was out of patience with Nick and his locks. She picked up the first thing she saw that was suitable and smashed the window with it. She tossed the marble sculpture of the rearing stallion right through the glass, venting only a small portion of her frustration. If only Nick had been open with her, none of this would be necessary. A tiny voice of doubt whispered in the back of her mind that it might be more necessary than ever, but she refused to listen.

She clambered through, her only thought that she had to save her mother. She had no plan of action, no thought of getting past the gate or of how to reach her mother in

time to protect her. She had no qualms about running into
the fury of a summer storm dressed in nothing but an
oversize shirt and her underwear. She didn't feel the jag-
ged shard that raked across her upper arm, tearing the
cotton shirt, as well as her skin beneath it. She didn't
flinch from the bits of glass that jabbed into the bottoms
of her bare feet as she made her way over the wet ground
and away from the house.

Chapter 8

When Nick walked through the third-floor study and found the bookcase standing slightly away from the wall, all the blood rushed to his feet. He moved quickly into the apartment, knowing already that he wouldn't find her there. He felt the emptiness in every room as if it were a presence in itself. He didn't need the flashing light to confirm it. He shut off the system before the alarm bell could start in.

He spun in a slow circle and pushed a hand through his hair. Where the hell was she? Somewhere on the grounds, he rationalized. She had to be—she wouldn't take off. Not now. Unless... Nick's gaze moved to the monitor. Unless she'd somehow overheard his conversation with Lou and believed his act. But she couldn't have. He had taken the remote...

...*and dropped it on the table in the study as he rushed through.* He turned now and went to find it still resting there, beside the unplugged telephone. He grabbed both items and ducked back into the apartment. He inserted the phone's cord into its jack, punched in Joey's number with one hand, thumbed the monitor to life with the other. He was scanning each room for a sign of Toni when Joey picked up.

"I'm calling it," he said without prelude. "Pull out, Joey."

"What do you mean, 'pull out'? Are you nuts? We just—"

Nick continued flicking buttons on the remote, his gaze intent on the screen. "Lou's too damn unconcerned about losing that shipment. Almost like he expected it. It stinks of a setup, Joey. Pull out now, and watch your back."

Joey sighed. "Okay. All right, if you say so. Listen, how's the leg? I—"

"Later. I have to move." Nick replaced the receiver slowly. He'd stopped flicking buttons when he'd seen the small sitting room with the smashed window. "My God, if she was in there..."

He closed his eyes slowly, opened them again. She had heard everything. And she'd obviously believed every word he'd said to Lou. He shook himself and went into the bedroom, yanked a dresser drawer completely out and flipped it upside down on the bed. Now that it didn't matter, she believed his cover story. Her timing was damn near awful. He tore free the envelope taped to the bottom of the drawer, ripped it open and took from it a small leather folder the size of a wallet. He slipped it into his pocket and ran back through the apartment and down the stairs, ignoring the stabbing pain each step sent shooting up through his leg.

In the little sitting room at the bottom of the stairs, the wind blew the curtains wildly. Rain slanted in, wetting the floor and the wall beneath the window. Nick paused only long enough to find a flashlight and then he clambered out the same way she had, noting the trace of blood on the pointed finger of glass at his right. On the ground, he squinted through the downpour to try to make out her shape in the darkness. He shone the beam on the muddied ground in search of her small footprints. If anything happened to that damn little Gypsy, he knew he would never forgive himself.

Toni slipped in the rain-slickened grass more than once as she ran from the hulking mansion. She decided not to go near the front gate, certain that would be the first place Nick would look for her. She headed for the woods in the rear of the house. Maybe the place wasn't as secure as he'd said. There might not be fencing all the way around, and even if there was, there might be some way over or under or through it.

The trees closed themselves behind her as soon as she breached the first cluster of them, hiding the house from her view. She stumbled onward, rain still streaming between her shoulder blades. It had plastered the shirt she wore to her skin and soaked her hair within seconds of leaving the house. Her limp curls stuck to her face and neck, heavy with cold. She had to blink raindrops from her eyes every few steps just to see where she was going. She pushed on, trying to keep to a straight course, refusing now to think or to feel. She focused her every sense on moving, on seeing through the rain and on putting as much distance between herself and Nick as she could.

She resisted the subconscious masochist that wanted to replay, over and over in her mind, the horrible things she'd heard Nick say. She didn't want to hear again the change in his voice from the moment Taranto had told him who she really was. She didn't want to wonder if that knowledge had made a difference to him...had made him hate her as much as it sounded like he did.

A sob tore at her throat as these thoughts ran through her mind, despite her determination not to let them. The seed of doubt grew larger. As the trees grew closer together, they blunted the force of the rain. Pines, she realized dully as their needles continued brushing her arms and their scent reached out to offer solace. The wind couldn't slash at her here. The rain still came through, though, but more gently, filtered through the boughs. The ground seemed to sink under her feet, as if she were walking on soft sponges instead of several inches of wet, browning needles. They made a soft carpet for her sore, bare feet.

She slowed her pace, beginning to feel the biting shards of glass on which she'd stepped and the painful scratch at her right shoulder. Eventually she had to stop. She'd walked for what seemed a very long distance and still hadn't come to a fence demarcating the border of the property. She braced one hand against the sticky trunk of a pine and heard its needles whispering above her head as the rain hissed down through them to sprinkle her. She glanced around but could see no farther than two or three trees in any direction. The glimpses of sky she could catch between the sheltering arms of the pines showed her only a bleak, gray thing—the perfect sky to match the way she felt. She couldn't understand the intense pain that seemed lodged in the center of her chest. But she knew it grew with every step she took...and each time she felt herself doubting him, it grew even more.

She bit her lower lip, and a chill raced up her as the wind found its way to her bare legs. Had she allowed herself to indulge in a silly infatuation? Had she deluded herself with a fantasy image of a man who didn't exist?

She thought about last night when her heart had iced over at the sight of his blood-soaked leg. She'd been overwhelmed with the need to ease his pain, to make him all right. She'd held him when his fever had climbed. She'd rocked him in her arms as she would her own child, and she'd felt the wrenching pain in him when he'd dreamed of his brother. She'd convinced herself that no man who'd loved a brother as he had could be one of Lou Taranto's cold-blooded hoods.

She simply couldn't believe it was all in her imagination. Even now she wished she could turn around and run back to him, fall into those big, iron arms and pour out her fears as he held her and promised her that it would be all right. Only fear for her mother kept her from doing just that...fear and a kernel of doubt that wouldn't let go.

She folded her arms against the tree and lowered her head to them. "God," she moaned softly. "Have I been wrong about him all along?"

"You weren't wrong, Toni."

His voice was so near her ear that she stiffened in shock. She pivoted, flattening her back to the wet, stringy bark to see him standing mere inches from her. "Don't try to take me back, Nick. I have to go to her...I have to—"

He caught her hand in one of his, turned it slowly and pressed the flashlight he held into it. He folded her fingers around it. She frowned and shook her head, not understanding. She opened her mouth to ask what he wanted from her, but his finger pressed to her lips silenced her. He caught her other hand and lifted it, palm up. He took something from his pocket and lay it flat on her palm.

Her fingers closed over the leather. She brought it to her face for a better look and caught the scent of it. It was folded in half. She looked at Nick, and a crazy hope leapt up in her breast. She opened the folder and lifted the light to it. The shield glowed in the white light, right beside the photo ID. Nick's face, unsmiling, beside his full name, Nicholas Anthony Manelli, and the words Federal Bureau of Investigation.

Every muscle went limp, and Toni swore her bones melted. Her hands fell to her sides, and her eyes closed. Nick took the folder from her unresisting fingers and then the light. His hands came back to her in a moment, huge and strong, closing on her shoulders, pulling her away from the solid tree. She gladly traded its support for that of his equally solid chest as his arms folded around her. She felt as if she'd been standing alone in a hurricane. She encircled his neck with her arms, pressed her head to his chest so that it rose and fell with every breath he took. Her goose-bump-covered legs were flush with his, separated only by a thin barrier of wet cloth.

When his arms loosened from her waist, she knew he would lead her back to the house. She didn't want to go. She didn't feel strong enough to stand if he stopped holding her now. She clung shamelessly. She felt his head tip backward, as if he were seeking help from above. A moment later his big hand cupped her head, cradling it more securely to his chest. His other arm closed once more around her waist, providing her with the support she'd sought, holding her tight against him. His head came down, and she felt his lips in her hair, at the very top of her head.

She tipped her head back and she saw his eyes, even darker than the darkness of the predawn. The emotion in them reached her and found its mate within her. She felt her response begin deep in the pit of her stomach before his lips claimed hers. And when they did, it became a fire that tried to consume them both.

She parted her lips to admit his seeking tongue, then parted them farther to take it in deeper. She clutched at his shoulder with one hand, while the other buried itself in his hair and pulled him closer. She kissed him hungrily, unable to get enough of him. He groaned deep in his throat as his hands slid down over her hips and beyond the edge of the shirt to her rain-slickened thighs. He brought them up again, lifting the shirt away, cupping her buttocks, impatiently shoving her panties aside to knead her bare flesh.

She felt his fingers slipping over her wet skin and she felt him growing hard against her stomach. She pushed against him, and when he shuddered in response she wondered at her ability to inspire such a reaction in him—a man so beautiful it hurt to look at him.

She worked one of her hands between them and flicked open the buttons of his shirt. When she gained access, she ran her hand over his chest, dragging her nails lightly over his nipples and hearing his ragged breath. Impatient now that she was sure of herself, she pushed the material over his shoulders and seared his chest with her kisses and her rapid, shallow breaths. He let her dampen his skin with her lips for a moment, but then his own patience seemed to grow thin. He pushed her back from him, gripping the lapels of the shirt she wore, one in each hand. He tore it open, and Toni didn't flinch.

He stared for an elongated moment, as if mesmerized. In slow motion, it seemed, he sunk to his knees, pulling her forward until her breasts dangled inches from his face. His lips closed over one throbbing peak, and she gasped in pleasure. He nibbled, suckled her until she threw her head back, unable to contain her responses. He moved to the other breast, his touch growing more urgent. He sucked it harder, tugging, closing his teeth on the tender crest and sending shocking ripples of awareness zinging through her. She felt the pressure of his teeth, the flick of his tongue, the damp heat of his mouth. She felt the cool rain on her flushed skin, her upturned face, and the chill breeze that played across her thighs. She felt everything.

He reached up to tug the shirt completely off her, then let his hands drift down until they rested just behind her knees. Their gentle pressure told her what he wanted. She lowered herself down to the cool wet blanket of needles until she knelt with him. He spread her shirt behind her and pushed her backward, his eyes glowing in the dark as she slowly lay down for him.

Still he knelt, his knees on either side of her. He hooked his fingers in her panties and tugged at them. She obligingly lifted her hips, and he slipped them down over her legs to her ankles. He took her feet from them, making each gentle touch a caress. When his eyes met hers, she felt no shyness. His hungry gaze moved over her, leaving no part of her untouched. She felt feminine in every cell of her body because of that gaze. She felt more attractive, more powerfully female than she had in her life.

She reached for the button of his trousers and tugged on the zipper. She touched the erect rod beneath them, and he closed his eyes. She closed her hand around him, and his body vibrated. He pulled from her only to rise and kick off his trousers and shorts. Only then did Toni remember his injury. The white bandage around his thigh stood out in marked contrast to his tight, tanned skin and defined muscle. "Your leg—" she began, sitting up as she spoke.

She stopped short when he shook his head once, dropped to the ground beside her, his hands on her shoulders, gently forcing her to lie back. He watched her in silent admiration until she wanted to squirm. He watched the rain falling on her, watched the droplets beading on her body. Finally he straddled her and leaned over her to put his lips to her collarbone, closing them over a raindrop there and drinking it in. The act made her shudder violently. He rose higher and similarly kissed the moisture from her eyelids, her cheeks, her chin and then her throat, where he nibbled the skin with his teeth before moving tantalizingly lower.

It was deliberate torment, she knew, but each moment of anticipation made his next stroke that much more thrilling. He sucked droplets from the skin all around her breasts before putting his mouth to them. He licked every trace of moisture from each one before quenching his endless thirst at her throbbing nipples. He saw how they hardened as he drew nearer. She watched the gleam in his eye when he noticed her reaction and knew that it pleased him.

He moved lower and dipped his tongue into her navel, drinking the raindrops that had pooled there. He prodded it hard with his tongue, as if he could enter it. The gesture was incredibly erotic, and Toni realized that her hips had begun to gyrate in slow, insistent circles.

He rubbed his chin over the curly mat of hair at the apex, then lowered it so his mouth hovered just above. She felt his thumbs touch the lips of her secret center and spread them open, exposing her to the rain, to the cold air...to him. He kissed her there, long and hard. He nipped with lips and then with teeth, driving her to a fever pitch of need. Finally he opened her still farther and applied the punishing lashes of his whiplike tongue.

She groaned loudly, every inhibition forgotten as her fingers tangled in his hair. Her entire being vibrated with sensation. He was going too far, she realized. She didn't want to experience the magic alone. She pushed his head from her, met his inquiring glance and simply whispered, "Please..."

He lifted himself until his body covered hers. He didn't need to position himself to enter her. It happened almost on its own. His heat found hers and nudged inside. He stiffened, hesitated. Toni gripped his buttocks and pulled him to her, groaning in satisfaction when he plunged deep. He drew back and plunged again, still deeper, filling her as she'd never been filled. She arched her hips to take more of him, and his next thrust sheathed him completely inside her.

She moved with him then, lifting her hips high to meet his powerful thrusts, which forced the air from her lungs. She kneaded his skin, kissed his chest, his neck, his face. When his rhythm pushed her toward fulfillment, she whispered his name over and over until he silenced her with a ravenous kiss. It was while their tongues were twined together that the climax threatened to rip her apart with its intensity. She realized vaguely that Nick had stiffened, as well, then bucked within her. He trembled violently before he collapsed on her with a long, shuddering exhale against her parted lips.

His mind kept telling him it was not possible. His body disagreed. It made no sense. It couldn't have been as explosive as it had seemed. Nothing could be... It had felt like being caught in a tempest and carried through its violence to the paradise at its eye.

Now he had the craziest urge to rock her small, curvy body against his—to kiss every inch of her until she either fell asleep in his arms or asked for more—to brush some of that wet, wavy hair away from her face and look into her eyes and tell her—

"What am I, insane?"

He rolled away from her as the words burst from him without permission. He sat up and held his head in his hands.

She sat up beside him, her shoulder pressed to his. "You think it was insane to make love to me?"

Make love. God, he wished she wouldn't call it that. It hadn't been that. He wasn't stupid enough to have let it be that. He said the first thing that came to mind, realizing she expected some kind of answer. "Out here, like this, yeah. Insane. You'll probably have pneumonia."

He turned toward her to see what she thought of that answer, and saw her sitting with her knees slightly bent, toes playing in the pine needles. Her breasts were already dotted with raindrops again. Nick closed his eyes. "Put your shirt on, Toni, you've got to be chilled through."

Frowning a little, she stood, shook out the shirt and slipped her arms into it. When she reached for her panties, he turned his back and busied himself replacing his own clothes. They were wet, which made it difficult, but he wasn't about to march back to the house stark naked. The way he felt every time he looked at her, he'd never make it. When he turned again, she was watching him, a puzzled expression on her face.

"Is something wrong?"

Good question, Nick thought. No, nothing's wrong; everything's just the way it should be. Good ol' gullible Nick has let himself care again, and sure as the sun will rise tomorrow, he's going to get left high and dry again. Toni would walk away from him. One way or another she'd leave him. He had no one to blame but himself, because he'd known it would happen. He'd told himself not to feel anything for her. The problem was, his "self" hadn't listened. The only thing left to do now was to prepare for the blow. He had a feeling it was going to be a tough one to take. Maybe too tough. Maybe this would be the one that brought him down.

"Nick?"

Her hand on his face sent a shaft of bleak pain through him. He nearly winced at the strength of it. The most he could hope for now, he realized, was a little damage control. He could only avoid total devastation by keeping his feelings for her from growing any stronger. He'd always been a man of action—never content to let anything slip beyond his ability to control it. He could do this, he told himself. He could keep this thing on a purely physical level. He could force his feelings for her to die quietly, before she had the chance to throw them back in his face. She couldn't reject something she'd never been offered. Right?

He cleared his throat and pushed the damp hair off his forehead. "We have to get back. It'll be light soon."

He didn't miss the slight sigh or the little shake of her head. She opened her mouth to speak, but closed it again without saying a word. She blinked twice in quick succession before she turned and started to walk away from him. When she put her foot down, he heard her suck air through her teeth. She didn't stop, though. She kept going, despite the limp.

He caught up to her. "Glass in your foot?"

She only nodded, and Nick scooped her into his arms and strode toward the house. She weighed almost nothing.

"Put me down, Nick. Your leg—"

"Relax," was his curt reply. He tried not to smell the scent of her hair drifting up to him or feel the curve of her hip against his groin. "Just relax." His tone was gentler the second time, and she complied, linking her arms around his neck and resting her head on his shoulder.

Nick gave up trying not to notice her—the feel of her in his arms was too much not to notice. The pain in his thigh as he walked back through the woods was minor compared to the exquisite torture his Gypsy was dishing up.

Chapter 9

Toni slanted another sidelong glance at him. He sat behind the wheel, as stonily silent as he'd been for most of the day. His chiseled jaw didn't move except for the occasional twitch. He'd been all business from the moment they'd returned to the hidden apartment. One hundred percent efficient, effective Federal Agent Manelli had taken over. The Nick she'd longed to know, the one she thought she'd finally uncovered, was gone.

With military precision he'd supervised the packing of her things to erase any trace of her presence. He'd gathered a sparse few of his own, including, she noted, the jeans and the high-tops, the basketball and the photograph. He left every one of those stuffy suits behind.

Meticulously he'd orchestrated her mother's safe departure from the country, just the way he wanted to orchestrate her own. She'd come very close to losing that round.

He stiffened in anticipation when another set of headlights broke through the darkness. The white beams moved eerily, pushing the shadows from outside the car into it and illuminating his taut face. They passed, and Toni heard his aggravated sigh. For over an hour they'd been parked here in the nearly empty concrete lot. The only other vehicles here were an abandoned '75 Chevy and a stripped-down framework that might once have been a Corvette.

"He should have been here by now." The worry in his voice came through clearly, and Toni longed to comfort him. He'd been so distant since this morning, she wasn't sure she knew how.

She knew he was worried about Joey. That was part of the reason for his icy demeanor. Joey should have been here to meet with him at dusk. It was an arrangement they'd made months ago. If it got to the point where they both had to pull out in a hurry, they'd go their separate ways and meet in this crumbling parking lot at dark the next night. He'd told her that. He'd also told her about the drug shipment that had been confiscated the night he'd been shot, and his feeling that Taranto had expected the police raid. He thought Taranto suspected Joey. If he was right, then where was Joey now?

Toni thought of the man's gentle voice and his obvious worry about Nick, and she bit her lip. If Taranto had him—

Nick glanced again at his watch. He shook his head and looked around the empty parking lot. Change the subject, Toni thought. Get him talking. At least the endless minutes of waiting would tick by a little faster.

"Mom should be safely in her hotel in Toronto by now. It's such a relief knowing she's away from all this."

He looked at her, his eyes narrow, his temper short. "If you had half a brain, you'd be with her."

She shook her head. "I told you, Nick, I have just as much invested here as you do. I'm not walking away until I see it through. If you'd put me on the flight out, I'd have caught the next one right back here."

"So you've pointed out—repeatedly. It's the only reason you're here. I couldn't risk you wandering around on your own. Lou would've had you in a matter of hours."

She rolled her eyes. "How *did* I ever manage without you? Must've been pure luck that I didn't bungle my incompetent self into an early grave last year when I took on those drug lords south of the equator."

"I didn't mean..." He shook his head and sighed loudly. "Okay. You're good at this, all right? You're just too damn gutsy for your own good. You rush headlong into situations that could be dangerous. That's all I meant, not that you were incompetent."

She blinked and looked at him. "Gutsy?" She felt the frown come and go as she digested that. After a moment she shook her head quickly. "No, I'm a big coward. Katrina's the gutsy one." His gaze seemed surprised. "I could never do the things she does," she said to try to explain.

"Oh. Things like following Mafia associates into dark alleys in the middle of the night? Or maybe things like slapping a six-two alleged hit man who's carrying a gun because he says something you don't like?" He looked away from her face. "You're no coward, lady. You wouldn't be doing what you've been doing if you were."

"You have it all wrong." She answered him quickly, the words tumbling out before she had a chance to think about them. "I do it because I'm a coward. I do it to make up for what I didn't do before."

"Before?" His dark brows drew together as he regarded her in the dim interior of the car. "Before what?"

She shrugged.

"You're talking about your father's death, aren't you? Toni, you can't possibly blame yourself for that."

She couldn't hold his gaze. She hadn't understood until now the connection between her guilt over her father's suicide and her need to fix society's ills in any way she could. She gazed through the window, seeing nothing. "I knew what was happening. I should have done something."

"You were still in high school. What could you have done?"

"Something. Anything. I shouldn't have let it go on so long. I shouldn't have let him . . ." She stopped and tried to swallow the lump in her throat.

"Shouldn't have let him what?" Nick touched her arm, but Toni couldn't answer him. "You couldn't have changed what happened, Toni."

"I could. I knew when he left the house that day . . . it was in his eyes. I shouldn't have let him go."

He was quiet for a long moment. Maybe he finally believed her, her mind whispered. Not that it mattered. She knew. She'd always known. When he took her chin in his hand and turned her to face him, she wished he'd just drop the subject.

"You know what I think?" She shook her head, and he went on. "I think you feel so guilty about it that you want to be punished. I think that's why you challenge death at every opportunity. Maybe you're hoping it'll beat you one of these times. Maybe you think, somewhere deep down in that pretty head of yours, that you don't deserve to live when he didn't."

In the dark, quiet car, Nick deftly opened the festering wound in her soul and let the infection begin to heal. Toni felt her lips tremble. She couldn't speak. How could he see so clearly the truth she'd kept hidden from herself for such a long time? The accuracy of what he'd said was so clear to her all at once. Why hadn't she seen it before?

"It wasn't your fault, Toni." He watched the changes in her face for a moment. "Do you think your father would've wanted you to spend your life paying for his decision that day?"

She shook her head. "No, but—"

"You know how badly you've felt since he took his own life?" His arms suddenly encircled her shoulders. He brought her close to him, until she was held like a child. "That's how badly your mother would feel if you followed his example, Toni. Do you want to be responsible for causing her that kind of pain?"

She shook her head hard, moving it against his shoulder where it was cradled. "No! I never meant . . . I didn't realize . . ." She released all her breath at once. She felt like crying. The huge burden she'd been bearing for so long suddenly grew lighter. It didn't vanish; some of it remained. For the first time in a very long time, though, she thought she understood it. God. This changed the scope of her very existence! She felt free all of a sudden.

She sat up slightly and studied his face in awed fascination. "You should have been a shrink. My God, how do you see so much?"

He shrugged. One hand stroked a wisp of hair away from her face. "You are transparent to me, Gypsy. Don't forget, we've been together constantly for the past week. I think I know you pretty well . . . except . . ."

"Except what?"

He released her and settled back in his seat. Toni settled back, too, but close enough so their bodies touched. "Did you ever want to do anything else?" he asked. "I mean, besides write tell-all books to clear your conscience?"

She allowed a small smile. "I love to write and I'm good at it."

"I'll let you know after I read the book," he quipped.

She smiled fully. Finally the easy, relaxed atmosphere between them had returned. "I had a plan, you know. A long time ago before I got so wrapped up in being a do-gooder."

He folded his arms, clasping his hands behind his head. "Tell me."

Toni closed her eyes and envisioned the life she'd allowed to exist only in her dreams. "Rural town," she told him. "Not suburban, *rural.* I'm not even certain my road is paved. The house is a rambling old Victorian—white with black shutters and huge open porches. I have a big office in the back with a window that overlooks the enormous back lawn. There are yellow roses growing there and a flowering crab apple tree. I write wonderful books with happy endings. When I get tired of sitting at the computer, I walk the dog."

She didn't need to look at him to know his brow shot up. "The dog?"

"Um-hmm. He's a huge gray-and-white sheepdog. He's so shaggy I have to trim the hair around his eyes every few weeks so he can see. His name is Ralph. We walk together every day, down the path to the duck pond, and—"

"This is one vivid plan," he said slowly.

"I'm a writer. I see details in everything." Headlights approached once more, and Nick sat up straighter. This time they veered into the parking lot. The car drew nearer, pulled up alongside, and the driver's window lowered slowly. The man sitting there was not Joey.

Nick lowered his window. "Harry, what the hell's going on?"

The man in the other car met Nick's gaze, all but ignoring Toni's presence. "It isn't good, Manelli. Joey's dropped off the planet. No one's been able to find a trace of him."

Nick flinched as if he'd been struck. The man in the other car kept on speaking. He glanced at Toni. "Her mother was not on that plane, Nick. We haven't been able to locate her, either."

"Damn."

Toni shook her head rapidly. "No. It isn't what you're thinking. I know my mother. She probably just set her heels and decided she wasn't leaving. When I talked to her earlier and explained the situation—" she swallowed and cleared her throat "—I should have known she agreed too easily. She's stubborn as a mule sometimes."

"I hope you're right," the man called Harry said. He returned his attention to Nick. "Why's she still with you, Manelli? You had orders—"

"She would have come right back and become a target," Nick snapped. "It was safer to keep her with me."

"I'd appreciate it if you two would stop talking as if I'm not here." She looked at Nick, feeling a dark terror creep into her heart. If Taranto had her mother...

"What do we do now, Nick?"

Harry reworded her question and put it to Nick. "Do you have enough on Taranto to make an arrest stick?"

Nick shook his head. "He paid me to kill Toni—but that's no good because I don't have enough to prove it and Toni isn't dead. He sent me to witness Vinnie's hit, but he never really confessed to that on tape. The man knows enough to talk in circles. He says all he needs to say without ever admitting a thing." He looked down and shook his head.

"What kind of evidence do you need?"

Both men looked at Toni. "What have you got?"

She eyed Nick for a moment. "I have photographs of Lou Taranto passing a large manila envelope to a man named Santos. Santos was later arrested in Colombia for murder."

"Right," Harry interrupted. "Last year. He'd tampered with the plane that was supposed to carry Juan Perez to the U.S. to stand trial for drug trafficking. The plane crashed after takeoff. Perez died, along with the three DEA agents who were escorting him back."

"Juan Perez was Lou Taranto's cocaine supplier in Colombia," Nick said.

Toni nodded. "That's right. And if he'd made it here to stand trial, he might have been offered a deal in exchange for his testimony against Taranto. Santos took that envelope from Lou and left for Colombia within six hours. And when he got there, a large amount of money suddenly appeared in his bank account."

"Toni, how the hell do you know all this?"

She met Nick's intense look. "I followed Lou for weeks, researching this book. One day I saw him meet with Santos in a little café. I slipped the waitress fifty bucks for her apron and got close enough to eavesdrop. I took the shots of Taranto passing Santos the envelope, and they never even glanced up at me. When they left the diner, I decided to follow Santos and the envelope instead. That's how I know he went straight to Colombia. I still had connections down there from the last book and I called one of them. Larry Wetzel. He has a lucrative little investigations agency going down there. He'll testify if you force him to. Anyway, he met the flight and tailed Santos on that end. He reported that Santos had checked into a motel and got himself a job at a small airfield. The next day Perez's plane took off from that same airfield and crashed.''

Nick stared at her and shook his head. "Slipped the waitress fifty bucks…" he mumbled, more to himself than anyone else.

"How much of this do you have documented?" Harry seemed eager.

"The photograph of Lou handing Santos the envelope is irrefutable. I have another one of Santos boarding the flight to Colombia. You already have proof that Santos sabotaged the flight. He would've been tried for that last year if he hadn't been found hanging by the neck in his cell."

"If that was self-inflicted, I'll eat my badge," Harry said softly.

"Still, it's not solid," Nick put it.

"I have the envelope. There's a coffee stain on it, identical to the one that shows in the first photo. My PI friend grabbed it out of a trash can where Santos had dropped it after lighting a match to it. Larry managed to douse the flame before it did too much damage."

Nick looked at Harry, then at Toni again. "Come on, Chekov, don't keep us in suspense. What was inside?"

She couldn't help smiling a little smugly. "A five-by-seven glossy of Perez, and a handwritten note with the name of the airfield, the flight number and the time and date of departure. The only thing that wasn't there was the money, and that is still in Santos's bank account."

Harry's long, low whistle came at the same moment that Nick asked, "Where?" She didn't answer. His hands clasped her shoulders, and he squeezed them between his fingers. "Don't play games, Toni. Tell me where to find the evidence."

She shook her head. "I'll take you to it." He frowned, and his grip tightened, but she only stuck her chin out a little farther. "If I tell you, you'll try to stash me somewhere while you go after it alone."

His hands fell to his sides. He nodded. "That's right." He glanced downward for a long moment, then faced her again. "Your apartment. That locked room, right?"

She shook her head, but not before he'd seen the answer in her eyes. His gaze pummeled her. "All right, yes. But you don't know the combination for my safe, and I won't give it to you."

"I'll get into it whether you give me the combination or not."

"But that will take time. Isn't time of the essence here?"

"She's got you there, Manelli," Harry interrupted. "Take her along, we're wasting time arguing. I'll get a team in place. You'll have backup. One hour."

Nick glared from Toni to Harry. "I don't like it—she'll be a moving target."

"We'll take precautions," Harry told him. "Beginning right now. Get out of the car." Nick hesitated. "Come on, Manelli, I don't have all night. You've been driving that one through this entire operation. Taranto knows it. We'll switch. I'll get that thing out of sight for a while. You have any vests on?"

"Not yet," Nick said.

"There's a pair in the back seat. Get into them." He got out of the car as he spoke and yanked Nick's door open. "Come on, let's not sit here all night." She could see that Nick didn't want to comply, but the moment he opened his mouth to argue the other man held up a hand. "Consider it an order."

Lou Taranto leaned back in his overstuffed chair. He took the cigarette from his lips and held it in front of him, studying the smoke that spiraled up from the glowing tip. He released what he'd inhaled, and his face became a blur in the center of the stark room. Viper stood at his right hand, his button eyes gleaming. He alternately clenched and opened his red-knuckled hand.

"Bring him around," Taranto ordered.

Viper shook his head. "He's had it, Lou." Viper thumbed a swollen, purple eyelid open and let it fall. The only things holding Joey upright were the ropes that bound him to the straight wooden chair. "He's told you all he's gonna."

"He's told me nothing. But he will, damn lousy cop. Bring him around!"

"I told you, he's had it. Damn near comatose. Be dead in a few hours."

"Stubborn little son of a bitch," Lou muttered.

Viper rolled his eyes. "You don't need Salducci to tell you what you already know. Nick's a cop, too. It's obvious. They came in right around the same time. They were both in on the shipment that was taken."

"Nicky took a bullet that night!"

"And Joey patched him up. You know he's a Fed. You think he'd have patched up my leg? Yours? No way, he'd have smiled while we bled to death. What do you need? A signed confession? Manelli's a cop. I say we off him."

Lou came to his feet as fast as his ample weight would allow and gripped Viper by the lapels. "We have to be sure, you little twit, because of the girl! If Nicky's a cop, then you can bet she isn't dead. She's still out there and she's got more on us than any cop does. We have to find out for sure."

"She saw my face," Viper ground out, jerking himself from Lou's hands. "And so did he. I'm on the line here, and I'll deal with it my way."

"Don't cross me, Viper, or I—"

"Don't you worry, Lou. I'll handle it. You'll thank me before this is over." Viper spun and left the room. Lou opened the door and bellowed after him, but he kept on walking. A moment later his car left the lot outside the Century.

A bulky man with a crew cut loomed over Lou a moment later. "Word is they have warrants to search the place. What do we do?"

Lou looked at the limp, bruised man in the chair. "Cop or not, Nicky didn't know who that broad was until I told him, I'd bet my life on that."

The overgrown hulk in front of him puckered his brows. "Huh?"

Lou turned, paced away from him, muttering to himself. "If he's a cop, he'll go to her apartment to see what she had on me. If he's loyal, he'll go because I told him to." He stopped in front of Joey and lifted the lax head by a tuft of hair. "What do you suppose he'll think when he finds you there waitin' for him?"

"I don't get it, boss."

Lou whirled. He yanked a small notepad from his shirt pocket and scribbled three letters onto the first sheet, then tore it off. "Here, pin this to his chest. Then take him to the Rio broad's apartment and dump him there."

"But how can I get him in there without somebody seein' him?"

"How the hell do I know? Roll him in a rug for all I care, just do it! We'll soon find out just how loyal Nick Manelli is to the family."

Harry Anderson shook his head slowly and tried to see it again in his mind. The way that bit of a woman stuck her chin in Nick's face and told him what was what—the way he *let her!* He'd finally met his match, the big jerk. It was about time.

He drove Nick's car toward the gloomy mansion they'd set him up in. He'd retrieve the videotapes just in case the del Rio girl couldn't produce what she said she could. They'd be better than nothing. At the very least they could be used to identify Viper. Then he'd head back to headquarters and get a team together to back Nick up when he went to the woman's apartment. Taranto would be watching, if Harry's opinion was worth anything.

He was within sight of those ridiculous iron gates, rounding a bend in the curving road, when he heard the glass shatter and felt the searing pain at his left temple. He clenched the wheel reflexively, jerking it to the right. He felt the front tires leave the pavement and realized he was airborne and heading down the steep drop alongside the road. He prayed the bullet that had hit him would kill him before he hit bottom.

Chapter 10

Nick circled the block twice, then turned to enter the parking garage. He drove slowly beneath the fluorescent tube lights on the low ceiling. His gaze scanned every vehicle, peered around every support column. The place seemed as still as a graveyard. The hair on the back of his neck bristled in anticipation. He could feel that he was being watched. His fear made him more careful than he'd ever been. Not fear for himself, but for the woman in the seat beside him, crouched low as he'd instructed. He knew he'd lose her. The cycle had repeated itself again today, just in case he'd forgotten the way things worked. Taranto had Joey. Nick had a grim knowledge in his gut that he wouldn't see his best friend again. He shouldn't have let himself care so much.

Now, like an idiot, he'd let himself care again, about Toni. He had to lose her. That was the way it always happened. He'd be damned, though, if he'd lose her to Lou

Taranto the way he'd lost Danny and Joey. Let her walk
out on her own the way his parents had.

He nearly drove past the stairwell, he was so absorbed
in his thoughts. He pulled up close to the heavy door, shut
the car off, pocketed the keys. It'll be all right, he told
himself. Harry must have a half-dozen men in the building, a dozen more outside, if he was true to form. Nothing could happen to her. He wouldn't let it.

He opened the door and stood for a moment, every
sense attuned. He saw no one, heard nothing but the
normal traffic noises and a car squealing on the level below. The place smelled of exhaust and hot pavement. He
glanced down at Toni, nodding once. She wriggled out his
door, staying bent low, just the way he'd instructed. With
his body blocking her from view on one side, the car on
the other, she hurried to the open door of the stairwell.
Her running shoes made no sound. She moved through
the doorway, pressed her back against the inside wall and
waited. Nick closed the car door and moved in beside her.
He pulled the heavy stairwell door closed. The place echoed like an empty church. If anyone opened the door, he'd
hear them. Then again, anyone already here would hear
him, too. Any sound would echo through the cool, hollow stairway. He pressed a finger to his lips to remind Toni
of that.

He pulled the Taurus from the holster under his left
arm, held it with its nose pointed up and began to move
up the stairs. He kept Toni close behind him. His caution
doubled when he reached a landing. He pushed her flat to
the wall behind her and peered around to the next flight,
taking his time to be sure it was safe before urging her to
come along. It seemed to take forever to reach the fourth
floor. In reality, it took less than ten minutes.

Nick glanced through the small square of glass, criss-crossed with wire between the panes, before he opened the door and stepped into the tiled corridor. Toni came out behind him. Her tug on his jacket brought his gaze around fast. She frowned at the gun in his hand and shook her head. Okay, she was probably right. He'd draw some attention sneaking through the corridors of an apartment building with an automatic in his hand. He slipped it back inside his jacket. She pointed a finger, presumably in the direction of her apartment, and Nick started moving again.

Trying to walk causally through the hall was the toughest thing he'd done in a long time. Moving steadily beneath the lighted ceiling panels, between the doors that lined both sides—doors that might swing open at any second to reveal a hard-faced man with an Uzi.

He swallowed. It wouldn't happen that way. Taranto still trusted him. Joey wouldn't talk, no matter what they did. Besides, Harry was here, somewhere, with an armed entourage.

They came to a T and Toni jabbed her thumb to the left. Nick moved no more than three doors down when her hand on his shoulder stopped him. Nick looked at her. Their gazes locked for a moment, and that unspoken *thing* passed between them—that connection he couldn't acknowledge and didn't recognize.

He pulled his gaze away and looked at the door she indicated. Nick's spine stiffened. He took the gun out again and put his hand out for the key. Toni was quicker, already leaning to slip it into the lock. When she touched the door, it fell open without a sound, and she jerked away from it, eyes wide. It hadn't been locked. It hadn't even been closed properly. Someone had been here. Maybe they still were. He pushed her to the wall and mouthed the words, "wait here." He let his gun lead him into the apartment.

His stomach clenched when he saw Joey in the middle of the floor. He wasn't sure he'd have recognized him except for the familiar clothes he wore. A slip of paper on his jacket had the word Cop penciled on it. His face varied in shades of crimson, blue and purple. His eyes looked like two fat grapes, swollen closed. From the looks of it, he'd never open them again. There was no doubt in Nick's mind that Joey was dead. His training helped him push the paralyzing grief aside, allowing only the cold certainty that Lou Taranto would pay dearly, to remain. He let the experience of years on the job take over and quickly checked each room of the apartment. When he was certain no one else was there, he went back to tell Toni it was safe to come inside.

She already had. She knelt on the floor beside Joey, tucking a blanket around him. He recognized the throw that had been on the couch and then the matching pillows she'd placed under his feet. Nick approached slowly, afraid to believe . . .

"We have to get him to a hospital, Nick." Toni's brows pushed against each other until they crinkled. Her voice was grim with fear.

Nick looked to see that she'd already closed the door, then knelt opposite her, over Joey. He couldn't credit what he saw when Joey shook his head slightly left and right. "No."

Nick felt a twisting sensation in his gut and a sudden rush of guilt to his mind. This has been *his* obsession. It should have been him lying on the floor, his face encrusted with dried blood, barely able to form a single word. It should have been him, not Joey.

The battered lips moved again. "Nick?"

Nick gripped his friend's shoulders to let him know he was there. Joey couldn't open his eyes to see for himself. "I'm right here, pal."

"Lou...watch—watching," Joey managed. His slurred speech had Nick more worried about brain damage than about Lou.

"To see if I help you," Nick finished for him. A white rage unfurled inside him.

"We should call an ambulance."

The tightness in her voice brought Nick's gaze back to Toni, and he saw tears brimming in her eyes. She leaned closer to Joey, keeping her voice soothingly low and soft. "We're going to take care of you," she was telling him. "You'll be okay."

It reminded Nick of the way she'd spoken to him the night before, when the fire in his thigh had burned bright. Funny, he'd barely felt the pain since arriving in this building. Adrenaline was a great anesthetic. "If Lou's watching, Toni, he doesn't intend to let Joey out of here alive. There's no way he'll let an ambulance crew in the building." Nick felt the frustration gnawing at him. He had to think! Joey needed serious help and he needed it fast.

"Didn't...tell...him," Joey stammered, "any-thing."

"I never thought otherwise. And I know what you're getting at. My cover's intact. You're thinking I should leave you here and keep it that way. I'm not going to do that, so shut up and let me think."

Nick felt Joey's hand close around his with surprising force. "He'll...kill you...both."

"Not if I can help it, he won't. And if we can get out of here in one piece, he's going down. Turns out Toni had the goods on him all along." He glanced up at Toni. "Get the file."

She got up and hurried into the room that was her office. He heard her moving around in there at the same time he heard the door opening. He yanked his gun out. The apartment door swung open, and Nick saw the barrel of a .44 Magnum staring him in the face. There was a small blond woman attached to it. She seemed vaguely familiar.

"What the hell—"

"Put that gun down and tell me what you've done with my daughter!"

Nick realized who she was. Somehow he wasn't surprised. He lowered his gun slowly and laid it on the carpet. "Come in and close the door."

She did warily. Toni chose that moment to emerge from the office with the thick folder in her hands. The two women spied each other at the same moment, and a second later both the .44 and file folder were on the floor as they embraced.

"You've had me worried to death, Antonia. Are you all right?"

"Fine." They pulled apart, and Toni seemed to drink in her mother's face. "I'm so glad you're okay. When you didn't get on that flight, I—"

"You didn't expect me to just fly off and leave you, did you?"

Toni shook her head. "Not really. Where on earth did you get that cannon?"

Kate del Rio glanced down at the gun on the floor, then at the man beyond it. "My God, what happened?"

"He's a federal agent, Mom. Taranto found out."

"How did you get into the building?" Nick inserted when there was finally a long enough break.

"Through the front entrance. Why?"

Nick blew a sigh and shook his head. "This is a real high-security place you picked, Toni. What the hell do you do with all that money your books earn you?"

"I—"

"She hoards it away like a pack rat," her mother inserted with a mock scowl. "Saving it for some rambling Victorian house and a sheepdog." She glanced at Nick and offered him a tremulous smile. "If you're who I think you are, I have to thank you for keeping her alive to spend it."

There was affection in her warm blue eyes. "Nick Manelli," he told her.

"Kate del Rio. Sorry about the gun before." Nick shrugged. Kate looked again at Joey on the floor. "Why isn't this man on his way to a hospital?"

"Taranto is watching. If I try to take him out of here, there's a chance I'll get him killed."

She frowned and shook her head. "What are you going to do?"

"I haven't figured that out yet."

"I have," Toni said.

Nick looked at her fast. He hadn't liked the slight waver in her voice, and he saw now the unnatural paleness in her cheeks. She was scared. "Tell me. I can see you don't think I'm going to like it."

"Doesn't matter if you like it. Joey needs help, Nick, or he won't make it. I'll wrap myself in a blanket. You can carry me down to the car, and we'll leave. Taranto will think I'm Joey and come after us. You just said he wouldn't let Joey make it to a hospital alive. He'll come after *us*. When he does, it will be safe for Mom to get Joey to an emergency room."

Nick rose from Joey's side, took Toni's shoulders in his hands and gazed into her bottomless eyes. "Listen close, little Gypsy, 'cause I'm only saying this once. No. It isn't going to happen."

She stood straighter. "Then I assume you have a better idea?" Her tiny chin jutted, and her eyes flashed with determination that overrode her fear. "We'll be all right, Nick. You know Harry and all his men are out there. They'll be right behind Taranto when he comes after us. We'll be fine."

His hands tightened. "You're offering to act as a decoy, Toni. A target. What am I supposed to do if Taranto manages to catch us? Stand there and watch him give the order to put a bullet in your head?"

"Are our chances any better by staying here? They aren't and you know it. The longer we argue about this, the closer Joey gets to having no chance at all."

Joey moaned low as if to punctuate her words. His body shuddered once, then went still. Kate tensed beside him, pressing the pads of her fingers to his throat. She sighed and took them away. "Antonia is right. He can't stay here, Nicholas. Every minute is pushing him closer to death."

"We'll leave the file here," Toni said quickly. "She'll keep it safe and give it to Harry when he gets to the hospital."

Nick shook his head. "*You* give it to Harry. I'll try and lead Taranto away myself."

"If you do, Nick, I'll get in Mom's car and come after you."

He closed his eyes slowly, opened them again. He felt like a projectile had lodged in his chest. She was offering him a way to save Joey. Joey, his best friend since he'd been no more than a smart-mouth kid. Joey—whom he loved. But her offer put her at risk. Toni, the woman who'd handed him the ammunition to put Taranto away. Toni—whom he...what?

He damn well didn't love her. It would be stupid to love a woman he knew he'd lose in the end. Stupid!

"You wanna tell me why you're being so stubborn about this?"

Her gaze held his as a magnet holds steel. "You'll have twice the chance of getting away if I'm with you." She shook her head. "Look, this might be your case—your vendetta, but it's my evidence. Whether you like it or not, we're in this together. I'm not going to walk away and let you take the heat alone just because things are starting to get dangerous. Taranto might not follow you if you leave alone."

Joey began to shake again, violently this time, his legs stiffening as his heels jostled off the pillows and tapped a beat on the floor. Toni pulled from Nick's restraining hands, disappeared into the bedroom and returned a second later with a blanket draped over her shoulders. She bent to pick up the gun her mother had dropped.

Kate got to her feet, wrapped Toni in her arms and squeezed. "You be careful—and take care of your Nicholas. I like him."

"I love you, Mom."

To his shock, Kate del Rio stepped away from her daughter and turned to fold him in a powerful embrace. "I'll take care of Joseph. Don't worry about him. And don't keep questioning yourself. This seems the only way."

Toni had to remain limp in his arms as he carried her through the corridors and into the chill concrete of the stairwell. She'd much rather have wound her arms around his neck and hidden her face against him. She felt a shiver of pure fear when she thought about what they were doing, yet she hadn't been able to stay behind. She'd let her feelings for Nick grow too quickly. The thought of staying behind and allowing him to face this alone had been unacceptable. She hadn't been able to consider it.

She told herself that it was because he'd done something so precious to her by making her see what drove her all this time. Recognizing that the emotion behind her recklessness had been guilt over her father's suicide was a major step toward overcoming it. He'd opened the shutters, spilling brilliant light in the shadowy corners of her mind, and forcing her to see what was there. Now she could begin to sweep away the cobwebs and dust that had built up for so long. She owed him for that.

Still, there was more than gratitude in her heart. She recognized that he had some musty, sealed-off rooms in his mind, too. Rooms he rarely allowed himself to enter. She knew the wound in his soul he'd allowed to fester since his brother's death. She knew that the abandonment by his parents had injured him deeply, and she knew he refused to admit that. She wanted to help him clean out those cluttered rooms and then fill them with warmth and happiness.

It was amazing how well she'd come to know Nick in such a short time. It hit her hardest whenever he looked into her eyes. It was palpable, whatever passed between them then—as if they were touching souls. She wondered if he felt it, too. He kept himself so closed off, it made it difficult to tell.

She felt his body tense, and shook herself. He'd come to the entrance to the parking garage. As he carried her through the doorway, she tensed, as well, but he moved quickly, lowering her into the front seat faster than she would have believed possible. She kept the blanket over her face, left her head limp and clutched the textured walnut grips of the huge handgun until her knuckles whitened. He was behind the wheel in an instant, gunning the motor and speeding away. She knew when they left the underground garage and turned onto the street.

"Is anyone following—" She began to sit up a little as she spoke and flipped the blanket away from her face. Nick's hand pulled her down again. Her backside was on the seat, but her head was pressed to his rib cage. He held her for a moment, his arm around her like a steel band.

When it came away, she saw him adjust the rearview. "Oh, yeah. They're coming, all right. Where the hell is Harry?"

Toni felt the car jerk and heard the squeal of the tires when he took a sharp corner, then another. She wished she could see his face. She heard the grim tone in his voice, though. "Harry isn't here. I can't believe this...." He took another corner, drew a breath. "Something must've happened to him before he could get back to HQ. I think we're on our own."

Toni tried to make her voice level. "What—what could've happened?"

"Don't worry about it now. Listen, I'm going to take a few quick turns, see if I can lose them for a second. Just long enough for you to get out. Slide over by the door and get ready—"

"I told you we're in this together, Nick."

"That was when we thought we had backup."

"And now I'm the only backup you have," she countered. "I'm not going anywhere."

He drove in stony silence then, never slowing down, his muscles tense. Suddenly he hit the brakes, and she heard him swear viciously. His thigh went rigid under her hand,

and she lifted her head very slightly to see what had caused him to skid to a halt.

A car had pulled across the street in front of them. Nick shifted into reverse and slammed the pedal to the floor, turning the wheel sharply. He was crossways in the street when the van skidded to a stop behind them. They were trapped. The only way out was a narrow channel between the vehicles. It would take them over the sidewalk and smack into a mailbox, but—

Before she could complete the thought, the men were out of their vehicles. She saw two barrels pointing toward her from behind the car. A frantic glance to her right showed two more from the van. Lou Taranto's voice came clearly. "Out of the car, Nicky. I don't have time to play with you. I count three and put a bullet in the gas tank!"

Nick looked down at her, into her eyes, and again she felt that powerful surge of some unknown force linking them together. "Stay down low," he instructed. His voice was deep and soft. "Count to ten, then shift into gear and put the pedal to the floor." His eyes shifted, indicating the same escape route she'd just recognized.

She frowned. "I don't under—" She stopped, eyes widened when she saw his hand close around the door handle. "No. Nick, you can't—"

"He means it, Toni. He'll blow us both to hell if I don't." He reached down, threading his fingers in her hair. "They think it's Joey in here with me. They won't be expecting it. Their attention will be on me. When I get far enough from the car, floor it. It's your only chance."

"No. I won't do it, you can't—"

"Manelli! I'm taking aim! Get out now or burn!"

Nick blinked. He leaned over and touched her face with his lips. "Do it. Don't look back." He forced a lopsided grin. "For what it's worth, Gypsy, it meant something with you."

He wrenched the door open and got out fast. Toni barely restrained herself from shrieking at him. She slid herself into his spot behind the wheel, still keeping her head lower than the seat.

"Move away from the car," Taranto yelled.

Toni saw Nick walk slowly toward the rear of the car, then past it. He stood several yards to the rear of the vehicle, and as he'd predicted, every gun was trained on him. She swallowed hard. This couldn't be happening. She blinked and when she opened her eyes, she saw a man coming toward the passenger side, his gun drawn and ready.

"If Salducci isn't dead yet, finish him." Taranto's voice echoed in her mind. She turned herself in the seat so she faced that door. She pulled the blanket around her, leaving a crack she could see through and poking the six-inch nickel barrel through another. She thumbed the hammer back.

The car door opened, and the tall, dark outline of a man filled it. She watched in horror as the gun barrel lowered toward her. She tightened her finger on the trigger, and the big gun bucked violently in her hands. The roar of it was deafening in the car's interior. The man reacted as if he'd been slammed in the chest with a hammer, jerking backward. His face went lax. The shock faded, and his body sunk limply to the ground.

She had to act quickly while the confusion lasted. At the moment, they must think his gun was the one they'd heard. She jammed her finger on the trunk-release button and shifted the car into reverse. She backed fast, hitting the brakes only when she was right at Nick's side. She heard the shots being fired at her now. The window to the left exploded, showering her with glass. The one at the right imitated it, seemingly at the same time. As soon as she felt the car sink with Nick's weight, she sped away, hitting the mailbox hard enough to rattle her teeth, jumping the curb and squealing over a stretch of sidewalk. The car dropped back to the street again on the other side of the parked van, and Toni pushed the pedal to the floor.

The lights around her blended into a single blurred haze. The traffic sounds became a buzzing drone as the adrenaline surged. They must be chasing her. She couldn't see them now, but they must be. Was Nick hit in all the shooting? Was he even now bleeding to death in the trunk? She'd killed a man. The weight of it dropped on her suddenly and powerfully. She'd taken a life. She hadn't even known him and she'd killed him. Her stomach heaved, and she bit her lip until she drew blood to fight off the nausea.

Tears pooled in her eyes, and no amount of blinking prevented them spilling over. She'd never been so frightened in her life! Her hands shook, partly from the force with which she gripped the wheel and partly from the remnants of her terror. She could barely see where she drove now, but she kept the pressure on the accelerator all the same...

...until she careened into an intersection and heard the blast of an air horn. The impact snapped her head back. She heard grinding, bending metal and shattering glass. She smelled diesel smoke and hot rubber. She felt a warm trickle at her temple and then she felt nothing at all.

Chapter 11

The collision sent Nick sailing from the trunk of the car. He felt the queasy sensation of being airborne, then the force of the ground that rushed up to meet him. A knife seemed to twist in his shoulder. Every trace of air gusted from his lungs with the impact. For an instant he couldn't move, paralyzed by the jolt. His head came up slowly. His gaze pinpointed the car, its front folded like an accordion, its windshield shattered. A diesel truck's long nose stood embedded in the side of the car, just to the front of the driver's door. The vehicles had met at the center of an intersection, where Toni had probably run a red light.

Nick struggled to his feet and shook his head to clear it. He had to get over there, had to see if Toni—

He sucked in a sharp breath when he saw her, slumped forward in the car, her wild hair obliterating the steering wheel. He moved forward at an uneven lope, not aware of the renewed bleeding in his unhealed thigh or the way his left arm hung limp at his side. He approached the car door, and a woman leapt to the pavement from the truck and hurried toward him.

"I never saw her. She ran the light— Oh, God, is she all right?"

He barely heard the woman's words as he wrenched the door open and bent over her. He saw the thin rivulet of blood and pushed the hair away from her face, careful not to move her. A tiny cut, perhaps from flying glass, bled only slightly. In the dim glow of the truck's marker lights, Nick searched for signs of injuries but saw none. Her skin was dusted thinly with a white powder that puzzled him at first.

He took her hand, felt her strong pulse thrumming beneath the skin of her wrist and breathed a sigh of relief. "Toni? Can you hear me?" Her eyelids flickered. "Toni? Come on, baby, talk to me."

Her brows drew together, and her eyes opened slowly. "Nick?" She lifted her head from the wheel. "What happened?" She looked around her, saw the truck and stiffened. "Oh, God... are you okay?" Her gaze pored over him.

"Fine. You're the one I'm worried about."

She seemed to take stock for a moment, then looked at him, her eyes clearer, and nodded. "I bumped my head. Other than that, I'm okay...." She stopped and fingered the powder-coated material that hung from the center of the steering wheel into her lap.

"The air bag. Looks like it burst somehow. Sure did its job first, though." He touched her face, studying her dark eyes. "You sure you're all right, Gypsy? Do you hurt anywhere?"

"I'm okay," she repeated. This time she leaned toward him, placing her feet on the pavement. Still sitting, she looked up suddenly. "Taranto. Where is he?"

"Not far, that's sure." She nodded, started to stand. Nick slipped his arms around her waist and helped her up. She took a moment to get her balance.

Behind him Nick heard the truck driver sigh. "She seems okay. Look, I'm going to find a phone, report this. Do you want me to call an ambulance?"

"No," Toni answered quickly before Nick had a chance to say anything. She met his gaze, and he knew they were both thinking the same thing. She'd be a sitting duck in an ambulance.

The slender woman nodded. Nick saw her reach into the truck and remove some flares before she hurried away. He held Toni against him with his good arm and urged her away from the scene. A crowd was already forming. He moved quickly, keeping to the shadows, ducking between buildings and emerging in a parking lot that must have been filled to capacity. It took only a minute to find an unlocked car. A '75 Mustang, with several rust spots forming in the cherry red paint. He reached under the dashboard, twisted the right wires together and smiled slightly when the motor came to life. He stepped back to help Toni slide into the car, but she shook her head fast.

"You said you were fine. Your leg is bleeding."

"That's not all that will be bleeding if we don't get out of here."

She shook her head, but got in and slid across the seat. Nick took the wheel and drove very slowly from the lot. As they gained the street, he glimpsed Lou Taranto's car pulled up at the curb. He scanned the crowd, catching sight of Lou's round body forcefully moving through toward the car in the intersection.

Toni pointed. "Nick, it's him!"

"I know. Take it easy, he won't be looking for a Mustang." He continued to drive carefully, causally. In a moment the accident scene was behind them, and he drove faster.

Toni glanced up at him, shook her head. "You aren't using your left arm."

He felt the relief wash through him. Her speech wasn't slightly slurred now, as it had been a few minutes ago. He looked at her. She sat back against the seat, brushing at the powdery residue from the air bag that clung to her. He had the absurd urge to pull off the road, take her into his arms and kiss her breathless. God, when he'd seen her in the car in those first moments after the collision, he thought he'd lost her. Again. The horrible feeling had hit him once before, earlier, when he'd seen Taranto's thug walk toward the car and heard that single gunshot. For just one excruciating moment, he'd thought the man had killed her. The notion had nearly made him sink to his knees then and there.

This realization put a whole new light on things. He thought he'd prepared himself for the inevitable time when she'd leave him. Now he knew nothing could prepare him for that. He'd felt only pure anguish in those moments. Desolation like nothing he knew could exist had enveloped him in blackness.

"Nick?"

He snapped out of his ponderings at the sweet sound of her voice. He knew he'd have to reassess this thing...later. Right now all he could feel was elation that she was all right. He looked at her again, at her smooth dark skin, her thick-lashed ebony eyes. He could look at her forever and not get used to her stunning beauty, he thought vaguely.

"Nick, your arm. Is it broken?"

"My—no. I landed on my shoulder when I was launched from the trunk. It's sore but not broken." He was having a tough time keeping his eyes on the streets, making the right turns to take them to the highway and as far from the city as they could get.

"But it hurts...a lot. I can see that." She shoved her hair back with one open hand. "Do you want me to drive?"

"You think I have a death wish? I will not ever be a passenger in a vehicle you're operating again, lady. Not even if it's a tricycle."

A laugh escaped, but she stifled it quickly. "I owed you a ride in a trunk, the way I see it." Her smile faded slowly, and worry clouded her hypnotic eyes. "Do you think Mom and Joey made it out of there?"

"Not a doubt in my mind," he told her without pause. "Taranto was behind us the minute we left. Your plan worked like a charm. There was nothing to get in your mother's way—not that I think it would have mattered."

She looked up quickly. "What is that supposed to mean?"

"I think you're a lot like her," Nick said. "Now I know where you get your brass." She shook her head, but he went on. "As soon as we put a few miles between us and Lou, we'll find a pay phone and check on them."

"Good." She studied her hands in her lap for a moment. "You're wrong about the brass, Nick. I was terrified back there."

"Only an idiot wouldn't have been." He signaled to turn and took them over the ramp to Route 95, heading east. "You could've left me there...should've. Instead, you backed the damn car right into the cross fire to pick me up." He shook his head, recalling the shock he'd felt to see the car coming toward him as the trunk lifted. "Until then, I thought the son of a bitch had shot you."

He swallowed the lump that came into his throat when he said those words out loud.

She cleared her throat, and he saw her blink rapidly. "I never . . . thought I'd have to . . . kill someone."

Idiot, he chided inwardly. He hadn't even thought she might be feeling the effects of that. "You know it was him or you, Toni."

She nodded. "I know . . . it's just . . ."

He forced his throbbing shoulder into action, lifting his arm and taking the wheel with his left hand. He slid his right along the back of the seat, encircled her shoulders and pulled her to his side. "Go on, tell me. I've been there, too, you know."

A tiny sob escaped, and she pressed her face to his shoulder. "I keep seeing his face. He looked so shocked at first, and then . . . then just nothing. Just dead." Her voice thickened, and her hand gripped his upper arm. "Dead, and I watched the life leave that man . . . I caused it. It's a horrible feeling. I took his life. He's gone, forever, because of me."

He nodded, hating the pain in her voice but understanding it all too well. "He'd have taken your life, Toni. It wouldn't have been the first. It certainly wouldn't have been the last. God only knows how many lives you might've saved by taking his. I know that doesn't make it right. But it's something to remember."

"Does it help?" She lifted her head and gazed up into his eyes.

"Not really. Nothing helps but time." He let his fingers run through her hair. "You can bet he wouldn't have wasted a single second feeling guilty if he'd been the one to pull the trigger first." Again that lump lodged in his throat, making his voice sound strained. "I know I'd have never got over it."

He met her eyes again, felt that jolt of elusive knowledge that disappeared as soon as he returned his gaze to the highway. He held her as they crossed the George Washington Bridge. He paid the toll and took them into New Jersey, still heading east. An hour later he pulled off the highway and into the parking lot of a low-rate motel. He drove the car around to the rear, where it wouldn't be visible from the street.

Toni collapsed into the nearest armchair with an exaggerated sigh. Nick finished speaking to Harry and hung the phone up, looking worried but better than he had before.

"How is he?" Toni asked.

"Which one?" Nick shook his head. "Joey's conscious and stable, but I'm sure your mother told you that."

She nodded. Her own relief at hearing her mother's voice on the other end had left her limp. "She says he's the world's most uncooperative patient."

"They want to keep him a few days. They still haven't ruled out brain damage, but they think it's unlikely. I always knew that guy had a hard head."

She smiled. "And what about Harry?"

"The bullet only grazed him. He was wearing a seat belt, or the crash probably would've killed him. A tree kept him from going all the way down. He's okay."

"I'm glad." She tipped her head back and closed her eyes. "So, what now?"

"Your evidence is being analyzed. Warrants will be issued before the night is out. Taranto, Viper and a few others will be picked up. Until they are, we have orders to stay put. They'll kill us without a second thought if they see us."

Her head came up. "What about Mom, Joey? Aren't they in danger, too?"

Nick shook his head. "They're safe. There are enough cops guarding Joey to fill this motel. Harry is still on top of things. He says your mother has made herself a fixture at the hospital and he thinks that's for the best. She'll be well guarded, Toni."

She felt a weight lift slowly from her mind. "Do you realize what this means?"

She saw him frown. "What?"

"It means we can relax." She shook her head. "One uninterrupted night of blessed normalcy. No one shooting at us, no secret midnight meetings with Joey, no spying on you with that monitor and thinking you're a slug."

He lifted his brows. "You thought I was a *slug?*" He placed a hand dramatically over his heart. She laughed with him at that. He came to stand over her. "What would you consider normal, Gypsy?"

She looked up at him, feeling absurdly close to him now. "A large pizza with everything." She broke eye contact to gaze around the room. "We have a VCR. What about some movies? And something to drink." She glanced down her powdery clothes. "I think I'll begin with a shower." She frowned. "Do we have any clothes?"

"Leave it to me, Toni. Take your time in the shower." She tilted her head to one side, but he didn't explain his remark.

Shrugging, she moved into the bathroom and adjusted the water. She found thin white towels on the racks. Not exactly the height of luxury, but they would do.

As she stood under the spray, Toni tried to figure out exactly when she'd reached the decision not to write any more Katrina Chekov thrillers. She wasn't sure. Now that she'd spent a few days living the life Katrina lived, she wasn't so impressed with it. She supposed she'd been living vicariously through Katrina for some time now. This had been different, though. This had been real. Instead of creating courageous deeds for a fictional heroine, Toni had lived through her own. It wasn't romantic or exciting. It was terrifying. She hoped she never had to go through anything like it again, even in her imagination.

The appeal of her long-ago dream of a big house, a big dog and a handful of small children was suddenly alive again. It was time, she realized. Maybe she'd needed to come to grips with her father's death before she could think about living a real life. Maybe she'd needed to see that she didn't have to be Wonder Woman to be happy. Maybe she'd only needed to find a man she wouldn't mind sharing that huge Victorian house with.

In her mind's eye, she saw Nick, and a little lead weight lowered itself onto her heart. He'd never feel for her the way she felt for him. He'd never settle for that dull sort of life she imagined. Something inside her told her she wouldn't want it anyway with anyone else.

She loved him.

The realization came to her from somewhere deep inside, where it had been for some time. It bubbled up to the surface and danced there, refusing to be ignored any longer. She loved Nick Manelli.

What on earth was she going to do about it? Should she tell him? No, she couldn't do that. It might scare him to the other side of the world. What if she could make him love her, too? Was it possible to do that? Could *she* do it?

A knock on the bathroom door jarred her. She twisted the shower knobs until the water stopped, yanked a towel off the rack and wrapped it around herself. "Come in."

Nick opened the door. The smile died on his lips when he looked at her. She didn't know why; she looked like a drowned rat with her hair still dripping wet, hanging over one shoulder, and rivulets of water running down her legs to make a small puddle at her feet. His eyes darkened, though, as his gaze traveled down her body, and there was no mistaking the desire she saw there.

He licked his lips, brought his gaze level with hers again. "I—uh—here." He held a black T-shirt out to her. "I found it in the video store across the street."

She took it from him, and when her fingers touched his she trembled. "Thanks." She held it by its shoulders, so it unfolded. Charlie Chaplin was depicted on the front, leaning on his ever-present walking stick. The shirt was large enough so it would come to midthigh on her. Just right for a nightshirt.

He nodded and backed out of the room, closing the door.

Toni hugged the shirt to her for a long moment, biting her lips. He wanted her. She could see it in his eyes. She remembered the time she'd spent with him beneath those pines in the storm this morning. The way he'd shuddered at her touch. The way he'd held her, touched her. He'd been cold afterward, but while they'd been together he'd been completely open with her—physically, at least.

If she couldn't reach out to him on an emotional level, at least she knew she could on a physical one. She'd have a last resort, if all else failed. She dropped the towel, pulled on her shirt and pulled her hair out of the collar. She opened the door.

"Your turn," she told him.

She noticed how he forced his eyes to stay level with hers this time. "Okay, but you have to promise not to eat the pizza without me when it gets here."

She shrugged. "If I were you, I'd make it a fast shower. I am starved." She saw the pile of tapes on the bed then.

"You got some movies! Let me guess. Schwarzenegger, Stallone, and—"

"Not even close, lady." He moved past her into the bathroom, and in a moment she heard the shower running.

She picked up the tapes and looked at the titles. They were comedies, all of them. Martin and Lewis, Abbott and Costello, Danny Kaye. "How did you know?" she called several minutes later.

"Know what?"

"That I love classic comedy? You've got all my favorites here."

The water flow stopped. "Those are *my* favorites. I didn't know what you liked, although I had Miss Marple in mind. You snoops tend to stick together."

She smiled, dropped the tape in her hand, and moved to stand near the bathroom door. "Don't bother getting dressed," she told him. "I want to take a look at your leg. Did you pick up any bandages on your excursion?"

The door opened, and Nick stood there in his shorts, rubbing his hair vigorously with a towel. "On the dresser." A knock at the door brought his head up. He motioned Toni to stand where she was, ducked back into the bathroom and emerged again with his gun in one hand and his wallet in the other.

He stood to one side of the door, opened it slightly and relaxed. He took a twenty from his wallet and slipped it through. "Keep the change. Leave the pizza." A moment later he opened the door wider, glanced quickly left and right and picked the square box up.

"Is it necessary to be that cautious?"

"Better safe than sorry." He crossed to set the gun on the nightstand, wincing when he moved his left arm to lower the pizza box.

She marched past him, picking up the bandages he'd bought and shoving gently at his chest so he sat on the bed. "You are in sorry shape. Sit still." She looked at the wound, satisfied that it was progressing, if slowly. She began to bandage it. Nick pawed the tapes as she worked.

"What do you want to watch first?" he asked.

She replied without looking up, "Abbott and Costello. 'Who's on first?'"

"I dunno," he answered, not missing a beat.

She looked at him, caught the glint in his eye. Together they chorused, "Third base." She laughed aloud, taped the bandage in place and reached for the cassette.

Nick pulled a triangle of cheesy pizza from the box as she slipped the tape into the machine. He handed it to her when she came back, then took one for himself. He surprised her by producing a pair of cold Cokes. For the next two hours, they laughed themselves sore, over jokes they'd both heard countless times before. They seemed fresh somehow when she heard them with Nick.

While the tape was rewinding, Nick choked back his laughter, eyed her seriously and said, "*What* is the name of the guy on first base?"

"Who," Toni answered.

"The guy on first. What's his name?"

"No. *Who's* on first."

"I dunno!" Nick yelled.

"Third base..." Toni broke down into gales of laughter that had tears brimming in her eyes. "If you ever get sick of cloak-and-dagger work, Nick, you have a brilliant future in comedy." She got her laughter under control with an effort and studied his face. "Will you, do you think? Give it up, I mean?"

He folded his arms behind his head and leaned back against the headboard. "I haven't thought about it."

"You must have," she countered. She sat on the opposite side of the bed, legs tucked under her, facing him. "You said once you'd waited your whole life to bring Taranto down. You must have known your life wouldn't be over when that happened. What will you do with the rest of it?"

He looked at the ceiling, apparently considering what she'd said. "Law enforcement is my only area of expertise. What else could I do?"

"Law enforcement is a very broad term. It encompasses a lot more than just being a deep-cover federal agent with his life on the line every single day." She shook her head. "Do you want to keep doing that?"

He sighed hard. "It gets to you after a while. The stress—the nerves."

"It must." She studied him for a long moment. "Try this. Close your eyes and think of your ideal life. The one you'd have if you could just snap your fingers and it would be real." She was surprised when he complied, his eyes closing instantly. "Okay, now tell me what you'd be doing."

His eyes opened again. "Andy Griffith," he told her. "I'd be sheriff in some speck-on-the-map town. I'd stop at a three-table diner for a cup of the world's best coffee and a homemade doughnut every morning. And every night—" He broke off suddenly and averted his eyes.

"What, Nick?"

He shook his head. "Doesn't matter. Pipe dreams."

She felt like stomping her feet or breaking something. Why wouldn't he open up? How could she get to him?

When he looked at her again, his emotions were well hidden. "How about another movie?"

She shook her head, opened her mouth and closed it again.

"What?" he asked, suddenly concerned. "What is it, Toni?"

God, she hated feeling this helpless. How did you get someone to see that it was okay to let go of past heartaches? That history didn't necessarily have to repeat itself. That just because everyone in his life had walked out on him, it didn't mean she would, as well.

That was it. That must be it; it didn't take a psychologist to see what was going on with him.

His forefinger hooked beneath her chin and lifted it. "Tell me," he said softly.

"Hold me," she whispered. She moved closer to him and sighed softly when his arms came around her. "Was I terrible?"

His arms loosened, he stared down into her eyes. "Were you what?"

"Terrible . . . this morning. I haven't had a lot of practice. There was a boy in college, and then two years ago, there was a man—but it didn't last. I thought it was wonderful, but what do I know? Was it that bad for you—"

"Whoa, wait a minute, lady. Where is all of this coming from?"

She pulled away from him, turned her back to him. Nick got to his feet and looked at her. "You've barely touched me since. I figured I must have been lousy."

He smiled broadly. "I didn't mean for you to think— Hell, if you want the truth, you shook me." He caught her face between his palms and tipped it up. "Are you listening? Unlike you, I've been with a lot of others."

She had to blink fast to hide the pain that remark brought.

"But it was never that intense before. It was never that good, Toni. You hear me?"

She felt her eyes widen. "Is that true?"

"Swear to God." He smiled a little. "Wasn't it for you?"

"Yes—you know it was, but I thought that was because..." She stopped and caught her breath. It had been that intense for her because she'd been in love with him. She hadn't been aware of it yet, but she had been. Could that possibly be his reason for feeling as he had? Could there be a chance? Maybe he did have strong feelings for her. Maybe he just didn't realize it yet. Maybe she'd just have to make him realize it.

"Because what?" He frowned down at her.

Toni rose from the bed, her hands on his shoulders, a tiny smile playing with her lips. She turned slowly, pushing him until the backs of his legs touched the mattress. She slid her hands to his broad chest and shoved him hard. All of a sudden, she'd recalled his words to her as he'd left the car before, when he'd believed he was about to be killed. *It meant something with you.* The question was, what? He fell back onto the bed, but clasped her wrists so she went down with him, landing on his chest.

"You could have said something sooner," she scolded. "All day I've been thinking how rotten I must have been."

"Oh yeah? And what are you thinking now?" She saw the desire flash to life in his eyes. A smile was her only answer.

Chapter 12

Something about that half smile and the sparkle in her liquid eyes scared the hell out of Nick. He couldn't have said exactly what. A moment later he no longer cared. She settled her tiny body more comfortably upon his and nuzzled his neck with her warm lips...and tiny flicks of her tongue.

A tremor quaked within him. It began at the core of his being and radiated outward until it enveloped his entire body and soul. The silken black curls tickling his skin were a potent, sensual torture, and he caught her head in his palms. He brought her face to his until she hovered just beyond reach of his lips. Her hair made satin curtains around his face. Its touch against his cheek thrilled him. Its scent, surrounding him, was an aphrodisiac.

Her mouth, so close to his, parted. He could see her small white teeth, feel her short, heated breaths. Her lips at that moment were two swollen, ripe plums whose nourishment he required if he were to survive. He craved those lips and he reached for them with his own. He captured them, suckled them, held them captive until he hungered for more. He starved for the sweetness beyond, and his tongue swept inside her, tracing her moistness, absorbing her drugging nectar.

She allowed him to taste her honeyed mouth for some time before her tongue forced his out and followed it. He felt its pointy tip run a path along the roof of his mouth, over his teeth, inside his lips. It tangled with his own tongue even as their bodies were beginning to tangle.

Her thighs straddled his, her knees bent so her calves ran back under his. He felt the soft center of her pressed tight to his throbbing hardness. He could stand no more torture. He had to have her—now.

Nick reached down her back, over her hips, until his fingers touched the edge of the oversize T-shirt she wore. He lifted it, letting his hands run over the bare skin of her back, a forefinger tracing the curve of her spine. When the garment bunched around her shoulders, she lifted her body slightly, allowing him to pull it over her head. She would have returned her body flush to his, but he caught her shoulders and held her away. His gaze moved over her full, round breasts, lingering on their melon-colored centers. Her nipples went erect beneath his hot gaze. He moved his hands from her shoulders to cup them. He pinched the hard little tips between thumb and forefinger, watching her face. Her eyes closed in obvious pleasure. He pinched slightly harder. She threw her head back, arching like a cat.

She drove him beyond gentleness. He gripped her shoulders fast and jerked her forward until her breasts dangled within reach. He caught one with his lips and sucked it hard, tugging and using his teeth on its stiff crest until small whimpering sounds came from deep inside her throat. With a shivering inhale, she pulled back, met his gaze, her own glazed with passion. She lowered her lips to his chest, scraping her teeth over his flesh, over his sensitive male nipple until he shuddered in response.

She'd thought she was lousy! Nick let his eyes fall closed as her fingers moved to the fly of his jeans. A moment later her hand dipped inside and gripped him tightly. The reaction to her touch was both instant and intense. Never had a woman made him feel the way she could. Her touch sent jolts of pleasure to his toes. She eased herself lower over his torso, and when he read her intent he thought he'd explode. He felt her hot breath bathing his manhood. Her lips went around him. He wanted to roar like a lion. Instead, he fought to catch his breath while she worked exquisite magic, and when he forced himself to speak the words came in broken, gasping fragments. "To—ni...I...I—need..."

She knew, he realized through the haze of need in which she'd immersed him. She knew she'd driven him to the edge, and she'd enjoyed it. She rose away from him, and the tidal wave he'd felt approaching receded just beyond reach. She shoved at his jeans, and he helped her to remove them. He caught her hips in his hands and pushed her silky panties down over them. She kicked them off and returned quickly to her former position. Her hands on his shoulders, her eyes holding his prisoner with a power he couldn't resist, she positioned herself over him. She willed him not to move as she sheathed him slowly. He heard her breath leave her in a rush as she took all of him. So small, he thought. So tight around him. It amazed him that she could hold him inside her. She lifted her body and began the achingly slow descent again.

He could hold back no longer. If she'd intended to drive him to the brink of madness, she'd already reached her goal. He gripped her hips and held her hard while he moved all the way into her heat. He withdrew, suddenly and completely, and plunged into her again, and again. She arched so far that her hair cloaked her back. Her hips rocked with his every stroke. She rode him like a goddess riding a storm.

He knew when her body began to tighten from the rapturous, desperate expressions that raced over her face. Her muscles clenched in the building tension. Her breathing quickened, grew ragged, and she slammed herself down onto him as roughly as he slammed himself upward into her. His own body traveled the same rocky path, gaining momentum as he approached the cliff that would land him in a sea of pleasure. He couldn't slow his pace now, but he wanted them to plunge over that cliff together.

He reached down to the place where they were joined and pressed the pad of his thumb to the quivering nub of flesh at her apex. She shook violently, her eyes flying wide. His other hand caught one jiggling breast and held it for his mouth to capture, his teeth to torture. He attacked her until each exhalation she released was a moan. Her body rocked. The spasms began, and she cried his name so loudly anyone outside could have heard. Her body squeezed itself around his in the rhythm of her climax, and he lost himself to the feeling of his own shattering release. The ecstasy of his seed spilling into her, of her body milking it from him, became the focal point of his entire being. He groaned with the force of it. Moments later her small body collapsed on top of him, and he closed his arms around her.

When his mind stopped orbiting his body, Nick cursed himself for feeling what he was feeling. He'd never had it so good. He knew he never would again—not with anyone but Toni. There was something that went way beyond the frenzied coupling of two bodies happening here. They connected on some deeper level. He'd sensed it before. The result was this incredible sex.

He knew he was allowing himself to get way too attached to his little Gypsy. He'd warned himself against it. He'd moved beyond that now. Now, dammit, he thought he'd move heaven and earth to keep her with him. It would no longer be enough to admit he'd be devastated when she left. He couldn't *let her* leave. He wouldn't.

Okay, so he'd admitted it. He cared about her…maybe a little too much, but he didn't love her. He wasn't stupid enough to have let that happen. Not again. A pain like he'd never known tightened around his heart, and past realities forced themselves to be acknowledged. He'd loved his father. He'd loved his mother, dammit. It *had* hurt when they walked away. It still hurt.

He'd loved Danny…like no one else, he'd loved Danny. Nothing he'd done, though, had ever been enough to make the people he loved stay with him or even love him back. He'd long ago learned that no one could. He simply wasn't capable of inspiring that emotion in another person. Even as a child, he'd given up waiting to hear those words spoken to him. He had no illusions that Toni might fall hopelessly in love with him. But could he inspire her devotion? Could he make her want to be with him? How?

He didn't have a lot of time to puzzle out the answer. She moved devilishly against him, and every sane thought went out the window. Nick tightened his arms around her waist, already hard for her again. With a soft growl, he rolled her over, covered her body with his. He'd have her tonight, and he'd be sure he was like no other man she'd ever had. He'd burn his touch into her soul until she could never forget that she belonged to him. She was his.

She'd never been so brazen in her life. She knew it and she understood it. She'd never been in love before. Everything she did was born of the burgeoning feelings inside her. She couldn't bring herself to tell him she loved him, but it poured from every cell of her body. She kept herself from saying the words, but she couldn't hold so much love inside—it burst from her like water from a broken dam. She couldn't seem to hold him tightly enough or closely enough.

Toward dawn she nestled into his arms, listening to the steady beat of his heart. This past week had changed the course of her entire life. Nothing would be the same—not ever. If she could find a way to unlock his heart, she'd have her dreams come true. She was only just beginning to realize that those dreams didn't necessarily have to include a rambling Victorian home or a sheepdog. She needed only Nick... having him with her to share whatever kind of life she ended up living. The other things had been symbols of the peace and security she craved and could find only in him. If she couldn't make him love her, she knew she'd spend the rest of her life grieving his loss. She sighed deeply.

"What's wrong?"

I love you, Nick, her heart whispered. I love you and I don't know what to do about it.

"Nothing, I...can't get to sleep."

"Neither can I. You'd think after all night long, we'd both be exhausted." His fingers continued threading themselves through her hair, as they'd been doing for some time. She didn't think he was aware of it. "You want to get up, then?"

She rose a little, propping her arms on his wide chest and regarding his face. She wished she could look into those tiger-striped eyes and see his feelings there. Had last night made any difference at all? Did he realize yet that they belonged together? "It isn't even light outside yet."

"I saw a truck stop back along the street. They'd be open. We could walk over there and have breakfast. What do you think?"

Dark beard shadowed his face. It made him look incredibly sexy, she thought. She lowered her face to his and rubbed her cheek over his stubbly jawline. "I think if you want to go, we'll go. I can't say no to you."

His chest moved with his soft chuckle. "That's one hell of an admission, lady. I might have to put it to the test." His fingertips moved over her spine, and she shivered. He lifted his head and kissed her languorously. "Will you join me in the shower?"

"Um-hmm."

"Scrub my back?"

"Yes, Nick."

"Give me a shave?"

She smiled. "Don't push it."

Toni placed their order at the counter and joined Nick at the pay phone in the back. Her stomach growled at the wonderful aromas coming from the grill. Nick frowned. "Funny. I got a recorded message when I dialed Harry, with another number to reach him."

"So dial it," she suggested. She caught a whiff of brewing coffee and licked her lips. "And hurry, I'm starved."

"I wonder why," he quipped. He punched another number and waited. "Harry? Is this phone secure?"

Toni thought he'd been in the undercover business for too long. She saw him sigh and shake his head. "A hospital pay phone?" He covered the mouthpiece and shook his head. "They're working out of Joey's hospital room.

It's the only way they can keep him down, and whenever he gets up he gets sick.''

She smiled softly. "Is my mother still there?''

He repeated her question to Harry, then nodded. "They can't get rid of her.'' He winked and went back to listening. He looked more worried after a moment. "You've checked his place in Jersey?'' He shook his head again. "Okay. Every four hours, got it.'' He replaced the receiver, his expression grim.

"Tell me,'' she said.

"The warrants have been issued, but they can't find Viper or Lou. It won't be safe for you in the city until they're both behind bars. We're stuck here for a while.'' He checked his watch. "We'll check in again at 10:00 a.m. Every four hours. Remind me, will you?''

"Okay.'' She bit her lip. She hadn't liked the way he'd phrased that, *we're stuck here for a while.* It sounded as if he were eager to get this over with.

He put an arm around her, and they moved to a small table. The young blond man came from behind the counter to fill their coffee cups. An older woman, who might've been his mother, turned sausage links on the grill beyond the counter.

An orderly with small, fishlike eyes watched the federal agent replace the receiver. He waited for the man to round a corner, heading back to his comrade's room, before he approached the same pay phone with an uneven gait. Despite the limp, he moved quickly. He punched the "O" and waited. When the operator answered, he made his voice as pleasant as it could get.

"I am sorry, but I was cut off in the middle of a conversation. Could you please reconnect me right away?''

"Certainly, sir. What number were you calling?''

"Just a minute." He paused, waiting, then said, "Damn—I had it here. I guess I threw it away when I got through the first time."

"Give me the number you're calling from, and I can check for you."

He read the number from the pay phone, and in mere seconds the helpful woman came back, read off the number and even connected him. When a young male voice answered, he turned on the charm again. "I'm afraid I have the wrong number. To whom am I speaking?"

"This is the pay phone at Tracey's Diner," the kid said.

He smiled. He already knew about the midseventies-model Mustang stolen from the parking lot near the intersection where the traitor's car got smashed. He thought he had him when he'd shot his boss, near the gates to that heap of stone he called a house. It turned out he hadn't even killed the boss, just nicked him. His nerves were showing. He never missed. He'd misjudged the nature of Salducci's injuries, as well. He'd been sure the rat would be dead by now. He was slipping, and it was not a good sign.

He cleared his throat. "Then I do have the right number. I'm supposed to meet a friend there later. Do you suppose you could give me directions?"

He smiled, jotting them down on a pad as the boy explained them. He nodded hello to a uniformed cop who moseyed past. The place was crawling with them. He wasn't worried about being recognized, though. Other than Lou, only two people alive knew what he looked like. The traitor and the bitch. He'd take care of them before the day was out.

She'd said she wanted a normal night. Nick figured he'd give her all the "normal" she wanted, although it had been far from normal for him. His feelings for her had turned into a runaway train last night. They picked up velocity with her every touch, her every breath, until he knew it would be impossible to apply the brakes. He had a feeling there was a brick wall looming somewhere ahead. He was afraid of what would happen when he hit it, but he didn't have a clue how to avoid it. He supposed he'd have to hold on tight and pray for a miracle. He didn't like feeling as if he'd lost control, but he knew that's exactly what had happened to him with Toni. He had no say over his emotions where she was concerned.

They lingered over their breakfast of pancakes and sausage, then walked hand in hand to a grocery store in the distance. They bought toiletries, and he promised they'd stop at a department store for a change of clothes after they left the motel.

She clutched her brown paper bag in one hand, while the other encircled his waist. "I thought you said we were stuck here for a while?"

He carried a small bag, too, and had one arm draped around her shoulders. "I think it would be best if we moved around a little. We'll check out, drive a little farther and find another motel."

She shook her head. "If Taranto's smart, he'll be on his way out of the country."

"I'm not sure about that. He places a lot of value on loyalty, and I betrayed him. He's not going to want to leave until he sees me pay for that." He felt her small arm clutch him tighter. "I know how he thinks," he went on. "He might have some idea that if he learns what we have on him, he can find a way out of it. He's done it before. It's usually a matter of eliminating witnesses, tampering with evidence or inventing alibis, all things he is good at."

"The man doesn't give up easily, does he?"

"No. As long as he thinks there's a chance of weaseling out of this, he'll keep trying. He has a lot to lose if he leaves. He's built an empire in this country."

Inside, Nick almost hoped Lou evaded them for a while. It would give him more time to find a way to keep Toni with him. He was unaware of his arm tightening around her shoulders or of the way his jaw went so rigid he grated his teeth. He was only aware of raw determination. He would make her want to stay with him. He could do it. He just hadn't tried hard enough with the others, his parents, his brother. This time he'd do anything. There had to be a way.

"Nick, what's the matter?"

She'd stopped and turned in his embrace to stare up at him, concern in her onyx eyes.

He tried to will the burning sensation away from the center of his chest and offered her a smile he was far from feeling. "Nothing. I . . . nothing." He shook his head and pulled her to him, kissing her to show her what he felt. He couldn't tell her. Not yet.

It had been two hours since they'd arrived at the diner. The sun shone brightly now, and the long walk had done him a world of good. They crossed the motel parking lot, and Nick opened the door to their room.

As soon as they walked in, all hell broke loose. The door slammed behind them. Toni was jerked from his arms, and a gun barrel poked into his temple. He saw another one held upright, under Toni's chin, forcing her head back.

Lou Taranto stood in front of Nick, smiling. "Well, Nicky, I'm glad you could join us. I was afraid you wouldn't show." His gaze slid away from Nick. "Miss Rio, I presume? Viper figured we'd find you with Nicky."

Viper held Toni, and Nick felt absolute rage for a moment. He felt a jab in his upper arm, and his gaze swung fast to pinpoint its source. David, the mousy little M.D. Lou had brought to tend his leg, was depressing the plunger of the hypodermic in Nick's arm. Instantly the room began to fade. Nick's head grew heavier, and his vision clouded. He saw the small man shove his wire rims up on his nose, holding another needle and moving toward Toni. Darkness loomed. He forced his eyes open just in time to see her slump lifelessly to the floor.

"Nooo," he moaned just before he joined her there.

Chapter 13

Joey had trouble focusing at first. When he did, he wasn't sure he was seeing clearly. Harold Anderson, the most miserable bureau chief he knew of, was handing Kate a cup of coffee and asking politely if there were anything else he could do for her.

"Where's mine?" he croaked, surprised at the dryness of his throat. "Cream and one sugar, Harry. I'll take a doughnut while you're at it."

"Why waste good food on a guy who can't keep it down?" Harry barked. His return to his normal state reassured Joey, oddly enough.

Kate came close to the bed, her intense blue eyes scanning his face. Her high, defined cheekbones and tight, unlined skin reminded him of another Kate—Hepburn. Her take-charge style did, as well. "You're awake," she said, smiling.

"I didn't expect to see you still hanging around."

"Mr. Anderson says I'm probably safer here than anywhere. I'd have been driving back and forth anyway, to keep tabs on Antonia."

Joey slanted a glance at Harry. "Mr. Anderson isn't always the best of company."

"He's been wonderful. He even sent some men to my apartment to pack me a bag."

"Did he, now?" Harry scowled at Joey, so he dropped the subject. Joey had no doubt Harry was as affected by Kate del Rio's presence, not to mention her looks, as he was.

She leaned nearer him now, thumbing the button to raise his head and shoulders. The light from the window danced over her golden honey hair. She wore it longer than was in fashion for a *mature* woman. It curled softly around her face and brushed her shoulders. "They said you could have water, weak tea, broth, gelatine...." She glanced up and caught him staring. "Just stop me when I get to something that sounds edible."

"Hmm?"

"His lights are on, but no one's home," Harry snapped. "She was asking what you wanted to eat, Einstein. The nurse on duty told us to let her know what to bring you."

Joey blinked and began to wonder about things that should have occurred to him before. "Why are you here?" he asked Harry. "What's happening? Have Taranto and Viper been arrested? Where the hell is Nick?"

Harry nodded. "That's more like it. Maybe Lou's steroid-fed thug didn't permanently loosen your screws after all."

"Please, Mr. Anderson!" Kate smoothed the white sheet over Joey. "Mr. Anderson has set up a command center right here."

"Why?"

"He didn't have a choice, Joseph. That assassin mistook him for your friend Nicholas and shot him. That's the reason no backup team arrived to help at Antonia's apartment . . . but you probably don't remember much about that, do you?"

"If you don't mind, Ms. del Rio?" Harry came forward, turned so Joey could see the white square bandage at the back of his head. "I'll give you the nutshell version, Salducci. I switched cars with Nick as a precaution. When I drove to the mansion to get the videotapes, Viper thought I was Nick and took a shot at me. Just a graze, no big deal. But big enough to keep me out of commission for a couple of hours. I was supposed to get a team and meet Nick at Rio's apartment. She had evidence on Taranto. I didn't get there. They did and found you. You with me so far?"

Joey nodded, trying to remember. Mostly what he remembered was pain. "Taranto was waiting to see if Nick would help me." He shook his head gently. "How did he ever get me out of there?"

"He wrapped the girl in a blanket and carried her to the car. Taranto thought it was you and went after him. When the coast was clear, Ms. del Rio here got some help and brought you in . . . along with all the evidence we'll need to take Taranto down permanently."

Joey glanced at Kate and frowned. "I can't believe Nick would do that—use her as bait that way—"

"He didn't want to," Kate said. "Antonia insisted."

"Where are they now?"

"Holed up in a motel in Jersey. Nick checked in at five-thirty this morning." Harry twisted his wrist and checked his watch. "He's due to call again any minute now. I won't give him the nod to come in until Taranto and Viper are in custody."

Joey felt his eyes widen. "God, they're still at large?"

Harry nodded. "We have the evidence and the warrants, but we're having one hell of a time tracking them down."

Joey opened his mouth, glanced toward Kate and snapped it closed again. "I—I think some tea. See if you can get them to bring me a slice of toast, too, will you, please?"

She smiled, nodded once. "That will do you a world of good." Her delicate brows touched. "I only hope you can keep it down this time." She left the room.

Joey pinned Harry with an angry stare. "You can't have Nick and Toni out there in a place as insecure as a motel while Taranto and Viper are free. They ought to be... guarded."

"Look, Salducci, if I had my ideal scenario, they would be. Problem is they aren't. He'd be liable to get them on the way in." Harry winced after raising his voice and touched the bandage on his head with probing fingers. "Listen, chances are Taranto is on his way south of the equator by now. He won't hang around with charges facing him just to try to get even with Nick."

"You're wrong. I know the man, I've worked with him. He puts loyalty above all else. Look what happened to Vinnie Pascorelli. Lou will want revenge on Nick for this. Beyond that, he'll be trying to figure a way out of the whole thing. He'll want to know exactly what we have on him, and knowing him, he'll come up with a perfect defence. He's always managed before. He's not going down without a fight, Harry. He has too much to lose."

Harry sighed and nodded. "I understand all that. I'm doing everything I can, Joey. We're systematically searching every piece of real estate Taranto owns. You just have to be patient. We'll find him.''

The door opened, and Kate came back into the room. "The nurse said she'd bring in a—" Her gaze jumped from one face to the other. "What's wrong?"

"Nothing. We were just discussing business." Again Harry glanced at his watch. "I'd better get to that phone. Nick ought to be calling about now." He nodded once to Kate and left.

She pulled a chair up to the bed and sat down. "Don't bother telling me you both aren't worried about them," she said. "Worrying about my headstrong daughter has become a way of life for me."

Joey shook his head. He'd barely had a clear glimpse of Kate until this morning, when the medications and ice packs had eased his swollen eyelids enough for him to see. "I can't believe she's your daughter," he mumbled, and was immediately embarrassed. "I mean, you, uh, look so..."

Her eyes narrowed. "Caucasian?"

"No! For crying out loud! I meant gorgeous. Too young to be her mother. Ouch!" Raising his voice sent a ringing through his head, and he lifted a palm to his temple. "Damn."

She came to her feet, one hand on his shoulder. "I'm sorry. Of course you didn't mean...I'm tense. It's...been a long night." She sighed long and low. "I'm afraid for Antonia. When I look at you—at what those horrible men did to you, all I can think of is what would happen if they got their hands on her, and I..."

Her throat seemed to close off in midsentence, and Joey saw the moisture in her sapphire eyes. "Oh, hey, nothing's going to happen to her. Not with Nick around." He sat up despite the rush of dizziness. Tears streamed over her flawless cheeks, and Joey could stand no more. He put his hands on her shoulders and squeezed. "Come on, sit down." She did, lowering herself gracefully to the edge of his bed, allowing him to close his arms around her and pull her head to his shoulder. "Nick won't let anything happen to her. If she were my daughter and in the same situation, I'd want her to be with Nick. He's the best."

She sniffed, straightened and looked him in the eye. "Will you tell me about him?"

"About Nick?"

She nodded. "I saw them together at the apartment before. Antonia—well, there was something different about her. And when she looked at him, I thought—"

"She's nuts about him," Joey filled in. He saw her eyes widen.

"I thought that might be the case. Do you think that he—"

"Oh, yeah. He's got it bad. I've never seen him like this."

She sighed hard and made herself more comfortable on the bed. "So, will you tell me about him?"

Joey shrugged. He didn't feel it would be any sort of betrayal to tell Nick's future mother-in-law about his painful youth. In fact, it might be good to get it out in the open right from the start. Besides, he had a feeling it would be useless to try not to tell her. If she looked at him with those tear-moistened jewel blue eyes long enough, he'd probably tell her about every top-secret investigation he'd ever worked on.

"Where do you want me to start?"

She opened her eyes and blinked them into focus. The floor where she lay smelled musty. The room exuded chill dampness. She knew it was a basement before she realized the floor was packed earth or the walls, chipped cinder block.

"About time, Manelli. I been waitin' all damn day."

The cold voice near the center of the room drew Toni's gaze. She barely stopped herself from gasping when she saw Nick, in a straight-backed wooden chair beneath a glaring bare light bulb suspended by a frayed cord. A rope lashed around his ankles kept his feet immobile. She thought another must be holding his wrists together behind his back, but she couldn't see for certain.

Lou Taranto stood a few feet in front of Nick, facing him. Viper was at his side. Nick's eyes seemed glazed, and Toni vaguely remembered the injections—they'd both been drugged. She had no idea how long ago or where they might be now.

"You disappointed me, Nicky. I trusted you. Like my own son, I trusted you, but you betrayed me." Lou released a short shot of air. "A Fed! A lousy, freaking Fed—don't bother denying it. No one fools Lou Taranto for long."

Nick wasn't looking at him. His gaze probed the corners of the room, and Toni realized that with the bright light on him and the shadows everywhere else, he couldn't see her. He searched for her, squinting hard. She wanted to call out to him, but didn't dare. It might be better to stay quiet for a few minutes. She might get an idea that could help if she could watch them while they thought her unconscious.

Viper lifted a hand, balled it and delivered a shocking blow to the side of Nick's head. The chair toppled to the floor with Nick in it, and Toni nearly leapt to her feet and charged the little weasel. A small voice warned her it would do more harm than good. What she needed was a weapon.

Viper leaned over, righted the chair with a rough jerk. "Pay attention when you're being spoken to, Manelli. Lou has a few things to say to you." He leaned closer. "And then it's my turn. You know how your pal Salducci looked when you found him? He looked good compared to what you'll look like, Nicky boy. You're gonna die slow."

"Big talk's easy when I'm trussed like a goose." Nick's voice came out even and low. "Untie me and say it again, weasel."

"Talk all you want, Manelli. You're a dead man. I don't pay much attention to dead men."

"I'm not dead yet."

Viper smiled, and it sent a chill right down Toni's spine. "Yeah, you are."

Toni reached out in the darkness, patting the damp dirt floor with her hands. They hadn't tied her as they had Nick. They must not consider her much of a threat. Her eyes strained to see in the darkness. A rickety wooden door hung at one side of the room. An ancient, molding pile of firewood was stacked in a corner. A broken wood crate, with a few dust-covered shapes in its bottom, sat beside a rusted water tank laying on its side. A weapon. She needed a weapon. A length of pipe, a hammer, anything!

"I need to know what they have on me, Nicky." Lou picked up the conversation again. "The warrant says I'm up on murder one. What are they basing it on?"

Nick shook his head. "My case was narcotics. The murder rap came from a separate investigation."

Viper hit him again, a straight-on drive of knuckles into his face. The chair rocked backward, hitting the floor hard. Blood spurted from Nick's nose. Toni heard him cough and spit. Viper yanked the chair upright again by grabbing Nick's shirt in both fists.

Toni was on her feet, fists clenched so her nails pierced her palms. Frantically now she looked around her, still cloaked in the darkness. She edged slowly along the cool wall, trying to work her way to the woodpile. A length of wood, if she could find one that wasn't completely rotten, would be good enough to split Viper's skull, she decided.

"Come on, Nicky. You can do better than that."

Nick shook his head. "I called the case as soon as I knew you were on to Salducci. We were packing it in."

"You're lying!"

Nick shrugged, lifting his chin and glared at Viper. "Isn't that your cue?"

Viper slugged him in the midsection this time, and Toni wondered how he kept from vomiting. The chair jumped with the force of the blow. Nick dragged air into his lungs.

"How am I going to prepare my defense if I don't know what the evidence is?" Lou spoke in a smooth, friendly tone. "Come on, Nicky, I can't let the business I've spent my life building go up in smoke like this. I need to know. You'll talk eventually." There was the tiniest waver in his voice. Toni heard it and knew it for what it was—desperation. A weapon, at last.

She stepped out of the darkness, forcing her face to appear composed, emotionless. If they knew what it did to her to see them hurting Nick, it would be over in no time. Her heart felt torn wide open and raw at the pain she knew he must be feeling. My God, she loved him. The pure power of the emotion awed her. She'd had no idea how strong her feelings had become until she'd been forced to see him suffer.

She drew on that strength now. She closed off the frightened, trembling part of her mind and focused on the strength. There—in one of those corridors within—she met an old friend. She held her hand, stiffened her spine. *Help me through this, Katrina.*

Haven't I always?

Toni blinked away the odd sensation and lifted her chin. "He's telling you the truth, Taranto. It wasn't his investigation that turned up the evidence against you. It was mine."

All eyes turned in her direction. Toni had to force her gaze not to linger on Nick's bruising, bloodied face. If she looked at him, she'd break down and cry. She'd throw her arms around him and kiss the pain away. She'd claw Viper's heart out for hurting him.

"Toni, don't—" Viper hit him again. The skin of his cheek split. Toni whirled quickly to hide her face.

"Fine, you don't want to listen to me, that's fine. You finish your little game with Manelli and want to talk, let me know. Of course, by then it could be too late to do anything, anyway."

"Just a minute, bitch." Lou's voice stopped her.

She didn't face him. She blinked rapidly to erase any trace of moisture from her eyes. She forced her features to relax.

"If you want to deal, you'll have to address me in some other tone, Mr. Taranto. I don't answer to 'bitch.'"

His chuckle filled the damp room, reaching all the way to the wooden two-by-six crosspieces supporting the ceiling and the thick cobwebs that covered it. "Viper," he said.

The clammy hands were around her body a second later, pinioning her arms to her sides, jerking her around to face Taranto. Nick strained against his bonds. She tried to send him a message with her eyes, but he continued struggling.

Her voice sounding nothing at all like her to her own ears, she said, "You don't need to pound on my face to get the information you want, Taranto. I'm no cop. I'm in this game for one reason and one reason only. Money."

Lou's head came up. "You want to deal?" He laughed again. "This one's bold as brass, isn't she?" His gaze shifted from Viper, who held her, to Toni again. "You got nothing to deal with, lady writer. You tell me what I want to know here and now, or I let Viper have an hour alone with you...no, not quite alone. I think I might watch."

Viper bent his head and closed his teeth on Toni's earlobe. It was no playful nibble. He bit hard, intending to hurt her, and he did. She sucked air through her clenched teeth and fought the pain. He let her ear go, and it throbbed angrily. He still kept her arms pulled painfully behind her. "I'm gonna like this, Lou. When can we start?"

Toni forced a smile and then laughter. "You've got to be kidding me! I thought you were a businessman. You're going to risk your entire operation just for a few hours of perverted sex?"

"Tell me what you know, sugar."

"I'll tell you a little. The murder charges on you are for the deaths of your ex-supplier and the two DEA agents who were escorting him back to the U.S. You remember Juan Perez, don't you? Your supplier in Colombia? He was the last man who refused the deal I offered. I brought him to his knees and I'll do the same to you."

Lou frowned. "You offered Perez a deal?"

"Before the book went to print, I offered to leave certain specifics out if he'd pay me well for my trouble. He refused. He thought I was bluffing." She met Taranto's eyes and felt an icy hand close over her heart. "A lot of men make that mistake. My book brought him down."

"What do you have, lady? Cut the games and spill it." Viper spoke near her sore ear, his lips moving against it, his breath hot on her throat.

She looked at Lou. "Tell him to let go of me."

Lou frowned and finally nodded toward Viper. "You'll have plenty of time to hurt her later on."

She chanced a glimpse toward Nick. His eyes on her were narrow, and she hoped to God he didn't think this bravado of hers was the real Toni. It wasn't. It was Katrina.

She faced Lou squarely. "I have photos of you passing an envelope to a man named Santos. I have documented proof that Santos left you and went directly to an airport in Colombia, where he somehow got a job as a mechanic. I have photos of him tinkering with Perez's plane moments before takeoff. I have evidence that Santos deposited a large sum of money into his bank account the day he arrived in Colombia."

Lou shook his head. "Nothing. It's nothing. Circumstantial, at best."

"I have the envelope."

Lou's brows shot up. "Impossible! Santos said he burned—"

"He put a match to it, dropped it in a trash can. A friend of mine pulled it out and doused the flame. It only blackened a bit around the edges." She saw his eyes narrow with skepticism. "Shall I tell you what was inside? A handwritten note with the name of the little airfield and Perez's flight number and time of departure. Your handwriting, Lou?" She shook her head. "Sloppy, sloppy. An expert analyst will use that, you know. There was a nice five-by-seven glossy print of Perez, too. The one of him in that tacky floral-print shirt."

Lou's eyes showed real fear now. "You gave them all of that?"

She laughed and shook her head. "You think I'm an idiot? What good would my book be if I gave them all of my surprises? It would come out in your trial, and all the juice in the book would be old news by the time it hit the shelves. I'd be lucky if it sold a dozen copies."

"But the warrants—"

"I gave them an envelope filled with bogus evidence. The photo they have is of my cousin Vito. All the documents are forged, and not very expertly, either. As soon as they realize it, which shouldn't be too far in the future, the warrants will be revoked. They have nothing."

Lou turned, paced the room slowly and came to stand close to her. "How could you know you'd need fake evidence?"

"I'm not new to this game, Taranto. The Feds are always leaning on me to give them what I have before it comes out in the book. I make up phony evidence on a regular basis, just in case. This time it paid off."

"So where's the real evidence?"

"Now, I'd be dead in a hurry if I told you that, wouldn't I?"

"Dead, maybe. Not in a hurry. Doesn't matter. You don't have a choice."

"I think I do. A lawyer is holding it for me. I can't even tell you who he is, because I had the arrangements made by my publishers. If anyone makes any attempt to get that envelope—other than me, of course—it goes straight to the federal prosecutor's office. If my publisher doesn't hear from me at least once a day, it goes to them even faster. Understand? Now, let's talk, Lou. I stand to make a cool million from the book. You want what I have, you'll have to make me a better offer.''

Lou lunged at her, gripped the front of her shirt and pulled her to his face. His rancid breath turned her stomach. ''There isn't gonna be any book. You either get me that envelope or you die right here. I guarantee Viper and I can convince you to cooperate.''

She tried not to show her fear and revulsion. Her false bravado was draining fast. She felt a tremor go through her heart. ''There already is a book. I delivered the final draft the day that jerk kidnapped me,'' she lied. ''The deal is, all the evidence goes to the Feds anyway, but not until the book is out.''

''Then you can't stop it?'' Lou asked, a little of the steel gone from his voice. He stepped away from her, releasing her shirt.

''There's a clause in my contract giving me the right to pull out up to ninety days before publication. That time runs out tomorrow. If you want me to help you out of this, Taranto, you better talk fast. I can make one call at 9:00 a.m. tomorrow that will put the brakes on this entire thing.''

Lou cupped his chin in one hand and squeezed. He met Viper's lecherous gaze, and she knew exactly what they were thinking. They'd humor her, offer her whatever she wanted, get the evidence in their filthy hands and then kill her anyway. She didn't care. It would only take a call to the publisher to tell them she'd made the whole thing up anyway. She was betting on its being after hours. They wouldn't be able to confirm her story until morning. She would have bought some time and nothing more.

''How much,'' Lou finally asked.

She shrugged. ''A million-five?''

''Done,'' he said quickly.

"And..." Lou glared at her. "Look, I'll do a lot for that kind of money. But if I'm going to get him killed, I'd just as soon not have to be here to know about it. I do have a few morals. I know you have to do it, but if you want my help you'll wait until I take my money and leave."

Lou turned a skeptical gaze on her, and she hoped she hadn't blown it by pleading for Nick's life. If Lou knew how much she cared, he'd have the best weapon against her he could've found. He eyed her now, and then Nick.

"You cold, greedy, lying bitch!" The vicious words exploded from Nick. He pulled again at his bonds, this time looking as if he'd like to wring her neck with his bare hands. "I'll kill you for this, you frigid little cat. If I get my hands on you, I'll—"

Viper smacked him in the gut again, knocking enough wind out of him so he couldn't go on. Toni heard the breath rush from his lungs. For just an instant Nick's scathing words stung, and she turned her back to him, her throat burning. She took one step away. She felt drained. All she wanted now was to slink back to her darkened corner and collapse. She'd done all she could, and if Nick couldn't see that, then...

She stopped herself and gave her head a small shake. What was the matter with her? Nick wasn't an idiot. Besides, he knew her better than to believe a word of that line she'd fed Taranto. He knew things about her that she'd only begun to realize about herself. Slowly she turned, and Nick lifted his mistreated face to meet her gaze.

"In the morning, then," Taranto said gruffly. She had to look away from Nick, but not before she'd glimpsed the reassuring glint in his eyes. "You'll make that call. I'll give you the money as soon as the envelope is in my hands. Deal?"

"Yes."

Chapter 14

Joey gripped the IV pole with one hand, his heaving stomach with the other. He closed his eyes slowly and waited for the nausea to pass.

"You can barely stand," she told him. "You're not going to be any help out there in this condition, unless you plan to apprehend Lou Taranto by throwing up on him."

Her scolding tone didn't hide the anguish in her voice. "Nausea is normal with concussion. It'll pass." He straightened, reached for the closet door and saw his clothes inside. He stretched his arm for the hanger, then paused when his balance deserted him.

She reached past him, retrieved his clothes and tossed them on the stiff white sheets on his hospital bed. "'Multiple concussions' was the term I heard them use. Joseph, you should be lying down. Harold is doing everything—"

"Yeah, but he hasn't found them yet. Damn Harry for not telling me when Nick didn't check in!" He sat on the edge of the bed and yanked his trousers on without removing the tie-in-the-back hospital gown he wore. He stood to fasten them, then offered Kate his back. She unfastened the ties without being asked. Joey turned again, picked up his shirt and poked his arms into the sleeves. As he buttoned it he heard her sharp intake of air. He looked up fast. Her ivory skin had paled considerably, and her blue eyes glistened beneath a thin film of tears.

Her gaze on his shoulders and chest reminded him the shirt wasn't exactly clean. He looked down and saw the spattered patterns of dried blood. His lips thinned. He met her gaze again. "I'm sorry. I didn't think—"

"He has them, doesn't he?" Her eyes seemed to beg him to deny what she knew. "They would have called in if they'd been able. I've racked my brain to think of a feasible reason they wouldn't have, but there just isn't one. Taranto has them."

Lying to her would be useless. She was an intelligent woman; she'd see right through it. "Probably," he admitted. "But don't think that means..." He broke off, searched his foggy brain, and began again. "He wouldn't kill them if he thought they had information he could use. He'd keep them alive until he got it from them. Nick knows that, and Toni—she seems like a smart girl. She's probably figured it out, too. They can use that knowledge to stall, and in the meantime we'll find out where he's holding them and—"

"I heard Harold say they'd checked every piece of property Taranto owned and found nothing. Where else can you look?"

"Every piece we know of," Joey corrected her. "Contrary to popular belief, we don't know everything. Toni already proved that."

A tiny glimmer of hope lit her eyes. "Antonia is very thorough in her research. She might know of other holdings—"

"If she did, how would I find out?"

Kate dove into the closet, her movements livelier. She retrieved his shoes and socks, his jacket and his gun. "It would be in her computer."

Joey nodded, his mind racing ahead of him as he mindlessly dressed his feet, checked his gun, adjusted the holster. "Okay. Do you have a key to her apartment?" She nodded. "Give it to me and—"

"I'm going with you," she told him.

"No." He straightened too quickly, and the resulting rush of dizziness nearly knocked him down. She came close to him, gripped his arm until it passed. "You'd better stay right here," he said finally. "Harry will kill me if I try to take you—"

"You know as well as I do that Harold isn't here. He's out looking for them along with everyone else. Besides, you wouldn't know how to retrieve the information. I do. Now, please don't waste time arguing over this. Where do you think Antonia got her stubborn streak?"

He sighed, pulled on his jacket and turned slightly to close the closet door. It was then he caught a glimpse of his own reflection in the mirror mounted there. He almost jumped. He looked like something from an old Saturday-afternoon horror flick. Dark-colored bruises with angry purple rings at their outermost edges covered most of his face. His nose bent at an angle near the center. His eyes were still swollen, their lids so blue they looked made-up. He shook his head, closed the door and looked at her again. "I'm surprised you didn't run screaming when you got a look at this." He indicated his face with an open palm beneath his chin.

"Yes, you do look fairly awful," she told him. Her gaze dropped. "I, um, made Harold show me your identification photo last night."

Joey's brows shot up. He opened the heavy door and held it for her to precede him through. "Damn. And here I was planning to tell you I normally resemble Clark Gable."

She looked up at him, and her lips curved slightly upward. That he'd managed to make her smile, even so slightly, in the midst of all this gave Joey an absurd sense of satisfaction.

She insisted on driving, and within thirty minutes Joey stood over her in Toni's apartment-office. Kate sat in a padded swivel chair, punching buttons on a keyboard. In a moment the words "Holdings: Real Estate" appeared on the electric blue screen. Letter by letter, line by line, a list took shape below. Joey scanned, his impatience nearing an all-time high. Then he saw what he was looking for.

"There! Number eighteen, that's one I've never heard of. I don't think we knew about that one."

Kate punched in 18 and hit the return key. "Farmhouse," the screen told them. "Rural. Chenango County—Upstate N.Y." Joey read that Taranto had purchased the property for back taxes, using his cousin's name on the deed. Toni suspected the place was a dispatch point for drugs being shipped to Syracuse, Binghamton and other surrounding cities. The house itself, she'd noted, was in a state of chronic disrepair, but ideal for Lou's purposes, being completely surrounded by state forest. Joey shook his head, a sickening feeling in his stomach that hadn't been caused by his concussions this time. "How do we find this place?"

Kate pushed a quick series of buttons then, and a map appeared on the screen. "Antonia is nothing if not scrupulously thorough," she said softly. She hit Print, and the machine nearby began making lifelike noises. A moment later she leaned over it and tore a sheet free. She shook her head as she handed it to him. "The drive will take hours."

"Who said anything about driving?" Joey folded the map and slipped it into his breast pocket.

It was several moments before Nick could speak again. The last blow to the midsection had struck a rib on the way in. He couldn't draw a breath. He forcibly clung to consciousness despite the pain that washed over him like a tidal wave and the dizziness it brought with it. He had to stay lucid. At least until he could be sure Toni knew why he'd said what he had. When she'd asked that he not be killed right way, Taranto got suspicious. Nick knew him well enough to recognize the look. He had to do something to convince Lou that there was nothing between them.

Taranto and Viper left the room, and he heard locks being slid home. A second later Toni was behind him, deftly untying his hands. Circling to the front of him, she dropped to her knees and loosened the ropes that held his ankles. She stayed there a minute, not looking up.

She drew a breath. "I hope I'm right about how well you know me, Nick."

He rubbed his wrists roughly, then placed both hands on her shoulders. "You put on one hell of an act, lady. And you'd better damn well know by now when I'm doing the same. Call it a supporting role."

Her head rose slowly, her eyes scanning his face. "You knew what I was doing?"

"Almost as soon as you did. It never entered my mind to believe a word of it, Gypsy." He closed his arms around her, but she stiffened and held herself away.

"Are you all right?" Her eyes danced back and forth as she studied his face. "I wanted to club that bastard with something . . . I almost jumped on him without anything but my hands to use as weapons."

"I believe that." He smiled to show her he was okay, but she touched his face gently with her palm, and her eyes grew damp again. "I'm fine, I swear to God. It probably looks worse than it is." Seeing the genuine concern in her eyes was a bit more than he could handle right now, so he tried to change the subject. "You were good with Taranto, Toni. You pinpointed his weakness and you nailed him with it. He'd do anything to save his organization."

She shook her head, getting to her feet. "I don't know. He'll be angrier than ever when he finds out I was lying."

Nick rose, as well, glancing around the musty room. "You bought us some time. Now all we need to do is find a way out of here. It's a basement . . . a cellar. A house, and not a new one by the looks. I wonder where the hell we are?" He walked as he spoke, examining the rotted wood, the toppled water tank, the broken wooden crate. He knelt beside it and pawed through the dust-covered bottom to identify the shapes there. He found bent nails, a broken screwdriver and some wire. He tucked the screwdriver into his rear pocket and rose again, glancing upward at the cobweb-coated ceiling. "Not a heating duct or a register in the place," he muttered.

"I don't think anyone's been here in a while," Toni observed.

"You're right. He had to bring us somewhere isolated. With warrants out on him, he couldn't risk hanging around where we could find him easily. He can't have had time to round up much help, either. I imagine most of his thugs scattered in panic."

He glared at the door, frustration rising within him. "If we could get through the damn door, we might have a chance." He paced the room. "What if I make some racket, get whoever's guarding the door to open it up?" He was thinking aloud, the plan coming together in his mind as he voiced it. "I could jump the guy when he comes in. You could run out, close the door so he couldn't yell or come after you."

She closed her eyes slowly and shook her head. "No." When she opened her eyes again, the look in them was intense. She held his gaze forcefully. "Listen to me for once, Nick. I will not leave you." He frowned, searching her face, and she caught his face between her cool palms. "I mean it. I won't."

He sensed she wanted him to read more into her words than what she'd said, and the idea awed him. Could she be trying to tell him that—

No. In his entire life no one had ever cared enough about him to stay with him. How could she? He shook his head at the impossibility of it. Still, some small part of him wondered. She hadn't left him yet, though remaining with him had put her at risk. She hadn't left him, even when he'd tried to make her go.

Again he shook his head. "Toni, this might be your last chance. I'm offering you a way out. I don't see any other options."

"He'd kill you," she said softly. "He'd have no reason not to."

"If you stay, he'll kill us both," he told her.

She sighed, looked at the floor. "You really think I could just walk away from you, Nick? After all of this? I can't, you know. I couldn't if I wanted to. I won't. Even..." She drew a steadying breath and brought her gaze up to his. "Even when it's over."

He couldn't believe what he saw in her eyes. It hit him harder than Viper had, rendering him speechless. He opened his mouth, and only air came out. Was she saying...?

The sound of a key turning in the lock startled him. Toni shoved him away, both hands flat on his chest. He knew she intended for him to sit down, as if he were still bound. He didn't, though. He couldn't take his eyes from her face. He couldn't stop his heart from pounding. The door opened, and two men he hadn't seen before stepped through it. Both held guns, and both barrels were trained on Nick.

"You!" The fiftyish one with the crew cut and brown teeth waggled his gun barrel toward Toni. "Come with us."

"She's not going anywhere," Nick said softly.

"What's a matter, Manelli? You want to keep her all to yourself, is that it?"

The one beside Brown Teeth shifted his stance. He was younger, with a pocked face and body like a bean pole. "I don't know about this," he muttered. "Lou said not to touch her until he'd had his turn."

"There won't be anything left to touch when he's had his turn, kid. You ever *seen* a woman after he's had her?" He shook his head and moved closer to Toni. His gaze moved down her body slowly, and Nick clenched his teeth. "I won't hurt you, babe. I know how to handle a woman. You might even like it." He licked his lips. "You don't come along like a good girl, though, and I'll have to put a bullet in Nicky. See, Lou would kill me if I hurt you. But I have permission to shoot *him* if he gives me a reason."

Nick saw Toni's eyes harden. It amazed him once again, the backbone she had. He knew at that moment that all his resolve hadn't amounted to a damn thing. He'd been in love with her all along.

"That's right, sweet thing. I can see you realize you have no choice. You give me trouble, you get to watch him die and then you do what I tell you anyway, right? So why get Nicky blown away for nothing? You just come with me and you keep what I said in mind while we're in the other room." He glanced at the younger one. "I think she's gonna be real willing to accommodate us, Ray. I think she'll do anything we tell her to. Won't you, babe?"

She didn't answer until the younger one lifted the muzzle of his gun to Nick's temple. Nick's eyes were on Toni as she stiffened her spine. "I'll come with you."

"The hell you will," Nick said.

"They won't kill me, Nick."

"They won't touch you."

He heard her stifle a sob. She swallowed. "I don't want to lose you like this," she rasped. "Let it go. It won't be me, I swear to you. They'll be touching an empty shell—"

"Enough of this damn talk. Anybody'd think you two had a choice in the matter!" Brown Teeth grabbed Toni's upper arm. "Come on, baby, I been waitin' for this." He yanked her toward the door.

The younger one pressed the barrel harder to Nick's temple, but Nick's eyes were on Toni. Her gaze sent him a silent message, begging him not to do anything. Aloud she whispered again, "It won't be me, Nick."

"You're damn right it won't," he growled. In one swift move, he'd pulled the broken screwdriver from his pocket and jammed it into the skinny man, just below the rib cage, angling upward and thrusting it clear to the handle. The shock and pain caused his hand to relax on the gun, and it thudded to the floor. Brown Teeth turned at the sound, saw his partner drop to his knees, gape mouthed. He released his hold on Toni and leveled his gun at Nick. Toni whirled, clasping both fists together and bringing them down on his forearms. The gun roared, but the bullet only embedded itself in the packed dirt of the floor. The deafening sound exploded in the small room. Nick used the split second Toni had given him to lunge for the gun at his feet. He had it in his hand when Brown Teeth backhanded Toni, slamming her into the cinder-block wall. He aimed at Nick once more, but not fast enough. Nick pulled the trigger, sending another earsplitting boom into the confined space. The man staggered backward three steps, then folded in on himself, ending in a heap on the floor.

Nick reached down, twisted the gun from his limp grasp and straightened again. Toni stood near the doorway, her sickened gaze on the bleeding skinny one with the screwdriver handle protruding from his belly. He was unconscious but still alive. Nick stepped over Brown Teeth, putting himself between them and Toni. He pressed the gun into her hand, gripped her chin, forced her to look at him. "We have to get out of here." He pushed her through the small doorway even as he spoke. Those shots must've been heard upstairs.

They entered the main part of an ancient, crumbling cellar. He felt her body tremble as he urged her through. Already he heard footsteps above. She resisted his hand pressing at the small of her back. "We can't leave him like that."

Nick glanced to the left and saw the rickety stairs that led upward, presumably to the house. To the right was another, less steep, set, with an angular hatchlike door that laid almost flat at the top. That set would lead outside. There were more footsteps from above, and raised

voices. He put his arm around her shoulders, tightened it
so she couldn't pull away. He mounted the first step and
heard the door at the top of the other set of stairs creak
open. If this exit were locked—

He shoved at the hatch, and it swung open, hitting the
ground hard. He pulled her out into the warm, fresh night
air and pitch dark. His stride lengthened. "Run, Toni!"
She did, clutching his hand tightly, and in seconds bullets
flew after them.

The first thing that hit him was that they were not in
New York City anymore. They crossed a dewy, overgrown lawn with weeds that reached above his knees. At
its edge, a dirt road twisted away into blackness. Nick
glanced back. He saw only a tall, sagging house silhouetted by the half moon—and muzzle flashes like murderous eyes. He pulled her with him again, crossing the dirt
track and heading for the thick woods opposite. They
were at the edge of the tree line when he heard her suck in
her breath and felt her hand clutch his tighter.

Fear hit him between the eyes with a fist of ice. He
paused just beyond the trees. "Toni?"

She didn't stop when he did. "Nothing—I twisted my
foot. Come on!" She tugged at his hand. He could hear
the men coming closer. They were going to chase them
right into the woods. He ran with her, heading more and
more deeply into the forest. The pain of the broken rib
screamed angrily.

They approached a sharp rise and took it at a brutal
pace. Nick began to worry. Just where the hell were they?
How far could this forest go on? Towering spruce trees
surrounded them, angling skyward even on this steep
hillside. The ground underfoot gave softly with their
steps, making little sound. They topped the rise and
started down the opposite side. A fallen tree caught his

eye, and Nick noticed the cavelike space formed by the awkwardly bent boughs and the steep incline. He pulled Toni to it, and they ducked inside. She sat down, and Nick glanced through the opening, seeing no one at the moment.

"How big can these damn woods be?"

She was breathing hard. Too hard, for a woman who was in as good condition as she was. "Thousands of acres," she said. "It's state forest."

He turned, frowning, and crouched beside her. Even in the darkness he could see the deep stain on her shirt. Her sleeve was soaked, dripping. "Dammit, why didn't you say something?" He forgot his own pain, that of his unhealed thigh and even of the broken rib, as he knelt near her. He unbuttoned the blouse quickly, shoved it down over her shoulders and yanked it from her hands. She winced when the material pulled away from the wound in her shoulder. Blood pulsed from a small hole. Nick swore. The exertion of running had only increased the bleeding. He tore the clean sleeve off her blouse, using his teeth to start the tear. He twisted it around her, under her arm and over her shoulder, and he tied it tight. He watched for a moment, unsure whether he'd stopped the blood flow or just slowed it. Damn the darkness. How much blood had she lost already? Angrily he tore the bloodied sleeve off and helped her slip her arms back into the now-sleeveless blouse. He buttoned it with badly shaking hands.

When he finished, he glanced up at her face. She leaned back against the sticky trunk, her eyes closed. "Toni? Talk to me. Does it hurt much?"

"It's okay. I'm just resting." She opened her eyes, but it seemed to be an effort. Her voice was weak. "I remember now—it's some rural county. I forget the name. Upstate."

He slipped his hand to the back of her head and pulled her forward until she rested on his shoulder. "You'll be okay." Was he comforting her or himself? "You'll be okay, Gypsy. I'll get you out of this, I swear I will." He couldn't lose her. He couldn't. He held her tighter.

She lifted her head. "We should go...farther. They'll come after us."

Nick studied her eyes, silently begging her not to leave him this way. "Just rest. It's dark. They'd have to trip over us to find us here." He pulled her head back down gently. "Just rest, Gypsy."

"I don't want to rest." She remained relaxed against him despite her words. "I have to tell you...not to feel guilty. None..." She drew a deep breath and seemed to steady herself. "None of this was your fault."

"Shh." He stroked her hair. God, how he loved her hair. "You can ease my conscience when you get stronger."

"But...what if I don't—"

"Don't even say it, lady. You aren't getting away from me that easy."

He felt her sigh. "You're right." Her voice was barely a whisper now. "I told you I wouldn't leave you, Nick. I meant it. You have to know that. I meant it." She lifted her head again, and it seemed to take an incredible effort. She gazed into his eyes. "I know it'll be hard for you to believe me...they all walked out. You don't trust anyone. But I won't...unless you ask me to." Her eyes closed slowly and popped wide again as if she'd forced them. "I love you, Nick."

He felt as if he'd been struck by lightning. "You—you're delirious."

She shook her head. "I love you. I thought I could make you love me...but it's okay. Maybe you need time."

Her head fell to his shoulder as if she could no longer hold it up. Nick caught her face in his hands and gently lifted her, but her eyes remained closed, thick lashes caressing her silken cheeks, tears glistening in the single shaft of moonlight that made its way between the boughs. He kissed her, but her satin lips were slack and unresponsive. He closed his arms around her and rocked her slowly as a burning dampness gathered in his eyes. "Hold on, little Gypsy. Don't you leave me now. I do love you, dammit. More than life!"

She loved him. My God, it was not credible. No one had ever uttered those three words to Nick before—not even his own mother. Yet Toni had. She said she loved him, and he believed her.

She shivered in his arms. She needed help; he knew that. She'd lost a lot of blood, running full tilt the way she had while her magnificent heart pumped more and more blood out of her body. He lowered her gently, then moved out of the sheltering boughs and paused, listening. He heard them moving, but in the wrong direction. Apparently they'd passed them and were still heading deeper into the woods. Nick ducked back inside, lifting her carefully into his arms. He'd take her back the way they'd come. There must be a vehicle, a phone, something.

He had no way of knowing that Taranto had guessed he would come back, or that he'd only sent his men into the woods to flush them out. He and Viper waited near the dirt road for Nick to emerge from the trees. When he did, they would blow him to pieces.

He'd carried her nearly all the way back. The dirt road should be just beyond his range of vision now. She hadn't stirred in all that time. Nick felt a sense of dread settle over him. To lose her now would kill him. He drew closer to the road, able to see it's writhing shape. He was about to step through the last line of trees when he heard the choppers. They approached fast, and in seconds hovered over him. Spotlights danced through the trees over the road and seemed to settle on a subject. An artificially amplified voice filled the air, all but drowned out by the pounding of the chopper blades, but audible and mad as hell. "We are federal officers. Stand where you are and throw your weapons to the ground."

There was sudden movement from the road, and a burst of gunfire. Nick lowered Toni to the ground and lifted his weapon just as Lou Taranto lunged through the trees directly in front of him. Nick heard one of the choppers touch down. Lou lifted his gun muzzle.

"Forget it, Lou," Nick said, his voice level. "You're going down this time. It's over."

The hand holding the gun wavered. "Like my own son, Nicky." His body shook now, as well as his hand. "I treated you like my own son. You're right, it's over. But not just for me." The change in his grip on the revolver was minuscule but enough. Nick pulled up fast and shot him. He pulled the trigger three times in quick succession, and each time Lou's fat body jerked as if electrocuted. He went down then and lay still on the ground.

Nick looked at him for a long moment. He'd awaited this second from the time he was sixteen years old, and now that it was here it was nothing. It meant nothing. All that mattered was Toni. He turned and bent low to lift her into his arms again.

"Not yet, Manelli."

Viper's voice came from just behind him, and Nick's blood went cold. He'd lowered his weapon too soon. To turn and fire before Viper could put a bullet into his back would be impossible. The chance Viper would miss his first shot was slim at best. Viper rarely missed.

Nick stiffened, not even breathing. He lifted his gun, ready to spin and fire.

The sudden crack that split the air behind him jolted him, but he felt no bullet. He whirled, ready to fire, not believing Viper had missed. He froze. Viper lay dead on the ground. Nick's gaze lifted and moved beyond the hit man to see Joey's garishly bruised face. He stood with one hand braced against a tree trunk and gave Nick a lopsided grin.

"How many times are you gonna make me save that overdeveloped butt of yours, pal? I'm getting kinda sick of it."

"By my count, that makes us about even, Salducci." Nick turned, holstering his gun, and bent over Toni again. He lifted her and walked toward the road.

"She okay?" Joey's voice revealed his concern.

"She has to be," Nick said. "I'm on a roll."

He stepped out of the trees onto the road and saw cops everywhere and several of Taranto's men being hand-cuffed. Kate del Rio ran toward him, shaking Harry's restraining hand from her as if it was nothing. She stopped in front of Nick, her hand smoothing Toni's hair.

"Antonia! Oh, God..."

"She's only unconscious," Nick said gently. "She's going to be all right."

She nodded brusquely, stepped to one side, keeping her hand on her daughter's face and walking along with him toward the nearest chopper. "Of course she will, won't you, Antonia?" She lifted her head, met Nick's eyes. "She looks better than you do, I can tell you that much." She glanced toward Joey, who hung back. "Come on, you

stubborn man. You can barely stand up. You're coming
with us.''

Nick heard the slight waver underlying the gusto of her
words. He saw her lower lip tremble and he spotted droplets forming on her lashes. What was it with these del Rio
women and their false bravado, anyway? "She lost a little blood—that's why she's fainted, Kate. But with the
chopper we can have her in an emergency room in a matter of minutes. She's going to be all right.''

She nodded, steadying him by gripping his shoulder
when he lifted Toni up into the waiting chopper. She
climbed in behind him. "You don't have to tell me that. I
can see she's okay.'' Joey clambered up after her and
slipped a comforting arm around her shoulders. He held
her close to his side as the chopper lifted.

Chapter 15

When Nick saw Kate del Rio's gaze jump just before she got to her feet, he knew the surgeon had finally come out of the O.R. of the tiny Community Memorial Hospital in the town of Hamilton. It was a good hospital. Nick had checked. And the guy was a good surgeon. He'd checked on that, too. He'd had little else to do in the four hours since they'd rushed her through the huge double doors with the signs proclaiming Absolutely No Admittance Beyond This Point. He got his rib cage wrapped and then he sat in anguish.

He tried not to think of her as she'd been when they'd wheeled her through the doors, pale and limp and so damn weak. She'd told him she loved him. He still wasn't over the shock of it. She'd meant it, too; he'd seen it in her eyes. She loved him. That beautiful Gypsy enchantress loved Nick Manelli. It was a miracle—the only one he'd had in his life. Maybe you were only entitled to one. He

sighed hard. He'd damn well like another one. He wanted
her to be all right. He couldn't lose her now.

"Mrs. del Rio, Mr. Manelli?"

He snapped to attention. The surgeon stood in front of
him. Nick didn't know when he'd stood. He looked at the
man's blue pouffy paper hat and at the mask he'd tugged
down so it hung around his neck. He couldn't seem to
meet the man's eyes. His fear of seeing the worst there
kept his gaze darting around the waiting room. The smell
began to get to him. He felt it must have permeated his
body by now. He felt as if he'd still smell it even if he
burned his clothes and took ten scalding showers. He
felt—

"Thank God," Kate whispered. She turned into Nick's
chest, and he knew she cried with relief. She wobbled very
slightly, and Nick put his arms around her small shoulders to steady her.

Nick realized in growing awe that the doctor had just
informed them Toni was fine. "When can I—can we—see
her?" he managed.

"She's in recovery. She won't wake for several hours.
I'd advise you to get some sleep. I'll let you know the
minute she starts to come around."

"She's going to be okay," Nick muttered as the doctor
strode away from them.

Kate straightened and looked up at him. "Yes, but are
you?"

He shook his head. "Two miracles in one day. It's hard
to swallow."

She smiled up at him. "I should go and tell Joseph. Are
you sure you're all right?"

He finally let it sink in. She was all right. She loved him
and she was all right. He grinned, feeling like a small boy
on Christmas morning. "I've never been better!" He

grabbed the tiny woman and hugged her hard enough to force the air from her lungs. "I have to go out, but I won't be long."

He walked on air through the corridors, found Harry and managed to commandeer a local cop's car for his purposes. He drove away from the neat, low brick building, through the college town and into the rural countryside.

He left the windows down so that wonderful fresh-cut-grass fragrance could waft over him, and he tried to imagine what on earth he'd done to deserve a woman like Toni.

As he drove, the houses grew farther apart. He passed green meadows, fenced fields and herds of lazy fat cows. He drove by a huge rambling Victorian house and he smiled, remembering the way she'd confided her secret dreams to him, afraid he'd think they were silly.

He didn't. He couldn't for the life of him imagine a better way to spend his life than with Toni in some big old house. They'd fix it up together, and she'd have a big office with lots of light. She could work on those warm, uplifting books she wanted to write. He'd join the local P.D. When he came home at night, she'd be there. She wouldn't walk out. She loved him.

He smiled, suddenly knowing exactly what he wanted to get for her. The doctor had said several hours. Would he have time to find what he needed?

The afternoon sun slanted in through a window and heated her face and eyelids. Toni wrinkled her nose. The smell was unpleasant and familiar. Her throat hurt. It felt dry and as if something had scraped it raw. There was no pain in her shoulder. Somehow she felt as if there should be.

She opened her eyes. Nick sat beside the bed in a chair. His hand held hers tightly, she realized. He looked better than he had. His cheek still looked swollen and purple, but not as bad as it had been. The blood had all been washed away from his face.

He looked relieved when she met his eyes, but nervous, too. "Hey, sleepyhead. Feel up to a five-mile run?"

She smiled at him, and her heart swelled when she thought of how much she loved him. She blinked. She'd told him so, hadn't she? When they'd been in the forest, and she'd felt so weak she'd wondered if it could be the end, she'd decided to tell him exactly how she felt, in case she never had another chance. Maybe that was why he seemed nervous. She'd scared him with the intensity of her feelings, just as she'd feared she might.

He smiled back at her. "You don't know how good it is to see that smile of yours, Gypsy." He leaned close and kissed her with exquisite tenderness. When he straightened, he studied her face as if he were drinking it in.

One hand—the only one she seemed able to move—lifted to run through her hair. "I'm a mess."

"You're gorgeous."

"My hair—"

"You'd be gorgeous bald, lady."

That remark elicited a giggle, but Nick wasn't smiling. His face was serious. "You remember what happened?"

Her smile faded. She nodded and glanced down at her arm. Her shoulder was heavily bandaged, her arm in a sling. "I was shot."

"The arm will be fine, Toni. No complications. A few weeks, you'll be as good as new." He cleared his throat, and his gaze dropped before hers. "Do—um—you remember what you told me out there?"

She drew a deep breath. "I didn't mean to make you uncomfortable. I was afraid I wouldn't make it. I wanted you to know—"

"Then you meant it?"

He seemed so insecure all of a sudden, so vulnerable. Frowning, she looked into his tiger-striped eyes. "I'm in love with you, Nick Manelli. Maybe I shouldn't have said it so soon, but I'm not going to take it back now."

"I'm glad you said it." He looked at her, and for a moment she thought there was a bit more moisture in his eyes than usual. "No one's ever said it to me before."

"Then you don't mind?" He shook his head. Toni sighed. "I love you," she told him. "I love you enough to make up for all the people who didn't. More than enough...if you'll let me."

"If I'll..." He caught her face in his hands and kissed her again. "Baby, I love you so much I would have died if I had lost you." He gathered her to him and kissed her deeply, letting his feelings rush over her and through her. She felt the lack of reservation or restraint and she gloried in it.

When he eased her down to her pillows, she felt caught in a whirlwind. "I'm not sure what this means, Nick. Where do we go from here?"

"Anywhere we want, that's the icing on the cake. Toni, do you realize how well our dreams mesh? Your big rural house, my small-town beat...and..." He bent low and scooped something from the floor. "And this," he whispered.

She frowned as he set the basket in her lap. She lifted the lid and peered inside. Her breath caught in her throat, and the tears she'd been holding back spilled over. She reached her good hand inside and pulled the tiny gray-

and-white fur ball out. She held him close to her, and the puppy nuzzled her neck. "Oh, Nick!"

"I'm calling him Ralph," Nick told her. "If that's okay with you."

* * * * *

HE'S AN

AMERICAN HERO

He's a cop, a fire fighter or even just a fearless drifter who gets the job done when ordinary men have given up. And you'll find one American Hero every month, only in Intimate Moments—created by some of your favorite authors. Look at what we've lined up for the last months of 1993:

October: GABLE'S LADY by Linda Turner—With a ranch to save and a teenage sister to protect, Gable Rawlings already has a handful of trouble...until hotheaded Josey O'Brian makes it an armful....

November: NIGHTSHADE by Nora Roberts—Murder and a runaway's disappearance force Colt Nightshade and Lt. Althea Grayson into an uneasy alliance....

December: LOST WARRIORS by Rachel Lee—With one war behind him, Medevac pilot Billy Joe Yuma still has the strength to fight off the affections of the one woman he can never have....

AMERICAN HEROES: Men who give all they've got for their country, their work—the women they love.

IMHER06

Silhouette Books has done it again!

Opening night in October has never been as exciting! Come watch as the curtain rises and romance flourishes when the stars of tomorrow make their debuts today!

Revel in Jodi O'Donnell's STILL SWEET ON HIM—
Silhouette Romance #969
...as Callie Farrell's renovation of the family homestead leads her straight into the arms of teenage crush Drew Barnett!

Tingle with Carol Devine's BEAUTY AND THE BEASTMASTER—
Silhouette Desire #816
...as legal eagle Amanda Tarkington is carried off by wrestler Bram Masterson!

Thrill to Elyn Day's A BED OF ROSES—
Silhouette Special Edition #846
...as Dana Whitaker's body and soul are healed by sexy physical therapist Michael Gordon!

Believe when Kylie Brant's McLAIN'S LAW —
Silhouette Intimate Moments #528
...takes you into detective Connor McLain's life as he falls for psychic—and suspect—Michele Easton!

Catch the classics of tomorrow—*premiering* today—
only from ❤ Silhouette

ROMANTIC TRADITIONS

Marriages of convenience, secret babies, amnesia, brides left at the altar—these are the stuff of Romantic Traditions. And some of the finest Intimate Moments authors will bring these best-loved tales to you starting in October with ONCE UPON A WEDDING (IM #524), by award-winning author Paula Detmer Riggs.

To honor a promise and provide a stable home for an orphaned baby girl, staunch bachelor Jesse Dante asked Hazel O'Connor to marry him, underestimating the powers of passion and parenthood....

In January, look for Marilyn's Pappano's FINALLY A FATHER (IM #542), for a timely look at the ever-popular secret-baby plotline.

And ROMANTIC TRADITIONS doesn't stop there! In months to come we'll be bringing you more of your favorite stories, told the Intimate Moments way. So if you're the romantic type who appreciates tradition with a twist, come experience ROMANTIC TRADITIONS—only in

SIMRT1

INTIMATE MOMENTS®
Silhouette®

Next month, don't miss meeting the Rawlings family of New Mexico. You'll learn to love them!

Look for

Linda Turner's exciting new miniseries.

Look for GABLE'S LADY (IM #523), October's American Hero title.

And look for his siblings' stories as the exciting saga continues throughout 1994! Only from Silhouette Intimate Moments.

What a year for romance!

Silhouette has five fabulous romance collections coming your way in 1993. Written by popular Silhouette authors, each story is a sensuous tale of love and life—as only Silhouette can give you!

SPRING FANCY

Three bachelors are footloose and fancy-free...until now.
(March)

Heartwarming stories that celebrate the joy of motherhood.
(May)

SILHOUETTE
SUMMER Sizzlers

Put some sizzle into your summer reading with three of Silhouette's hottest authors.
(June)

SILHOUETTE
Shadows

Take a walk on the dark side of love—with tales just perfect for those misty autumn nights.
(October)

Silhouette
CHRISTMAS Stories

Share in the joy of yuletide romance with four award-winning Silhouette authors.
(November)

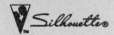

Silhouette®

A romance for all seasons—it's always time for romance with Silhouette!

PROM93

Silhouette Books
is proud to present
our best authors,
their best books...
and the best in
your reading pleasure!

Throughout 1993, look for exciting
books by these top names in
contemporary romance:

DIANA PALMER—
Fire and Ice in June

ELIZABETH LOWELL—
Fever in July

CATHERINE COULTER—
Afterglow in August

LINDA HOWARD—
Come Lie With Me in September

When it comes to passion,
we wrote the book.

BOBT2

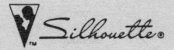

TAKE A WALK ON THE
DARK SIDE OF LOVE WITH

October is the shivery season, when chill winds blow and shadows walk the night. Come along with us into a haunting world where love and danger go hand in hand, where passions will thrill you and dangers will chill you. Silhouette's second annual collection from the dark side of love brings you three perfectly haunting tales from three of our most bewitching authors:

Kathleen Korbel
Carla Cassidy
Lori Herter

Haunting a store near you this October.

Only from 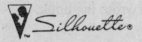 where passion lives.

SHAD93